Best wishes!
Phil Pople.
January 2018

FORTUNE
FATE
AND
FREDDIE MERCURY

Phil Page

Printed in the United Kingdom

First Printing, 2017

ISBN 9781787231160

Published by Completely Novel.com

www.philpage.org.uk

For Ralph and Alan.

To Bernie

With all best wishes

Alan (a.k.a. Al Mansfield)

What You Gave Me
Marvin Gaye and Tammi Terrell. Easy. Tamla Motown.

The cellar is hot, dark. Bodies crowd the dance floor. I catch glimpses of the girl I am dancing with, her black hair swirling wildly around her face. The music is irresistible, absorbing me into a world of noise, movement and sweat as the bassline thumps into my chest. I can't breathe, but a collective energy drives me on as stroboscopic flashes light the clock on the wall telling me it's 5am. The girl falls into my arms laughing, and we squeeze through the crowd up the steep, narrow steps out into Hardman Street and the welcome, cool air of a July morning. There is no alcohol, no threat, just people together, still intoxicated by the music, their adrenaline releasing into the quiet streets.

The first rays of sunlight fall on the slanted frames of the club's window, illuminating its sign above the door. 'The Sink Club. Liverpool's Premier Soul Venue'. The last bars of 'In The Midnight Hour' drift up into the street. The needle clicks off the turntable. Emptiness! I'm alone in my bedroom. It's September 1st, 1969 and I'm heading for school.

ONE

At The Crossroads
Mott The Hoople. Debut Album. Island Records.

There are plenty of crossroads in Widnes but none where you can just hang around and wait for the Devil to turn up. There are plenty of highways, but no one I know has any keys to them, except Dave Shuttleworth who drives a milk float. And anyway, the places they go to, Warrington, Wigan, St Helens, are hardly towns you'd want to disappear to or write songs about. There's nowhere in England which is twenty-four hours from Widnes and the haze in the air isn't purple just an invisible smell from Laporte's Peroxide Plant which gives the warm, autumn air a heavy, sickly taste.

A decade of unprecedented social, musical and political change is crawling exhaustedly towards its close, but there's little to suggest the changes of the Sixties have touched Widnes. Folk haven't really bothered about what's been happening outside South Lancashire and, even though the Beatles played at the Queens Hall in 1963, they've never been back. The clubs and pubs are still full of crooners belting out classics by Pat Boone, Bobby Vee and Frank Sinatra with occasional performances by beat groups left behind in the wake of the Mersey Sound's success. Widnes watched it all happen on the telly and read about it in the papers, but just got on with its everyday existence, clutching tightly to values locked safely away behind the scrubbed steps and solid front doors of its red, Victorian terraces. Hair has got longer, flares wider and, in Deacon Road, the Banjo Boutique adds a psychedelic splash of colour between the dowdy green of the Co-op and the middle-aged pastels of Calverts front window. But, for the most part, the town is still slowly recovering from the austerity of the Fifties. Life in Widnes is pretty grey.

I'm in the final year of the sixth form at the local grammar school, planning my escape down one of those highways and away from the bleak, weathered vision of a lifetime in a small industrial town. I've been suffering regular episodes of this worrying scenario every day on the bus journeys to school and back. It's the Ronnie Hurst story, and it beats Coronation Street hands down because it's real and frightening and has built up in fifteen-minute dialogues over the last two years.

Ronnie is our bus conductor, a friend of mine from junior days, who left school at sixteen. I know all about his life, from the excitement of starting work at the bus depot, meeting the girl of his dreams (Sandra, from 'Accounts'), saving enough money to buy a season ticket for the Chemics and joining the golf club. More recently he's been getting over the deaths of his pet dog, Rover, Buster the rabbit and assorted hamsters and gerbils, and saving with a view to getting married in a few years' time. Week by week Ronnie's life has unfolded before me, his prospects as jammed as the ticket machine he struggles with each day, and his horizons barely covering the three-mile bus journey from Widnes town centre to Hough Green housing estate where I live.

Our house is in a redevelopment scheme; one of those ideas that the council decided would improve the town by bringing the housing stock up to twentieth century standards. We were turfed out of our homely Victorian terrace in West Bank, with its cosy rooms, roaring coal fire and neighbours who chatted to each other while popping in and out of my Uncle Nuck's corner shop. In exchange, we were herded into one of the new modern semis, thrown up in the quick-build manner of the Fifties, with an electric fire and an inside toilet. I miss the misty streets where the night air swirled up from the banks of the Mersey clinging damply to the walls and pavements as it flitted silently, around street corners, through alleyways and over backyard gates, making a winter trip to the outside toilet a silent, spooky experience. I loved the persistent dripping of the rainwater and the wind rattling the slates, which created a half-belief that there was always something outside trying to weasel its way in. Now there are just the voices of the people next

5

door, drifting into our living room through the paper-thin walls, like some distant soap opera continually clawing away at my subconscious.

Moving to the new suburb took me to a better life. Well, almost. There were bright new streets and plenty of green spaces where I could play football and cricket all day in the school holidays or raid the ponds dotted around the miles of green fields, but the price was a new conservatism brought into our family by this clean, modern living. My Mum's aspirations rose so much that she left home for a man, a bit better off than my dad, who ran his own business. Now, when I'm round for Sunday lunch with her side of the family, the well-worn conversations click into place. Ronnie Hurst's future is alive and secure and reinforced to me every time we gather at my Mum's house in the wealthier part of Hough Green.

It usually starts with a seemingly innocuous comment by my Aunty Joan about how Karen, my cousin, has got herself a 'nice little job', is learning to drive, has money in her pocket, and is contributing to her keep. The theme will be taken up by Uncle Reg who then relates how he left school at fourteen, with a sound knowledge of the Three Rs, started sweeping the floor for twelve hours a day at a woodturning company and rose, 'through bloody hard work', to become managing director. Within minutes, the whole lot of them will have joined ranks against students, ('National Service would sort them out.'), hippies, ('Drug-crazed.'), rock bands, ('You can't understand a word they sing.'), the Labour Party, ('Bloody Communists.'), and the unemployed, ('Idle layabouts.'), while my mum will nod knowingly in my direction no doubt hoping that my shoulder length hair will shrink overnight and I'll wake up with an overwhelming desire to pack in my academic aspirations and get myself a proper job.

She thinks I'm a dreamer and she's right. It's her fault really. It all started with the transistor radio she bought me for passing the Eleven Plus. This was no small pocket size radio but a huge, spaceship gold, RCA Victor Globe Trotter, Model

3-RG-81 which could pick up radio broadcasts from hundreds of stations. As soon as I switched it on the dreams started. They were an irresistible force filling my head with images of places out there, wherever out there was. There were stations with people talking very fast in strange languages and people talking very slowly in even stranger languages and weird languages which had bits of English in them. There were news broadcasts from places I'd never heard of, with mysterious words and phrases like 'coup', 'fanatics', 'apartheid', 'boycotts', 'martial law', 'segregation' and 'civil rights'. The world out there had seemed a pretty scary place but, for me, it was the music, and not the stuff you got on *Uncle Mac's Radio Show* about elephants packing their trunks or crackpot kids losing their echo. On one level it was the music of back door men, midnight ramblers and people stealing away into the night, on the other, it was songs which found their way into the secret places of your soul.

Mum got the radio from her friend, Marie, who was married to an American stationed at Burtonwood Airbase. After dark, its eight transistors omitted a hypnotic hum from under my bedclothes as the rest of the house slept, producing enough heat so that, even on the coldest winter nights, my hot water bottle lay discarded on the lino floor. Calm nights were best when the reception didn't crackle or fade, discovering stations which were there one night and gone the next. Tiny, almost invisible spaces on the tuning band. Welcome visitors who brought the soul and blues of America into my life.

Along with the radio came a steady stream of American science fiction comics. Copies of 'Strange Worlds', 'Weird Tales', and 'Action Comics' stacked up in the corner of my bedroom. The TV chipped in with 'The Outer Limits', 'One Step Beyond' and any number of American B-movies as my mid-teen angst about not being alone in the universe grew. There were the uneasy feelings about walking home at night hoping the clouds gathering ominously in the sky were not concealing alien craft waiting to whisk me off to some planet at

7

the edge of the universe to be displayed in a huge glass vial for the next hundred years, and my Dad's casual comment about some people on our estate, 'not being right', had me believing there was an alien living just next door.

Bernice Flynn is a bit older than me and has a false eye and a bit of a gammy leg. A couple of years ago after watching *Invasion Of The Body Snatchers,* I got it into my head that Hough Green could be an offshoot of Santa Mira and that Bernice's ailments were a result of an alien's inability to assimilate itself properly into her body. I was convinced the real Bernice had perfect eyesight and could run like an Olympic athlete and it was the alien who was pulling pints in the Upton Tavern, it's monosyllabic grunts of 'Ta!', 'What?', 'Yeh!', and 'Nah!', a sure sign of its inability to engage in any meaningful inter-galactic communication.

Still, I've just about grown out of the fantasies, which were a product of being captivated by Clarke Kent, Lois Lane, Lana Lang and Jimmy Olsen, as they routinely battled it out with extra-terrestrials on the streets of Metropolis, and my English Lit course has taught me that escapism is not the sole domain of comics and radio broadcasts. *Tess Of The D'Urbervilles* is my favourite A-level text, and recently, in one of Herbie Gravitt's tutorials, we discussed the concept of the 'ache of modernism', how Hardy was sick of progress and just wanted to maintain the simple and uncomplicated ways. Like most northern towns, Widnes succumbed to the industrial revolution and the changes were riveted and welded into its identity. Now it's the finished product, bolted together and polished; a gritty, galvanised example of a town which knows its place. The more I read, the more I want to escape from the clanking of steam engines, factory hooters, chemical dust, and the steel-plated life, played out in its factories, docks, working men's clubs, pubs, bookies and the terraces of Naughton Park. I want to meander down lanes in Dorset, watch clean, white clouds sweep in over the Blackmoor Vale and roll home from the Pure Drop Inn with the locals in the silent hours of a midsummer's morning, the smells of blackberries, hazel and dogwood drifting from the hedgerows. And then there's Tess, of course, my heroine, who's tucked between the covers just waiting for me to leap into the storyline and rescue her from the hands of fate, so we can head off together over the green fields, thumbing our noses at chance, and changing the course of her life forever.

Sadly, my best friend, Al Morefield, is unimpressed with my romantic ideas to save Hardy's tragic heroine. He believes she's beyond redemption, her life already mapped out by Clotho, the Greek seamstress, who sits up in the clouds weaving the tapestries of our lives before we ever set foot on Earth. Like Herbie and Hardy, he believes Tess is powerless to save herself as she hurtles towards her predetermined end. This belief in predestination has recently become one of his new philosophies.

Having undertaken the move south from Bishop Auckland in the fifth year, seeking out new friends, and making his North East accent intelligible to the locals, his other life changing moment came when his sister, Avril, bought him a copy of *On The Threshold Of A Dream* by The Moody Blues for his seventeenth birthday. This was the moment Al said goodbye to the simplicity of life and started searching for a deeper meaning in everything. Now, locked in his bedroom, with his small, but rapidly growing collection of prog-rock albums, he disappears for a few hours each night into the surreal dark lands and philosophical whirlpools of King Crimson, Pink Floyd and Quintessence. Most days are a quest to find a connection with reality by expressing his feelings through his newly acquired wisdom and his favourite song of the moment is 'The Weaver's Answer' by Family, played loudly on his family's old Dansette record player. Had Hardy had access to such technology he'd have loved it. Dorchester would have rocked to the narrative of one soul's struggle against the tapestry of his life, already woven.

From about fifty yards down the road, I can hear the gravel-throated Roger Chapman painfully spitting out the last lines through Al's bedroom window. After several loud knocks, Mrs Morefield opens the door and smiles knowingly at me. 'He'll be down in a minute, pet. He's just lookin' for 'is mind.'

Seconds later Al appears, his school blazer stuffed into a plastic Adidas bag, his white shirt hanging loosely over his school trousers, and his tie knotted firmly around his wrist.

'I think that record is so pretentious.'

'You've got it wrong, Man! The Fates are part of literary heritage. It's inevitable that progressive, intelligent music is going to pick up on Man's futile struggle against irresistible forces. Anyway, it's better than that crap you were playing last weekend.'

This is a reference to my small collection of Motown records which I no longer possess. I was having a sort out when Al unexpectedly came round; just playing a few of the tracks that had taken over my life during the summer holidays, widening my musical horizons, but provoking ridicule and torment from my mates. I was thinking of keeping some of them but, after an hour, I'd got so fed up of his exaggerated puking noises and comments about 'bopper music' that I'd tipped the lot into a plastic bag and carted them off to Blue Mountain Records on Widnes Market.

A couple of days later I'd gone in to buy some of them back but 'You're All I Need', 'Two Can Have A Party', 'Your Precious Love', and others had gone. The memories of my summer love, Lesley Hutchinson, and most of my soul, had disappeared into somebody else's bedroom.

I've just about got over Lesley. The pain has disappeared, and I've stopped leaving the arm up on my record player, preventing our song from playing over and over again, and inviting a twisted, turntable of emotions to spin around inside my head.

Our song was 'Ain't Nothing Like The Real Thing' by Marvin Gaye and Tammi Terrell. Lesley had given it to me on our third date and, when I took it home, I didn't want to play it in case it got scratched or I spoiled the crisp, brown, starry Motown cover. I stood it on the shelf in my room and every night I lay on the bed and looked at it, a wonderful warm feeling washing over me. She said the words were really relevant because it was a reminder that when we were apart nothing could take the place of us being together. She was all long, dark hair and flimsy limbs and when she finished with me, she left a large, empty hole in my life.

There had never been any holes in my world before. I sat around in it for weeks before it slowly began to fill up with other things and now there are just the memories floating on top of the junk of everyday life which lies in a flat, grey mass beneath.

She was from Warrington and heavily into Motown. I'd taken some stick from Al for going out with a bopper but I'd have bopped anywhere for Lesley, and I didn't care that I looked out of place at the discos and had to hide the Motown records when Al came round to play Subbuteo and pretend I was still unequivocally into King Crimson, Pink Floyd and Caravan. Soul seemed to slow me down and take me away from that ache of modernism. There was no thinking, no analysis, no striving for complicated hidden meanings, no debates about the meaning of life and the pressure to be deep and thoughtful. For four months it was as if I'd taken one big breath which had slowed me down with all the distractions of life pushed somewhere over the horizon.

Then she finished with me for a soul DJ called Curtis. She said we were too different and she was probably right. In the beginning, you put up with anything when the magic's there, adapt yourself in all sorts of ways you'd never imagine. Then the real you begins to resurface and you've got to start to compromise. Lesley couldn't understand why I liked to sit and listen to records. For her, music was for dancing to, and you couldn't bop to most of the bands I liked.

11

Our first date had been arranged via the grapevine which fed on signals and messages picked up at The Dell, a tuck shop outside the school gates. Lesley had joined the sixth form gang which met each break. There'd been looks and smiles and a general weighing up of compatibility, processed by the girls in the group, and then one break time Lesley was there, chaperoned and presented, half pushed in my direction by three of her mates. We had five minutes to chat and arrange a date, and that was that.

Three days later I met her on the train from Warrington, her smile beaming out through the scratched and steamed up windows of the two-car diesel, and we had twenty minutes to get to know each other before we arrived at Lime Street. We'd spent the evening on the soul deck of the Babalu Club dancing to songs I didn't know while Lesley sang every word.

Looking back, our relationship was never going to stand the test of time. Curtis was always around feeding her the latest releases and Northern Soul classics. I don't know how long she could have accommodated me in her social circle, and I don't know how long Motown would have been enough.

After we'd finished, during an umpteenth playing of 'our song', I'd thought about having my hair cut short and spending some money on smart clothes, but I was too tall. Tight jackets with wafty, turned-up trousers look ridiculous on anyone over 5'9". I'd seen these lanky misfits in the clubs and discos, jackets stretched tightly across wiry frames, arms and legs protruding from clothes which looked two sizes too small. Their centre of gravity was all wrong and when they attempted to dance they looked like they'd been coached by Norman Wisdom. Soul is the domain of the small person, the evidence is all there; Little Stevie Wonder, Little Eva, Little Anthony. Big people belong to the other side.

I guess the simplicity of Motown was fine when everything was drifting along happily but now it's all ended I can't really sum up our relationship, or how I felt, in soul lyrics. I need a bit of the complexity back. Once you're past dwelling on how great and everlasting your love was there isn't much left to go on. Soul is all about feelings and not meanings. You had your girl, and you were in love. You lost your girl and you were sad; really, really sad. You wanted her back and were waiting with open arms but she was with another man. It's strong stuff. I've had a taste of it all but I need to move on. Now my feelings about Lesley are grasped from snatches of rock lyrics swirling around my head, and they aren't pleasant because they take me to cold places, hard times and loneliness. In rock, you have to put distance between yourself and your girl and suffer the hurt alone. You have to travel, move away, and re-invent yourself before the healing process can begin.

TWO

Something In The Air
Thunderclap Newman. Single Release. Track Records.

Al hasn't got anyone on his horizons at the moment. Well, he likes a girl in the Banjo Boutique. Not a real girl, the one dressed up in the window who pretty much matches his ideal. She's perfect for him, really. She has a lovely pale complexion, perfect figure, sky-blue eyes and blonde, silvery hair which glows even on the darkest mornings. She dresses in the latest gear and is about his height. She'd like everything he likes and she'd still have that Pleasant Valley smile even when he came up with all his usual contrived reasons to finish with her. He goes on about her quite a lot when we pass her on the bus and I can sympathise in a way. Two-dimensional relationships are much less complicated and I've often imagined walking into the bars and clubs of Metropolis with Lois Lane clinging to my arm after she's ditched Superman.

We are both in need of new beginnings. Judith Adamson is a girl in the upper sixth who I met briefly at a party a few months ago. She lives on a farm just off Long Barn Lane, on the outskirts of Warrington, and has the innocence of Hardy's heroine and the style of Julie Christie. However, I don't hold out much hope of dating her, having my own Tess, and a manifestation of Talbothays Farm on which to spend long, crisp autumn evenings. I have no connection with her and she stands aloofly outside my social circle. She does, though, have a place in a lot of rock songs which are buzzing around inside my head. The ones about leaving and travelling off into the sunrise are best, stealing away in the early morning light, leaving the quiet streets behind and heading off into a new life.

Of course, it's all fantasy. I'm just wandering between two worlds hoping that a new one will rise while the old one weakly lingers and fades. I'm not really sure how to move on but if Al, Herbie and Thomas are right there's no point in worrying about it, everything's already been mapped out and the story's told.

This morning we're heading for school, skipping today's episode of the Ronnie Hurst Story, and travelling the dusty footpath which leads out of our estate hugging the railway line next to the golf course. Across the fairways is the hazy outline of Wade Deacon Grammar School for Boys rising like a ghostly, Gothic clubhouse from the mist. We can just make out some third years kicking a football around the yard taking care not to let it stray onto the First XV rugby pitch which has been meticulously prepared for the new season with its white markings seemingly ironed into the lush, green surface.

Back across towards the fairways, and sloping at a ridiculous angle, are the football pitches. Bald patches in the goalmouths are still visible, the remedial sprinkling of grass seed long since blown away or eaten by passing birds. Bunches of yellow weeds dot each penalty area like memorials to matches lost and I wince at the prospect of the turned ankles and bleeding knees of the season to come. Wade Deacon is a rugby school, and Jock Laidlaw will soon be delivering his annual address to the first years leaving them in no doubt of the hard labour awaiting them in games lessons over the next five years.

I'm unsure where Jock comes from. Scottish accents all seem the same to me, but he's more Jimmy Shand than Andy Stewart, so I guess he's from way up in the remote regions more associated with Vikings and Nordic hoards than the soft borderlands. Actually, Jock is not a man, he's a piece of Jurassic rock which has been left out over the centuries to weather in the wind and rain of the remote Highlands before being transported on an articulated lorry south to Widnes and rolled into the PE department demolishing everything before him. Jock rules like a Scottish warrior, patrolling the changing rooms and showers, never missing the chance to make some disparaging comment about your kit, lack of skills, or his pet hatred, football. Jock is a rugby union man and spits the word 'football' from his mouth like a poison thistle head. His red

15

and black hooped jersey gives him a passing resemblance to Denis the Menace, apart from his shaved head replacing the shiny black curls of the comic book hero. To Jock, football players are softies who deserve to be exiled to the corners of the changing rooms, pinned back by the growling menace of his mantra; 'Gentlemen, we play a man's game at Wade Deacon, there'll be no mention of football in these lessons until the third year.'

We sit on the wall, outside The Dell, waiting for the 8.34 from Liverpool, which usually arrives at the same time as the one trundling west from Warrington. The shop's owned by Arthur and Vera who I've only ever seen glowering from behind the scratched plastic divide which protects their limited range of stock from disappearing into blazer pockets. The choice is pitifully narrow, mainly loose sweets from sticky jars, misshapen bars of chocolate, a few cartons and tins with faded labels and the contents of a freezer which are rapidly vanishing behind a growing ice floe. Under the counter are packets of Park Drive cigarettes which they open and sell as singles to maintain their profits at subsistence level.

The mass of white cloud billowing under the sandstone railway bridge indicates the arrival of the trains. Thomas Hardy hated steam engines. He saw them as grey, hissing monsters, destroying the old ways and threatening the order of the natural world. For us, though, they're a lifeline. Our means of chugging along through the whistle-stop events of teenage life.

The pupils spill out from the cream and maroon carriages mingling into one mass on their way up the station approach but it's easy to identify where most have set out from by the way uniforms are adapted into watered-down versions of their everyday clothes. The soul scene is still strong in Warrington, and the boys' blazers are tightly buttoned, ties shortened and fastened smartly to Ben Sherman shirts, with baggy trousers ending in turn-ups just above well-polished shoes. Their girls wear perfect school uniform and are every inch the smart equivalent of their alter-egos from the Warrington discos.

In contrast, the pupils from Liverpool have a worldlier look. Ties hang loosely around open-necked shirts and there is the occasional glimpse of baseball boots between the wafts of wide, flared trousers. Blazers are slung over shoulders or have been discarded completely into rucksacks which have superseded the satchels, now the sole possession of first years. The older girls wear longer skirts with cheesecloth blouses instead of the smart regulation cotton favoured by their peers from the other side of the tracks.

Last off the Liverpool train, and easily picked out against the generally clean, white faces and slim bodies, is Ralph Clayton. His mass of black hair falls lazily against the lapels of his fading school blazer complementing the thick, wiry beard he's been cultivating since the fifth year. Ralph is the star forward of the First XV, a positive force both on and off the field, and he flashes us a thumbs up before heading across to his girlfriend, Anne Woodley. They have been going out together since they were thirteen and have been a constant in my life, untroubled by the physical and emotional revolution of their teenage years. He sweeps Anne off her feet in a manner reminiscent of Fay Wray disappearing into the arms of King Kong, delivers the sort of kiss usually reserved for darkened bus shelters, drops her down, and ambles over.

'Big P! Big Al! I've got a proposition for you.' He ushers us around the side of The Dell as if to find a safe haven in which to impart a dark secret. A smug smile spreads across his face. 'I've got us a gig at St Mary's Autumn Fair. Des Wilcox, the vicar, has been let down. He'd booked a band and they've pulled out. So I said we'd fill in, no problem!'

I glance across at Al. The vicar's daughter is one of the most attractive girls in the sixth form. Nobody has ever been out with her which is not surprising as we all accept that getting past Des' vetting procedures is an impossibility. She's the only girl in the school with the bottle to write, 'Cliff Richard, Disciple of Pop', on her school bag. I look at Ralph pityingly.

'You've done this to impress Lisa Wilcox.'

'Bollocks!' He pauses. 'Well, yeh! Ok.'

'So it's all over with you and Anne, then? Was that the farewell kiss?'

'Don't be friggin' stupid, Man! I know Lisa fancies me. I just want to get up there on stage and show her what she's missing. It's the sort of thing all rock stars do, spread their irresistible persona out into the audience, driving the girls wild knowing that they're untouchable.'

'You'd have to be exorcised before her dad would let you anywhere near her.'

'St Mary's Autumn Fair?' says Al. 'Let's see. Home-made cakes? Tombola? Second-hand Christian bookstall? Marijuana tent? Satanic Bible reading? What does he want us to do?'

'Des doesn't mind so long as we just fill in!' Ralph pauses. 'But no sex, drugs, supernatural or blasphemy in the lyrics.'

'So three from Cliff's catalogue, then? Hardly the road to serious musical recognition.'

Ralph grabs Al in a headlock. 'It doesn't matter if it's a bleedin' garden party, Morefield. St. Peter's Church Fete, Woolton, 6th July 1957, possibly the most important date in rock history. Cakes, craft stalls, the crowning of the Rose Queen, and in the middle of it all The Quarrymen are belting out some rock'n'roll covers. McCartney turns up and meets Lennon and the whole world of music is changed in an instance. This could be our beginning, Men. We might not be the next Beatles but we can be the next Colour.'

He's alluding to our mates who have already made it down one of those highways. John Taylor and Mike Bersin got together three years ago with Mick 'Miffer' Smith, our local milkman, and turned themselves into a respectable blues band gigging around the clubs and pubs of Warrington, Widnes, and Liverpool. They even made it into the Widnes Weekly News and I've still got the cutting in my bedroom, somewhere.

18

The article predicted stardom and suggested that the band would soon be hearing from Stuart Henry at the BBC or from The Beatles' Apple label. It quoted John as saying, 'Blues is not music, it's a way of life', and they headed down to London just before summer, changing their name to Ibex because one day Miffer said he was hungry enough to eat one and the name just stuck.

I've seen them a few times in the clubs around Liverpool. They do a pretty accomplished set playing covers of Cream, Hendrix and Ten Years After, laying down blues as it's meant to be, mean and moody, unforgiving and raw, along with a sprinkling of sounds from those trans-Atlantic airwaves. John's taken to learning the flute, using one he 'borrowed' from the music department, so a bit of Jethro Tull also surfaces from time to time. He's even got himself a rock star's nickname, 'Tupp', because of his long, fleecy, golden locks. Mike looks like Hendrix with his bushy, Afro hair and Mick plays the drums like he's battering milk bottles into submission.

But, whatever Ralph's intentions, the prospect of being part of a band is an attractive invitation to help me travel to a better place, overdubbing the memories of summer and burying them beneath new layers of experience.

Ralph releases Al from the headlock.

'Sounds good, but I've not picked up my guitar for months.'

Ralph is undeterred. 'Friggin' Hell, Man, you've been livin' the blues so you should have no problem playing it. See you on the seven o'clock train to Sankey tonight. I've set up the first rehearsal at the Young People's Federation.' He casts a critical eye at our scruffy, black blazers. 'And try to look the part when you turn up. Image is everything, Men!'

THREE

Good Lovin' Ain't Easy To Come By
Marvin Gaye and Tammi Terrell. Easy. Tamla Motown.

Since my Mum left home three years ago the house is always
quiet and not particularly welcoming. My Dad usually arrives
home from his shift driving lorries for the crisp factory, has his
tea, lights his pipe, turns on the TV and settles for the night in
his comfy armchair. I usually spend the evenings in my
bedroom. I've grown into this room over the years and jigsaw
pieces of my life fill in the gaps between my bed and a small
wardrobe wedged behind the door. On a shelf next to the
window is disorganised stuff: a few books which are mainly
sport, selections from my pile of Action Comics singled out for
re-reading, football programmes and newspaper cuttings from
United matches. Alongside them are A-level notes scribbled
into various exercise books and copies of *Tess of the
D'Urbervilles, Romeo and Juliet, Macbeth* and *The Oxford
Book Of English Verse.*

Under the bed is a Subbuteo pitch on which Al and I spend
hours playing whole imaginary seasons of fixtures. There's a
huge poster of the crowd from Woodstock pinned to the wall
which serves as an audience when I'm miming away to rock
songs.

Lodged on top of my wardrobe is a Bush record player
accompanied by a neatly arranged collection of LPs, the latest
addition being a second-hand copy of *Electric Ladyland* by
Jimi Hendrix, the cover turned inside out so as not to offend
my Gran when she cleans the room. At the back is my red
Hohner guitar. It stands on top of a copy of *Play In A Day*, a
guitar book by Bert Weedon. Bert doesn't look like a rock star.
On the cover of the book, he wears a smart suit and stands
smiling cheesily from behind a huge electro-acoustic guitar,
looking uncannily like George Butterworth the right wing,
reactionary steward at Widnes Golf Club. Bert's promise of

mastering the guitar in one day had appealed. The book promised to teach me solos, skiffle, Latin American Rhythms and Jazz but 'lack of perseverance and poor concentration' are phrases which crop up regularly on my school reports. Still, I've managed to master all Bert's chord shapes, which allow me to strum along to most of the less demanding rock songs of the day.

I've not done much practice since Lesley packed me in. There's nothing like a broken relationship to slow you down. It takes a while to pick up the pieces again when you've lost those things you enjoyed doing because life was full of excitement, energy and anticipation and you always had that feeling that you were up and running and would never stop.

Suddenly, it's flat with all the meaning wrung out, but slowly it's coming back, and the pinpricks of light are starting to shine through the darkness. I lift the guitar carefully out of the wardrobe. Along the fret board is a thick layer of dust and the strings feel heavy and dull. I play a few chords in the vain hope that the instrument has somehow re-tuned itself during its exile. It sounds awful. Frustrated, I twiddle with the machine heads and shove it into its plastic case.

My band of the moment is Free. They don't collide with your brain like Led Zeppelin, stir up your blues like Cream, or swagger about like the Stones. They sort of shuffle and slide, possessed by Paul Kossoff's tortured guitar, Andy Fraser's mellow bass, and Paul Rodgers' seductive vocals. I flip up the top of the record player and put on *Tons of Sobs* while I sort out some options on dress for the rehearsal. I've been trying to cultivate this Rogers' image for a few weeks now: long hair, ribbed jumper, shrunk to skin tightness, the sleeves ending somewhere between wrist and elbow. Two inches of bare midriff separate the jumper from the top of my blue, flared Wranglers and an old pair of bumpers completes the look. I haven't managed to perfect the raw sexuality of the man, but I can dream.

I head out of the front door carrying the guitar and bump into Bernice who is on her way to her evening shift at the Upton Tavern. She looks at the guitar case quizzically as if her x-ray vision is trying to penetrate the cover and work out the function of the wood, metal, and plastic inside.

'It's a guitar, Bernice. I'm off to rehearse. Forming a band!'

'What?'

'A band! Rock group! I'm the guitarist.'

'Oh, nice?'

She ruffles my hair and heads off down the road walking at a slight angle and squinting into the late evening sun. There's still a small doubt, a nagging worry that the pat on the head was a way for the alien to extract critical information from my brain. Will she turn the corner, slip down a deserted alleyway and return to her hideous, cosmic life form, transmitting information about the fatal flaw in our makeup; that human hearts can easily be split in two, broken by an emotion abandoned during their aeons of evolution. A mysterious destructive force, more powerful than their death-ray guns, sonic vaporisers and anti-matter machines.

Despite this sense of foreboding, I feel good as I stand on Hough Green Station waiting for the train to Sankey. I'm beginning to feel ok about developing a new image and a conversation with Paul Rodgers drifts into my head. It's a few years down the line and we're sharing beers backstage after we've supported Free at the Liverpool Philharmonic.

'Great set, Phil. Where did it all start?'

'Well, Paul, it was three years ago at a church fete in Sankey. There was an A&R man from Island Records in the audience. He signed us up straight away and the rest is history.'

'Love your first album, Man. Kos loves your guitar playing. Who's your chick?'

'Oh, this is Jude. We've been together since it all started.'

The express from Manchester to Liverpool thunders through on the opposite line and snaps me back to reality, but I have a sudden surge of anticipation. On Widnes North Station, the

22

only stop between Hough Green and Sankey, Paul Simon wrote 'Homeward Bound' when, as a young unknown, he'd toured the folk clubs of Northern England. Everyone must have gone through this stage: Hendrix, Kossoff, Clapton, Beck. They'd all carried a guitar seriously somewhere for the first time.

Al arrives at the top of the station approach and he looks the part all right. He's borrowed his sister's cheesecloth blouse and squeezed into his newly-purchased, denim flares. He's washed his hair and, for the first time, it's starting to look really long. He makes a leap onto the platform, striking an exaggerated lead singer pose with his bottle of water serving as a microphone.

'Better not be a bloody waste of time, this. I've got that essay on Macbeth to finish by Wednesday.'

I tell him what I've been thinking.

'Forget it, Man!' he laughs. 'The odds against two adjacent British Rail stations each spawning a world famous pop star must be astronomical. Anyway, you've got zero in common with him.'

'Why?'

'Well, he had a ticket for his destination. You never buy one.'

'Right,' I say, as the train pulls in.

Ralph has boarded the train at the previous stop, Hunts Cross, and on the journey we talk about girls. Rock star bravado has got the better of me and I tell them about Judith.

'You've got no friggin' chance with, Adamson!' Ralph's voice reverberates around the carriage. 'She's untouchable. Normal lookin' guys like us just don't ask girls like her out because we're scared we'll be rejected and ruin our self-image. Girls like her always end up with ugly bastards who haven't got any image to worry about and nothing to lose if they're rejected. Look at the proof! How else would Cher have ended up with Sonny or Jane Birkin with that ugly French get?'

'You're talkin' crap, Man!' says Al. 'Judith Adamson could have anyone in the sixth form.'

'You understand friggin' nothing about female psychology, Morefield,' speaks the voice of five years' experience. 'Girls like Judith don't think they're attractive. Most women think other women are more attractive than them. Most guys set their sights too low and that's why loads of average looking girls don't have any trouble getting boyfriends. The Judiths of this world see all this and start to get worried when nobody asks them out. Then some ugly sod comes along, they say yes out of desperation, and we all sit around feeling pissed off.'

'Guess you and Anne prove the theory, then.'

'Piss off, Stephens. I was friggin' ugly when I was thirteen. I've just grown into my good looks. Shall I ask Anne to put in a word for you?'

'Thanks, but no, I'll do it myself. I'm just waiting for the right moment.'

Al slides down into his carriage seat. 'Ah, the unhappiness of unrequited love, deserving better at the hands of fate.'

'What?'

'You need to do some revision, Man! Chapter 34 of your favourite book, where Retty Priddle and Marian get legless and chuck themselves in the river because they've lost Angel to Tess. Bonnets found floating downstream, all the milkmaids going out of their minds. Mowtownesque melodrama at its best.'

Ralph puts his arm around my shoulder and stares disapprovingly at Al. 'He's over her, Man! Stuff Motown and Tess of the friggin' D'Urbervilles. We're bluesmen heading east and this train is bound for glory.'

24

FOUR

Dreams
Allman Brothers Band. Debut Album. Capricorn Records.

Young People's Federation is based in the church hall down the road from St Mary's. At one end is a small stage, flanked by some tattered, maroon curtains edged in gold. The hall itself is empty except for a few benches, battered canvas chairs, a small snooker table with ripped baize and a table football machine. The latter once sported two proud teams in red and blue strip but countless matches have taken their toll, and the players hang naked from the rusting metal shafts. The ball has been replaced by a giant glass marble which has already broken four of the players' legs.

The three windows high above the entrance allow dusty shafts of late evening sun to fall onto the stage. Almost reverently, they illuminate three large Marshall amplifiers which hum steadily in the grainy light. Next to them is a set of drums. Nothing else can be seen.

From one of the small rooms at the side of the stage, we hear a guitar strumming and girls singing.

'Come on,' says Ralph. 'Let's go and sort the band.'

We head into the small kitchen at the back of the hall. Sat on the floor, strumming his immaculate, Fifties Stratocaster is Ray Williams. He's a small, weedy-looking lad who's a bit of social recluse, spending most of his time perfecting the guitar styles of Muddy Waters and John Lee Hooker.

Jean Taylor and Carol Knowles are cocooned in huge Afghan coats. Turning to us, they deliver the final lines to 'Badge' in perfect harmony, spilling into laughter as Ray sounds off the last chord.

Jean is the sister of John Taylor. Like Tupp, she has long, wavy hair which spirals down and becomes indistinguishable from the fleecy collar of her coat. She shatters my stereotype of Warrington girls and has a cool confidence born out of having an older brother on the threshold of rock stardom. She's planted her musical allegiances firmly within the domain of Led Zeppelin and Deep Purple and she's a rock girl. I'm a bit wary of her because she knows about music and probably sees us as pretenders; a band left behind to replace the ghosts of Colour, playing in front of audiences of fifty or so for a few weeks, getting nowhere, and eventually replaced by the next hopefuls.

She smiles a sort of 'seen it all before' smile.

'How's Tupp, Jean?'

'You mean John, Phil.' She reprimands me with her eyes. 'He's fine. Really fine! In fact, he's back in Liverpool doing a gig next Monday. I've got some tickets if you're interested.'

Ralph's eyes light up. He wraps his arm around her taking the three tickets which are on offer.

'Smart,' he says. 'It'll be good to see the competition.'

Jean reaches into her bag and pulls out a crumpled photograph which shows a number of figures standing around a large, white Comma van. She tells us it was taken a couple of weeks ago in Bolton when Ibex had to honour some bookings which were arranged before they went to London.

It's a good picture. Apart from Tupp, Mick and Mike, there are another eleven people on it but I don't recognise most of them. There are two old school mates, Geoff Higgins and Ken Testi, next to five girls who are a year ahead of Widnes fashions. There's no denim or cheesecloth, just long, kaftan tops and trousers which are colourful, straight-legged or tight-waisted, ballooning out into huge flares. The guys are trying to look cool and there's one at the front wearing an eye-patch looking like Johnny Kidd. Tupp stands on the right. He's not wearing any shoes, and neither is the girl on the left who's next to a guy with his arm around her shoulder.

Jean tells us it's their new singer, Freddie, who they've picked up in London. He looks different to the others and wears a white, granddad shirt, and a pair of stylish trousers, with a belt tied at a loose angle across the bottom of his shirt.

27

Jean says John's glad he's arrived in the band as it means he doesn't have to sing and he can concentrate on bass and the borrowed flute.

The flute was a personal possession of Arthur Berry, our music master. We know him as 'Pom Pom'. He's a character. Unlike other masters, who use their capes as protection from the clouds of chalk dust, Pom Pom uses his as an aid to defy gravity, sweeping gently around the room like a daintier Zorro, swirling his cape in perfect time to the rise and fall of the great symphonies.

In our final lesson in the fifth year, he was in full flow, pompoming the Toreador's Song by Bizet when his eye caught the empty space by the side of the music cupboard. He was thrown, and his tempo went all out of time. He did a few more off-beat poms, checking again to see if it had magically reappeared before the grim realisation it was missing caused a final pom to slip out of his open mouth. But the flute had gone, into the arms of Tupp, for him to dexterously tease out the notes of Jethro Tull's 'Bouree', captivating his audience, and building his musical credibility.

I stare at the photo. It's not an image; it's how they really are. They're a band on the road and, even though we're at the point of forming a group, I feel a bit of a cheat. This is my first real go at stepping out into a new identity, with our band giving it some credibility, but I'm not sure I want to turn it into a way of life.

My worry though is the Shakespearian cauldron of Ronnie's world. It bubbles hisses and spits around in my head inviting me to peer into its depths, presenting me with the frightening prophecy that I'll be clawed back from my dreams to become a passenger for life on his red, Leyland PD2 cruising the bus routes of Widnes.

The main door opens and then closes with a mighty slam which echoes across the hall. A familiar figure enters the kitchen. Al and I exchange glances.

'Is this fuckin' it then?'

It's Dave Shuttleworth. He's older than us and left school two years ago. He plays the drums for any local band who'll give him work and most of the time leads a nocturnal existence going straight from a gig into his early morning milk round which he's taken over from Mick Smith.

Dave doesn't give us a second glance. 'Let's Go, Ralph!' He's impatient, jittery and creates the impression he's living on the edge, tapping out the moments of his life in complicated rhythms. He looks like he hasn't been to bed for a week. 'I've got a shedload of milk to pick up in three hours.'

I sense a slight shift of who is in charge. I'd assumed the band was Ralph's and that the garden party was just going to be a bit of a laugh. Dave has added an edge. He's not the sort of guy who takes well to direction, particularly if things aren't going his way, and he constantly has that demonic Keith Moon look in his eyes.

Ralph swigs a bottle of Coke in one, wipes his mouth with the back of his sleeve, and continues. 'We've got four songs to try out: 'Roll Over Beethoven' to get the place rockin', 'I'm So Glad' because that's the message Christians are always pushing, and a slow blues version of 'Eve Of Destruction' to add a bit of religious reflection for the audience to take away.'

'Isn't 'Eve of Destruction' a bit miserable for an autumn fair?' says Al.

'No, Des believes it'll be a suitable warning to all his parishioners who are straying from the path. And he loves the message; says it reminds him of the massive job he's got staving off the evils of the decade and possibly preparing thousands of us for premature entry through the Pearly Gates. He thinks it'll remind everyone that if they don't get their act together, take up praying and follow Jesus, they're all fucked.'

He hands me a piece of paper with the chords on. 'You'll be ok with these, Phil, mostly A, E and G with a few sevenths and minors.' He sees the look on my face. 'I've drawn them out for you. Let's go.'

'There are only three songs here, Ralph. You said four.'

'Oh yeh,' adds Ralph sheepishly. 'We're doing 'Toad' as well, so Dave can do his drum solo.'

'Toad' is my least favourite track on *Fresh Cream*. It rightly comes last on side two after the uplifting 'I'm So Glad' and is written by drummer Ginger Baker, for Ginger Baker, designed to thrust him into the spotlight for five excruciating minutes. Clapton and Bruce start playing and then fade away leaving Ginger to drum like some demented road warrior before they jump back in to rescue the song from exploding into oblivion with a few final bars easing it back into something resembling musical sobriety.

'Toad's an instrumental?' says Al. 'What do I do in that?'

'Just strut around a bit, Man. All the best front men strut. You can jump into the crowd and be carried off in a wave of hysteria down to the cake stall.'

Dave has walked off into the hall. I take Ralph aside. 'Why a drum solo? It'll go on for bloody yonks.'

'No choice, Man. He wouldn't come if he couldn't do it, egocentric bastard that he is.' He looks in Dave's direction. 'We can just leave him to it. We'll put some towels around our necks like all cool guitarists and piss off backstage. I'll bring some cans.'

I'm not convinced. Dave is the sort of guy other guys really hate. He's ugly, his hair is greasy and unshaped, and his skin is a battleground with acne. Despite these physical aberrations, he is somehow attractive to girls. Not just a few girls, but all girls. If you are with your girlfriend in his presence, you have an air of unease, a suspicion that if your back is turned, she'll be riding off on his milk float into the sunset. Al and I have come to the conclusion that mutant bacteria from the bottom of dirty milk bottles have given him some sort of hormonal aroma which masks his ugliness and sparks off sexual feelings in females. He is the ultimate 'ugly get' of Ralph's cop-off philosophy yet every girl he meets seems to fancy him, even Anne.

He exudes power, which is part of his attractiveness. He's short, stocky, plays the drums aggressively, and drives his milk float like Stirling Moss. While other teenagers aspire to scooters, Honda 50s or old Cortinas, Dave turns up for dates in his milk float, the bottles cleared from the deck and replaced by a mattress complete with pillows and sheets. This mobile four poster can often be seen disappearing down country lanes around Sankey with the phrase, 'Your Milkman Comes Daily' displayed ominously on the roof.

'Ok, Men,' enthuses Ralph, 'We'll start with, 'Roll Over Beethoven' 'cos it's the easiest and we've not played together before. Al's got the words, Phil you just play the background rhythm, I'll play bass and Ray will follow me with the lead. Let's go!'

Without looking up Dave hits the drums and a steady beat fills the room. 'When you're bleedin' ready!' he shouts over the noise. I hit the opening chord in time with the drumming, and we're off.

An hour later we've knocked it into shape. Al was in good voice and Ray's lead playing masked over my odd clumsy chord change. There's no time to continue, Dave is getting twitchy about his milk round, so we finish early and agree to meet in a few days' time to give the other three songs a go.

Ray heads home and the three of us make for Sankey Station.

'Where is Anne, anyway?' I ask Ralph. They are usually inseparable outside school hours.

'At the Upton Tavern with her mates, Man. We'll just make last orders.'

The Tavern stands overlooking fields at the end of a long lane of Thirties housing on the urban fringes of the town. It's a cosy place split into two halves with the bar on the left and the lounge to the right of the front door. We never go in the lounge, it's full of people my Mum's age, and it doesn't allow

31

jeans, so we pack into the bar filling the spaces around the small, hammered copper tables.

Predictably, for a Monday night, it's empty apart from Anne and her three friends drinking lager at the end of the lounge. Bernice stares blankly out from behind the bar her false eye glinting in the half-light while her other focuses on her nails which she's filing nonchalantly.

'Three pints of Guinness, love.' Ralph's command draws her reluctantly from her bar stool and without saying anything she arranges three glasses and sets the pumps in motion.

Ralph turns his back to the bar. 'Strange one there.' He rolls his eyes back in Bernice's direction.

'My next door neighbour,' I say. 'She's probably an alien.'

'From Runcorn?' says Al.

'Andromeda, round the back of The Milky Way. The alien's inside. That's Bernice's shell. The body-snatchers have her.'

Bernice plants three pints on the bar. 'Six bob!' She fixes Ralph with a myopic stare.

Ralph pulls a ten shilling note from his jeans.

'Live long and prosper!' Bernice gives him a quizzical stare which slowly turns into a smile.

'Oooh! Ta very much!' She places the ten shilling note in the till, takes the change, and drops it into the staff tips jar.

'Shit,' says Ralph. 'Can either of you lend me the train fare to Hunts Cross?'

We head over to the girls. Anne's friends are all members of the chaperone party and presumably have followed mine and Lesley's troubled romance over the summer.

Al chats comfortably to the girls. I envy his Geordie accent. He is attractive enough as it is but the added mystery of coming from the north and the fact he has no history in the school, give him a bit of romantic intrigue which draws girls to him. I sit on the edge of the conversations until Anne breaks away and plants herself on the seat beside me.

'Ok, Phil? Sorry to hear about you and Lesley.'

'Yeh, you're losing your touch as a matchmaker.' I smile at Anne. She looks back at me sympathetically, her soft brown eyes and pale features framed by the waves of her blonde hair. Five years of going steady make her look older and wiser than her eighteen years. She is definitely off-limits and, as far as I know, they have both remained faithful to each other since they met at the third year Christmas party in 1964 when Ralph literally swept her off her feet and carried her screaming and giggling over his shoulder, out of the school hall, and onto the bus home.

I think about Ralph's attraction to Lisa Wilcox. Maybe the first splinters are beginning to appear and the boredom is starting to menacingly creep in without Anne knowing. How long does it take to get over a five-year relationship? Neither of them has felt the first ice of rejection. I hate breaking up, all that stability, trust and sharing obliterated, preceded by the awkward silences which creep into conversations and a hand unoffered as you walk home together.

'She wasn't for you.' Anne reaches over and takes my hand. I suddenly realise what a length of time four months can be. We've all got older. The last of those summer holidays when you know things will carry on the same into a new school year has gone.

'We can talk whenever you want to.'

'What about?'

It's a stupid thing to say but Anne's remark has thrown me slightly. We're good friends but I only ever speak to her through Ralph. We've never spent serious time together. Chatting to her in the pub with Ralph's ever dominating presence a rugby tackle away is as close as we get.

'Things,' she whispers and releases her hand.

'Watch it, Stephens,' jokes Ralph. 'No snoggin' else you're a dead man.' He downs his Guinness in one. 'Your round, Man. We've a train to catch in thirty minutes.'

33

I can see the charcoal-grey outline of the engine, clouded in steam, as it labours up the line from Sankey. Ralph emerges from his goodnight wrestling with Anne.

'Big P. Can you walk Anne home and get the last bus from Widnes. She went to see *The Cremator* with her mates last night and doesn't want to walk past the cemetery in the dark on her own.'

I look across at Anne who is putting on a vulnerable look from back in the shadows.

The train heaves into the station drowning any further conversation and, in an explosion of steam, Ralph and Al disappear into a carriage.

I walk out through the waiting room with Anne. She links me and huddles close because of the cold. I pray we'll meet Lesley and Curtis on their way back from a soul night. I want Lesley to see me with someone who is the antithesis of a soul girl. I want to see the look in her eye as she realises she's no longer part of my life and been replaced by a different kind of girl, but the streets are empty and cold with just the two of us braving the wind as we head for Anne's house.

'You made it up about the film.'

'I need to ask you something, Phil. Do you think Ralph is ok?'

It's a pointed question, and I know what's coming, but I have no proof Ralph is going to make a move for Lisa. I mean lads always look at other girls when they're going out with someone. It's just how lads are. It doesn't follow that they're going to ditch their girl and run off with the next one who comes along.

'Yeh. He's fine. Why?'

Anne pulls me around and looks me in the eye. 'What do you know about Lisa Wilcox?'

I don't know anything about Lisa Wilcox except that she's beautiful, confident, aloof, a religious nutcase and, if Ralph's girl philosophy is right, she'll end up dating the ugliest boy in

Sankey. I only have a brief admission from Ralph that he finds her attractive. But we all do. It means nothing.

But Anne is a girl. Girls know, according to my cousin, Babs. Anne knows, but I can't think where the information has come from or whether she's just an expert at reading between the lines.

I take a deep breath and the cold air clears my head. 'Look, he wants to impress people at the concert, and I think Lisa will be there, so I guess he just wants to look good on stage to.... well, impress people who are there....like Lisa, I suppose....and others who might be there.'

Anne's male-to-female meaning translator kicks off in her head and she knows exactly what I've meant. Then I say something completely and utterly stupid. I don't know if it's a diversionary tactic or whether I mean it.

'If you and Ralph ever split up would you perhaps, well, maybe, come out for a drink with me.'

'Why would we split up?'

It's a moment where I realise how stupid I've been and how smart girls are and the best thing is to shut up. I shrug my shoulders, probably looking pathetic. I just want to see Anne home, get back to my bedroom and close the door, but it's also thrown Anne a bit. It's the first time in five years anyone has asked her for a date, even if it's an advance booking for something which probably won't happen.

'You're just getting over Lesley,' she says. 'It takes time.' We are outside her house. She gives me a quick hug and heads up the drive

FIVE

Gimme Shelter
The Rolling Stones. Let It Bleed. Decca Records.

Tommy Branaghan is a gunslinger with his finger permanently on the trigger ready for the next shoot-out. He's Wade Deacon's Man In Black, lurking in the shadowy outposts of the toilets, bike sheds and changing rooms waiting to ambush his next victim and satisfy his lust for blood and revenge.

There are five reasons why you'll become one of his victims:

1. He thinks you are laughing at him.
2. He thinks you are talking about him.
3. You won't share your sweets/cigs/homework or money with him.
4. You make accidental eye contact with him.
5. You can't answer the question, 'Who are you lookin' at?' satisfactorily.

The wrong answers being:

a. Nothin' much! (You are insulting him.)
b. What's it got to do with you? (You are challenging him.)
c. Why? (You are getting cocky.)

We're in the form room. Tommy's returned for another year, like an annoying complaint you can't get rid of. He's got no interest in pursuing any academic career. The main focus of his life, apart from beating people up and organising the protection racket he runs for the first years, is working in Karalius' Scrapyard after school, straightening out bits of copper and metal while the rest of us are trying to unravel Hardy and Shakespeare. Still, it's good news for the First XV, if he can keep his temper. Last year he was sent off six times, twice for threatening masters who were refereeing.

He'd not materialised for the first few days but, depressingly, he's back in his corner of the form room, dressed in his fading uniform, tainting the atmosphere like a toxic, grey cloud. Tommy can't get through a day without taking an illogical dislike to someone and, spotting a group of fifth years in the corridor, he leaves his mates in mid-conversation, wades through the desks and chairs, drags open the door and disappears. Almost instantly, a blurred, grey shape shoots back into the form room, hits an upturned desk, and sinks in a crumpled heap onto the floor. Tommy strikes a John Wesley Harding pose across the door frame looking down at a fifth year who lies at his feet and, almost as an afterthought, delivers a kick between the already stricken lad's thighs.

Nobody speaks. Tommy's victim gets to his feet using one hand to support himself against the wall and the other to staunch the flow of blood still coming from his mouth. Some classmates help him out of the room and pull the door shut. Only bright red spots on the polished oak floor and smeared, bloody handprints along the wall remain as evidence of the incident.

There is a minute's silence before one of the First XV speaks.

'What was up with him, Tommy?'

'Looked at my bird on the bus this morning,' he mumbles, adding to the list of things not to do in his presence. With that, he pushes the desks out of the way with one foot and ambles over to the window where he proceeds to drop slimy missiles of spit onto some third years who have gathered underneath.

After a few minutes, the common room door opens. The noise level in the room drops and fades to silence.

'Good morning fellows.'

It's the voice of William Arthur Bonney, our headmaster, known to everyone as the WAB. In a changing world, he's managed to keep the school firmly rooted in the values of the

Thirties. Demobbed from the R.A.F. in 1945, he went straight into teaching, and now he circles the corridors of Wade Deacon, the heavy tread of his brogues an instant warning for bullies to stop bullying and for staff to fear anything within their classrooms which might bring him displeasure.

He is scrupulously fair. If you do your best and play the game of life in the best traditions of the school, this is enough for the WAB. The sight of him striding up and down the touchline on a Saturday morning, his black cloak flowing around his wiry frame, and his steel-blue eyes lighting at every tackle won and point scored, is enough to drive every boy to find an extra yard of pace and strain muscle and sinew to new limits. Then, over the weekend, there will be the hope that, on Monday morning, a chance encounter on a lonely corridor might result in the ultimate accolade. 'Well done, old boy! You were a credit to the school.'

'Old Branaghan, you have an appointment in my office at break.'

'Sir,' grumbles Tommy. There is no defence against the WAB's commands.

The WAB scans the room, presumably to check for other miscreants hiding in its dusty corners, turns briskly, and like The Lone Ranger, is gone.

Tommy reclaims his place on the window ledge where he sits muttering never to be revealed threats against the WAB. Mugga McKenzie assumes command of the troop of rugby players who have resumed indulging in the kind of behaviour which would send homophobic shock waves through their jock straps had anyone outside the First XV dared to indulge in the touching, hugging and groping which is a traditional part of their post-summer male bonding.

Mugga is Tommy's right-hand man. He is the clown half of the double act; a stooge without brains. 'The most consistent academic achiever in the school,' the WAB had called him after he'd failed all his O-levels at the third attempt and, while he lacks the maliciousness of Tommy, he is still a danger to himself and others.

Towards the end of the previous term, he'd found a role model in Sandro Mazzola, the Italian centre-forward who had starred for his country in the 1968 European Championships. Mugga's reason is not subtle as they bear an uncanny resemblance. Both are of short, stocky build with close-cut, wiry hair, swarthy complexions and rugged features. Sandro, who was born and brought up in Northern Italy, has a cast iron genetic excuse for his appearance. The reason why Mugga, whose ancestry should be easily traced to the town's Anglo-Saxon past, came by his looks, must be rooted in the days before the Mersey silted up and cargo ships from the Mediterranean made it as far as Widnes Docks.

I thought the love affair with Sandro might have faded over the holidays, but I am wrong. Prising a white 'Frido' football out of his shoulder bag, he announces to the class that that we are having 'a game of Mazzola' before Don Hutchinson, our form tutor, arrives. I have witnessed several of these games before. They are based on the star's forte of arriving at blistering pace in the opposition penalty area and flinging himself horizontally to bullet an unstoppable header past a hapless goalie.

Almost before the image has turned over in my mind, the game is in motion. Mugga, who has a problem pronouncing his 'F's, announces, unsurprisingly, that he will be 'Puckin' Mazzola'. The diminutive Widge Wilkinson has been chosen to be the keeper, standing, quivering like a sacrificial goat in front of the blackboard on which Tommy has chalked an enormous white goalmouth.

Mugga is already at the far end of the classroom, his face glistening, shouting instructions to Tommy as to exactly where he wants the first cross to land. As I blink, Mugga is off, pounding down the aisle like a Pamplona bull. The rest of the form crouch behind desks and I say a silent prayer for Widge, which seems to be answered, as Mugga arrives a fraction too late sending the ball from the top his head vertically into one of the Perspex lampshades which hangs from the form room ceiling. Sharp, white splinters rain onto Mugga's head as he looks across at his winger.

'Puck, me, Tommy! Get it right next time.'

It's a sign of Mugga's place in the hierarchy that he can mildly criticise Tommy without an immediate threat to his physical well-being and ten minutes later the game is over, the shattered remains of the lampshade and Widge's glasses are kicked under the desks at the back of the form room.

The door opens and a young man, looking not much older than ourselves, wanders in carrying a smart leather briefcase and heads for the raised podium at the front of the classroom. He wears no black, dusty gown and has a stylish checked shirt with no tie. He is jacketless and, after placing his briefcase on the desk, has both hands free as opposed to one brandishing a cane. His dark-red, corduroy trousers are of the sort Al and I had coveted when we were last shopping in Liverpool.

'Ok, lads, settle into your desks. I'm Mr Rothwell and I'll be taking over from Mr Hutchinson who's tutoring 5 Gamma from now on.'

The rugby team moves as a pack into their seats at the back of the room. Ralph is the exception. He stays with me and Al and fires a question at the new master.

'Are you a teacher, Sir?'

'Hope so! My first week here. I'm the new Art and Drama master. Now settle down and I'll take the register.'

As our names are called out I glance across at Mugga who is dripping sweat onto the desktop. A thought enters my mind that maybe the WAB's appointment of a new Arts teacher might be part of an ingenious educational strategy to accommodate the Muggas of this world outside the academic curriculum.

There's no doubt he has a certain artistic streak. It was back in the third year when he introduced us to the possibilities of creative landscape photography. He'd been given a Polaroid

40

camera for Christmas and produced an original self-portrait, snapped outdoors, against the backdrop of a brilliant blue sky.

All that appeared in the frame was his penis, protruding upwards towards one passing cloud. Had the wobbly phallus had a bowler hat balanced on top, it would have given a passing imitation of a Magritte painting, and there was much debate as to how he'd achieved such a perfect perpendicular while struggling with the controls of his camera. None of us wanted to believe that Miss Jennings, the school nurse, had assisted him, as he had actually boasted.

'Right, before you head off, I'm giving you advance notice of the sixth form drama group which I'm setting up jointly with the girls' school. It's Friday evenings, 4.30 until 6.30, in their hall. First meeting this week. I'm leaving some leaflets on the table. If you're interested fill in your details and drop them in at the staff room. And you rugby mob at the back! Clear that mess off the floor before first period.'

'Not our mess, Sir.'

'Didn't say it was your mess, Branaghan, but there won't be a trace by the time I'm back this afternoon. Have a good morning, lads.' He picks up his briefcase and sweeps swiftly and confidently out of the room.

Ralph's eyes light up. He quickly picks up all the leaflets, stuffing them into his jacket pocket.

'Friggin' great news. You know what this means.'

Al and I look at him blankly.

'We're gonna be rock existentialists, just the three of us. Wade Deacon's answer to the Velvet Underground.'

Mugga has been listening to our conversation and edges towards us, stepping over Widge who is on his hands and knees picking up the sharp shards and dropping them into a waste bin. As he draws level with us he thrusts his hand into Ralph's blazer pocket and pulls out one of the crumpled leaflets.

He screws his eyes, struggling to make out the message now camouflaged by several creases.

41

'Puckin' drama! I'm puckin' good at that, me.'

'It'll be full,' says Al.

'Yeh, full of puckin' birds.' He turns and, bursting into a chorus of 'Tossing and Turning' by the Ivy League, performs an exaggerated pelvic thrust in the direction of the girls' school.

SIX

Bad Moon Rising
Creedence Clearwater Revival. Green River. Liberty Records.

We're in William Eric Gleave's after school, art workshop. We like to refer to him as the WEG, continuing our tradition of affectionately naming masters by their acronyms. We've got a few minutes before he arrives and we need a name for the band before tonight's rehearsal. Ralph's scrabbling through the WEG's library trying to draw inspiration from names hiding in the colourful pages of art history.

'We need a bit of mystery and magnetism.' He's thumbing through an old volume on the Pre-Raphaelites. 'What about something like *Dante's Dream* or *Light Of The World?*'

'Too psychedelic, Man,' says Al. 'We need something more earthy, gritty, a name that echoes our roots. This is the creative hub of the school. Keep your ears open and if anything grabs you write it down.'

The WEG enters. He is our crisp, groomed man about the classroom, a suitor to style, our very own John-Paul Belmondo. He doesn't actually engage in teaching as such. His approach is more that of a knowledgeable tour guide from the Louvre, taking his time to plant artistic seeds of knowledge into our fledgling brains and water them with occasional showers of creative critiques about his life, the great artists or, in today's case, Miss Elder, subject of the life drawing class. She's about to sit naked for a full hour while we try to replicate the female form hampered by hot sweats and shaking fingers.

We've not met Miss Elder before; this is an extravagance provided by the WEG for those of us he considers capable of getting good A-Level grades. As usual, we have a briefing during which he lights a cigarette before puffing his way around the studio, checking we have the correct pencils and paper onto which will appear dramatic sketches teased from our minds by his subtle glances and asides. The small thin

Capstan is a disappointment. A cheroot, or at the very least, a pastel-coloured Balkan Sobranie, would complement his air of scholarly sophistication.

Miss Elder is in her mid-40s and enters the room draped in a bright blue kimono that clings to her body, giving the impression that she is hiding a full set of secondhand Dunlop tyres somewhere in its folds. With difficulty, she reclines on the chaise longue before letting the kimono drop slowly from her body revealing the challenge for the following sixty minutes. A dozen pairs of eyes peer in disappointment from over the tops of the easels taking in the rippling waves of flesh shimmering in the fluorescent light.

Ralph sighs with dismay and pushes back on his chair, arms dangling by his side, pencil angled towards the floor.

I decide to make a start but Ralph reaches across and grips my arm.

'Give it time to settle, Man, otherwise, your perspective will be all wrong.'

Miss Elder strikes an affected pose, tossing her hair across her shoulder.

'We could do with some props, Mr Gleave.'

'Could we Miss Elder?'

'Yes Mr Gleave, They've got a barrel and a fishing basket at the Tech.'

'Have they Miss Elder?'

'Yes, Mr Gleave. I can do wonders with a fishing basket.'

'I bet you can Miss Elder.'

'You don't offer a girl much, Mr Gleave. You don't by chance have some drapes, a pedestal or a few remnants of cloth residing in the stockroom?'

The negotiations are interrupted by the WAB who enters the room with a well-practised flourish. The WEG self-consciously conceals his cigarette, curling his hand around it and dropping his arm behind his back.

'Old Gleave, I was wondering when you might have the posters done for the PTA barn dance next month.'

The WEG hovers on the balls of his feet almost leaning deferentially in the WAB's direction. From behind we can see the smoke from his cigarette travelling up the inside sleeve of his suit and reappearing at his collar creating a Da Vinciesque halo in the sunshine slanting through the windows.

'They'll be ready by the end of the week Headmaster.'

'Jolly good, thank you.' He turns to leave the room, pauses dramatically, and peers back over his shoulder. 'By the way Old Gleave, you appear to be on fire.'

The WEG exits into the stockroom to soak his burning hand in the clearing-up sink.

'Not much to go on,' says Al. Pedestal? Fishing Basket? Remnants is ok, it gives a washed up feeling of the salvaged pieces of some once-great entity. I can see the three of us on the front of the album cover, stumbling up a deserted beach silhouetted against a blue, triple sunset, having escaped from some apocalyptic nightmare.'

The WEG returns, his hand wrapped in an old, soggy tea towel.

'If you don't have any props, would it be possible to open the curtains, Mr Gleave? They like to do that at the Tech, it creates a kind of luminescent ambience.'

'I'm sorry Miss Elder. Mr Bonney insists they remain closed to protect those outside from temptation. The loss of the school window cleaner was a considerable blow. I believe he's still awaiting his summons from Widnes Magistrates Court.'

'Such a pity Mr Gleave, my folds and curves are enhanced when naturally bathed in moonshine.'

'I think you mean moon light, Miss Elder.' He turns around and addresses us quietly.

'The last time I encountered moonshine was in a small American bar near the Sorbonne, Paris, 1968. Oh, quelle nuit. Carry on boys.'

Two hours later we're back at YPF for our second rehearsal. 'Moonshine' has approval from Ray but Dave is already distancing himself from the rest of us. He thinks he's a professional, which I suppose he is, as he gets a few quid for playing around the pubs and clubs, and Anne is here, sitting on an old, battered chair next to the stage, isolating herself from Ralph.

We perform three of the songs reasonably well. Al's in good voice and has made the tambourine his own, even managing to beat it in time with the drums and avoid upsetting Dave, but there's tension in the air. Even though Lisa's not here, she's stirring the atmosphere which is getting thicker with every twist and turn of Dave's drumsticks. Now we're playing the intro to 'Toad', and it's slow. Dave is getting impatient. I can't understand his rantings about time signature and beat, and it's got to the point where Ralph has had enough.

'Why do pissing drummers always think the whole fuckin' band revolves around them?'

'This fuckin' band does,' spits Dave. 'I'm holding it together and carrying the rhythm section. You're playing too fast and Phil is half a beat behind.'

Ralph takes offence and slams his bass on the floor, making a grinding sound of discordant notes.

'If you're so bleedin' brilliant you don't need to hassle us, do you? Piss off and we'll rehearse on our own. We don't play in your friggin' drum solo anyway, so sod off.'

Being an egocentric, arrogant bastard, Dave doesn't usually react to any sort of verbal onslaught but, on this occasion, he grabs his drumsticks and kicks over his snare. It joins Ralph's bass in a tangled heap on the floor, and he disappears into the kitchen, slamming the door like a final drumbeat.

'Dickhead!' Ralph picks up his bass and catches Anne's eye. She's been sitting there, arms folded since we started the rehearsal two hours ago, and her look registers to Ralph that she's had enough. She rolls her eyes to the ceiling, snaps into life, and follows Dave through into the kitchen. We play on, thrashing out the beginning of 'Toad' up to the point where the guitars break off and we leave the stage. We have no idea how long Dave wants to drum for. Presumably, he'll give us some sort of cue to return and we'll finish the song with a few power chords. We've had enough and decide to head off to the station.

Ralph goes into the kitchen to get Anne. There's a gap of about ten seconds before I hear shouting and scuffling and the heavy thud of a body being manoeuvred against a door. It bursts open and Dave shoots backwards, losing his footing against the discarded snare drum and falling clumsily onto the floor. There's more shouting inside the room before Anne emerges, backing away from Ralph as if she's dealing with a caged animal.

'Just, fuck off, Ralph!' I've never heard Anne swear before but the words are spat out bitterly and undoubtedly meant. 'We're fucking finished, Ok! Don't come near me again.'

She helps Dave from the floor and they leave arm in arm.

Nobody speaks much on the train. I gaze into the blackness between Sankey and Widnes, straining to see the lights of Dave's milk float, but realising he probably has the arrogance to drive along with them switched off to save power. There is blackness. All I can see is the glazed reflection of the rest of the carriage. It's our own Phantom Zone; the place in Superman where criminals are sent to float around until they've served their time. I can just about make out three two-dimensional figures, one staring blankly out, one dozing, and one sitting back thoroughly pissed off with life. The phantom Ralph turns and stares back at me from outside the carriage, his face occasionally obliterated by flashing street lights and housing estates, but instantly returning, gazing through the glass as if pleading to be freed from his oppression. As we pass through the darkness towards Hough Green Station two of the phantoms rise. They utter an almost inaudible, 'See ya!' to the remaining phantom before alighting from the still moving train, onto the platform, and drifting, released from their twilight world, up the bright slopes of the station approach.

'Typical band stuff,' says Al. 'Nothing to do with musical differences. Chick trouble within the group. We should only get to this stage after years of drinking, drug taking, hotel-wrecking and mind-sapping tour schedules. Perhaps we'll split up and then re-form.'

'Bit hard to re-form when we haven't even really formed.'

'I suppose it'll be ok. All the best bands have a violent streak. The Kinks are always fighting and Ginger Baker and Jack Bruce hate each other. It's a sort of bonding thing, especially if their blood mingles while they're leathering each other. Oh yeh, and I forgot, Ralph gave me these.' He pulls out the tickets for Tupp's gig on Monday. 'Be good to see how a real band pulls together.'

'Where's it at?'

'Sink Club in Hardman Street. Isn't that where you and Lesley used to hang out?'

I can hear the express from Liverpool thundering down the slope from Hunt's Cross and my first thought is to take my ticket, shred it into pieces, and hurl it from the railway bridge as the train roars underneath, watching it swirl and disintegrate in the passing vortex. But it wouldn't be the act of a person who is moving on, so I sigh reflectively and stuff it into my pocket.

'Yeh, we went there a few times. A bit of a soul dive No atmosphere.'

'Ralph says we're meeting up with the band for a drink first. And they're bringing the new singer Jean mentioned, Freddie somebody or other. Strange name! Sounds foreign, so he'll probably be crap. All the best frontmen are English.'

SEVEN

All I Have To Do Is Dream
Bobbie Gentry and Glen Campbell. Single Release. Capitol Records.

I'm glad to get to Friday and the last lesson of the week with Kenny Walker, the tyrannical head of Latin and Greek. He's actually Adolf Hitler. Instead of dying in the bunker he slipped down a secret passage, shaved off his moustache, nicked a de-mob suit from a local charity shop and applied to be taken on at Wade Deacon. Most lessons are terrifying ordeals, or entertaining cameos, depending on how much whisky he's drunk, but it's guaranteed that in each lesson one of us will be beaten by the thick, wooden stick he keeps lodged in his sweaty armpit.

Today it's Widge's turn to draw the short straw. As I dream of rock stardom on the back row, Kenny is caning him for not knowing the complete pluperfect tense of some obscure Latin verb before retiring back to his desk, the heavy burden of a week's drinking and thirty-nine periods of Latin weighing heavily upon him.

Seconds later he's snoring at his desk and we've all pulled out *NME*s or *Football Monthlies*, leaving our Latin dictionaries within grabbing distance should Kenny wake from some Caligulan nightmare. I find a full page spread of Mama Cass and draw a line down her flowing white smock from her cleavage to her moccasin saddles. I decide to review the last few months and scribble 'Achievements' across her right breast and 'Ambitions' across her left. There is plenty of room.

Achievements.

1. Got over the trauma of breaking up with Lesley?

The question mark is added because I'm not entirely sure it's true, but for now it stays firmly scribbled and underlined. Now I'm stuck. I haven't achieved anything else, so I move across to ambitions.

Ambitions.

1. Work out a way of asking Judith for a date. Manipulate fate to prove Al and Thomas Hardy wrong.

2. Rid my room of all memories connected with Lesley. Bin 'Ain't Nothing Like The Real Thing'. Rip months of June, July and August out of my diary.

This will be hard, but it has to be done. I might need Al's help here. Maybe it could happen before a Subbuteo match, a rapturous celebration from the crowd as the teams enter the arena, with the torn fragments of our relationship fluttering like ticker-tape down onto the lush, green surface. Then they could be swept away under the bed and hoovered up with the dust and debris when my room is cleaned ready for a bright new beginning.

3. Solve the riddle of Bernice forever.

I know I've grown out of it but there's this nagging doubt that I need to exorcise. If the worst comes to the worst and she is cocooned in a pod in her dad's shed, then I'll find fame as the first human to make intergalactic contact and Widnes will be the new Roswell.

4. Practise guitar and image.

I've got to develop these hand in hand. I need to learn five new chords before the next rehearsal, and I need to look like a bluesman. My Paul Rodgers image is ok, but a new Wrangler jacket would be good; short, tight-waisted, with the sleeves turned over once, ending just below the elbow, top pockets full of stuff, like cigarettes and dope. But I don't smoke and, although I've experimented with dope, it's not really for me, so it'll have to be plectrums, chewing gum and a comb, which are all ok.

5. Join Drama Group

It's Ralph's idea but it'll be part of the healing process and drama is all about self-discovery and building confidence which I could do with at the moment.

The bell rings. Kenny is still asleep. As we file quietly past him, Mugga lifts his gown and folds it back over his head, covering the sleeping master in a black shroud. The end of the gown is spread out in front and Mugga with the daring of Mucius Scaevola thrusting his hand into the flame, carefully arranges twenty copies of *Cassell's Latin Dictionary* along the edge of the gown securing Kenny's head in a tight, black cocoon. Silently he ushers everyone out of the room and slams the classroom door with enough force to wake Somnus from his slumbers. From inside there's a muffled yelp and a noise like a desperate animal trying to avoid suffocation followed by the rumble of the pile of Latin dictionaries tumbling to the floor. Tommy and Mugga leg it down the corridor snorting with laughter. Al and I side-step into the library to lay low.

'What can I do for you, gentleman?'

It's the voice of our English master, Dr Bailey. A year or so ago he'd left his house to post a letter but on the way to the postbox his eyesight had failed and he'd stumbled back home clutching gates and garden walls for guidance. For most teachers, it would have been the end of the line, but the WAB had persuaded him to stay on fearing his academic prowess would have been too much for the school to lose. Now he teaches only the sixth form using an ingenious machine; a

Braille textbook contraption onto which roles of books are loaded. As the Doc reads in class he advances the book by turning the handle on the barrel. The book passes through his fingers and trails out onto the floor ready to be re-wound at the end of the session. It's worked well apart from, on one occasion, when it unravelled close to Mugga's feet. He'd taken a metal compass out of his blazer and stabbed holes in the first four pages changing the beginning of Macbeth forever.

'It's Stephens and Morefield, Sir. We've just got half an hour. Then we're going over to the girls' school to join the Drama group.'

'Ah, Mr Rothwell,' sighs the Doc. 'He has some absorbing interpretations of what Drama actually is.' He raises his face from the machine staring at us blankly with empty eyes. 'You have acted in our plays before, Stephens. Morefield, you have not had the pleasure of treading our boards.'

The Doc is referring to the last play produced by the school when, before he became sightless, he'd directed a production of *Androcles and The Lion* in which I'd had a walk-on part as a hideous Etruscan mask man.

'It was only a small part, Sir.'

'There are no small parts only small actors!' roars the Doc. 'Stanislavski! Have you heard of him?'

We both shake our heads but then realise the Doc can't see our responses.

'A Russian actor and theatre director. Co-founder of the Moscow Art Theatre. Emotion memory was his passion. He believed actors could not play any part successfully until they had experienced what they were playing in real life. No doubt Mr Rothwell will enlighten you. He is one of the new breed of drama teachers.' He says the word 'breed' with some venom, leaving us in no doubt of the pedagogical gulf that exists between the two. Without saying another word he rolls up his book, packs the machine into a large cotton bag, and sets off through the library doors tapping his white stick rhythmically.

I can't remember the last time I set foot in the girls' school. The atmosphere is different. It's clean, sanitised. It smells new. A sign in the foyer gives directions. *The Sixth Form Drama Group. Room 11. 4.30 pm.*

From down the corridor comes the sharp sound of a scraping mop bucket. The cleaners are arriving; one is Maud. She is a well-known figure in the boys' showers, leering at your private parts while at the same time apologising for being there. The sight of her bony fingers stretched tightly around the mop handle, is enough to make even the likes of Mugga wince and, as her eyes transfix on your nether regions, her mop performs an involuntary movement from the horizontal to the perpendicular. Her actions have given rise to the euphemism, 'swinging your mop', at which Tommy is currently world champion.

At first glance, Steve Rothwell is indistinguishable from the rest of the group gathered for the inaugural meeting of the Drama Society. He doesn't look like a teacher, threaten like a teacher and, after the initial embarrassment, when he insists we all call him Steve, it seems like we've found a friend.

It's a small gathering. Anne is here, but the only other girl is Jean Taylor who has starred in several school productions already.

Steve and the rest of us sit in a small circle on the floor. 'I'm not worried about the group being small. In fact, it's an advantage. I've got a suitable production in mind if things go well tonight. Right, what does everybody think Drama is?'

I've got an answer drawn from some muddled memories of Kenny's Roman History lessons and the Doc's pre-production pep-talks. I don't know if it might sound like I inhabit a world on the same pretentious level of Al's record collection but it's a chance to impress, so I give it a go. 'Isn't it something to do with Aristotle's theories that there should be three unities of action, time and place?'

'That's pretty impressive, Phil. Could you explain that to the rest of the group?'

I'm suddenly in a hole and the group is staring at me waiting for the answer.

'*The Alchemist*,' chips in Jean. 'Ben Johnson. It's one of our A-level books and an example of one of the few English plays which sticks to the three unities; action without sub-plots, a time period of no more than twenty-four hours and the stage representing only one place.'

I feel small. I've been rescued by a girl on a different cultural and academic level. Not only is she a cool, laid-back, rock chick but she's a bloody expert on Renaissance Drama and, much as I like her, she's a walking manifestation of my self-doubt. She flashes me that reproving look, the one she gave me when the date with Lesley was being arranged. I wonder if there's anything I could do that might eventually impress her.

'You're absolutely right,' says Steve, and it's just what I have in mind if things go well, but Drama is also a lot about concentration and the ability to focus your mind. Let's give it go. Stand up, drop your hands to your sides and relax. Now I want you to empty your minds of everything except a single thought on which you will focus. Ralph will try to break the bridge between your subconscious mind and the real world. He can't touch you but can use any other tactics he wants. Two minutes to get your concentration and we'll start.'

I concentrate hard, falling away into the summer of '69, repeating the words of 'My Girl' until they disintegrate into nothingness Ten minutes later, I realise I'm the only one left standing with Mugga's advice to Ralph of, 'Knee him in the bollocks for God's sake!' bringing me sharply back to reality.

'Well done, Phil, you lasted out really well there. What were you concentrating on?' asks Steve.

Surprising myself, I tell the group the truth. It's a sort of trust thing I suppose, not the type of confession you'd make in the changing rooms after a match. Anne goes a bit dewy-eyed, Jean stares blankly through me and Al sits cross-legged on the floor nodding supportively. Mugga mutters, 'Dickhead!' under his breath.

We are winding up the first half of the session with some deep breathing exercises. Ralph has fallen asleep and is snoring and Mugga's heavy grunting is embarrassing. The door opens and two stocky figures squeeze through the small gap. They are friends of Ralph. Billy Smith and Graham Johnson are not rugby players, which is a relief, and both look as if they have a genuine interest in joining the group. I'm just about to roll my eyes back up to the ceiling when I notice a third person lingering behind the lads. It's Judith.

I thank God she didn't arrive ten minutes earlier to hear my spontaneous outpourings. Suddenly Lesley seems a long way off. Anne calls out a welcome to her and Ralph wakes up.

'Best mates,' he enthuses, clasping my hand in a horizontal grip which nearly breaks my wrist.

I take this as confirmation that the whole thing had been set up by him through Anne before their split as a sort of favour designed to get my love life back on an even track. I wonder what Anne has said to Judith, but these thoughts are quickly obliterated by the need to get myself together and re-establish a positive image.

'Right! Great to see we've got a few more bodies and the numbers should just about fit what I've got in mind,' says Steve. 'It's a short one-act play by Tom Stoppard called *The Real Inspector Hound*. I'm a big fan of the Theatre of the Absurd and this one's a bit of an existential whodunit. Let's read through the script and see who fits the parts.'

After the reading, Steve feels the parts fall naturally to the members of the group. Jean takes the part of Mrs Drudge, the eccentric housekeeper, whose humour comes through her inability to distinguish between lines and stage directions. Ralph is to be the Upper Class, crippled Lord Magnus Muldoon and Anne, Lady Cynthia Muldoon. Al is to be the existential and mysterious Inspector Hound which leaves me with the part of Simon Gascoigne, a sort of philanderer and friend of the family who turns up for the weekend. Billy and Graham are Moon and Birdboot, two theatre critics who get drawn into the action, and Judith is given the part of Felicity Cunningham, a house guest of the Muldoons. Mugga is provisionally allocated the part of the dead body which remains on stage throughout the play, but Steve says he will have to audition as it's a crucial part and needs immense concentration. If he can lie prostrate throughout the next three meetings of the group, then the part is his.

As the meeting ends, I notice Anne in deep conversation with Steve. I catch the last few words of their conversation as Anne's voice raises slightly, 'I am not playing the wife of that bastard.' After a few moments, they call Judith over and there are furtive whisperings before it's announced that Anne and Judith have swapped parts.

It's a beautiful, warm, September evening. The last track on *Electric Ladyland* drifts away into the fading light. I flick open the cover of *The Real Inspector Hound,* pencil in hand, ready to underline my part.

I skim through the story. Simon is apparently in love with Lady Muldoon and they'd had a bit of an affair behind the old Lord's back. It is only when I get to page 22 that the full consequence of the casting changes dawns.

Simon (me) and Lady Cynthia (Judith) have to kiss, not once but twice within the space of a few lines of dialogue. The first kiss is brief but the second has to be sustained over seven lines of dialogue between Moon and Birdboot; about fourteen seconds in my estimation. It will have to be real. Stanislavski will decree it. No stage kisses. Fourteen seconds is a long time.

This is all wrong. I'd imagined how it was going to happen. We'd go out on a date, probably to a concert in Liverpool, then the train back to Padgate and a moonlit walk down Long Barn Lane to the five-barred gate. We'd sit talking for a bit as the late evening farmyard sounds added the romantic backdrop. Then the kiss and she'd turn and walk off back to the farmhouse, her white dress reflecting in the moonlight. But not this, no courtship, no soul. Simon Gascoyne and Lady Cynthia, two impostors, are going to highjack this moment. They don't have the right. It isn't fair. Our whole projected relationship is going to shatter apart in the dim, unheated, dusty hall of Wade Deacon, becoming a public event, with Maude and her mop handle performing all sorts of contortions to a cold, false passion.

I jump off the bed and, book in hand, head round to Al's. Ten minutes later we are sat in the Yew Tree Pub. Al is philosophical.

'There's no way out, Man. If you reject the part, you reject Judith. She won't see it as Simon and Cynthia. She'll see you as someone who doesn't want physical contact with her. Then we know what'll happen; ugly bastard syndrome. How would you feel? We could swap parts.'

I tense inside, suspecting some Machiavellian reason behind Al's offer. He's single and who wouldn't be attracted to her? They'd make a great looking couple. I trust Al with my life. I'd even lend him my Free records, but I don't trust him with girls.

'No,' I try to sound casual. 'Steve's fitted us to the roles and I like the character.'

'Then you've no option, Man. You can't do your first kiss as fictional characters. What's that crappy song you like, 'Ain't Nothing Like The Real Thing'?'

58

Saturday Sun
Nick Drake. Five Leaves Left. Island Records.

Saturday is my favourite day of the week. It's a day when I can connect with people without having to trek to the phone box to ring them up or walk miles round to their houses to find they're not in. Saturday morning is like condensing my entire social world into a couple of hours. On the half-mile walk from Calverts Coffee Bar to Widnes market, I'll encounter friends and family bobbing like pinballs in and out of the shops. I'm a lingerer more than a bobber though. Thirty minutes in Calverts for a coffee and then about the same in The Music Shop before hitting the second-hand record stalls in the market and hopping on the bus home in time for the football results. However, today the weather's closed in and there aren't many people negotiating the rain-polished streets of the town centre. All the shop doors are shut, and the only sound is the slushing of dirty water as cars and buses hurl the contents of deep puddles onto the pavements.

Calverts is warm and cosy but the tinkle of the doorbell draws a disapproving glance from the immaculately dressed, middle-aged assistant in charge of the men's outfitters. I sense a definite tightening of the tape measure in his hands with the realisation his receipt book can stay tucked away under the counter, his flannel blazers, Wolsey socks and Clydella pullovers untroubled by another two Wade Deacon sixth formers heading to fill up the spaces in his coffee lounge.

Sat in the corner, hogging a four-seater table, are Joe Hayes and John Hall. They are in my form group but live in what Joe would describe as a 'plushier' part of the town. His house is near the station, which is actually the only plushy part of Widnes, a dozen or so streets into which are crammed the aspirational middle classes. They've been playing badminton, a sport denied to us less plushy residents who haven't got the money to join the ICI club. They've just finished a two-hour stint. Joe looks as if he has taken his dog for a stroll around the park, John looks at the point of exhaustion, his long, frizzy hair matted with sweat which drips from his forehead, watering down his orange juice.

Slight hand movements and nods are woven into a code of greeting. Al heads over to talk to some girls and I sit down next to Joe with the promise of a frothy Cappuccino to come.

'Destroyed him, 2-0, 2-0.'

Joe's comment is predictable as his only sporting mission in life is to thrash his opponents mercilessly and then sit back smugly watching them deteriorate into silent suffering. He drinks his Coke ceremonially out of the bottle in much the same way as others would savour whisky or fine wine to celebrate their moments of triumph. Subbuteo matches at his house are pressured, with every flick and shot scrutinised and challenged. He is the only person I know who has committed the Subbuteo rule book to memory and whose every excuse for a defeat is that both Al and I abuse P.A.Adolph's strict instructions as to the correct and allowable movements of our right index fingers.

Joe is the ideal person on whom to sound out the potential of our group and the feasibility that we might step into Colour's shoes. There will be the inevitable derision but perhaps somewhere deep within the soulless look, which stares at me from behind the Coke bottle, there might emerge a tiny acknowledgement of respect.

Joe considers himself a rock music aficionado. As well as owning a high-quality badminton racket and an expensive pair of Green Flash trainers, he has a stereo system; a real system with separate speakers which stand like sentinels in the corner of his front room. He's also placed the settee at the exact point in the room where the stereo effect is at its optimum. The last time we were there a dozen of us clambered onto it. The lights were dimmed, and Pink Floyd's, 'Set The Controls For The Heart Of The Sun', filled the airspace with a buzzing timpani which swirled around the cornices and bounced strange metallic sounds off a radiator somewhere deep behind us. It stole our consciousness and transported us through uncharted dimensions, as Joe's Mum and Dad drank tea in the garden, unaware that their front room had disappeared into a deep, black void.

Al was so impressed he swore that lying in the living room was equivalent to being cocooned in some giant rocket ship blasting away from Windsor Road. When he eventually came back to earth he was too scared to open the front door in case he was confronted with a cavernous, black infinity and pieces of Widnes orbiting like satellites around number 23. That is Al for you, though. Over summer, I even went along with his idea that, as we had no money, we should try to create a stereophonic sound using the equipment at our disposal.

His first attempt was to wire our two mono record players together in the hope that our brains would somehow separate the sounds entering our ears from different directions. His next experiment was to place the same album on each record player but start one off slightly in advance of the other. The result was a disturbing echoing effect that took me back to my worst nightmares of childhood. Al told Joe smugly that both systems were a success at a fraction of the cost of his Leak Amplifier, Thorens Record Deck and custom-made speakers. A demonstration, however, was never offered, thus ensuring both of his new theories of stereophonic technology could not be disproved and leaving a lingering doubt in Joe's mind that perhaps, just perhaps, he had wasted his money and that the plushy part of Widnes could, on occasions, be upstaged.

John is interested in the band. He is always interested in new things and even hints that he may come along to St Mary's for the gig. No light shines from Joe's eyes. After finishing his Coke, and slamming the bottle down firmly like some judge's hammer, he removes a ten shilling note from his pocket and places it on the table.

'Ten bob says you won't do three gigs before Christmas.'

This is typical Joe stuff, a tantalising bet given that three gigs is not completely out of the question but is on the cusp of being extremely unlikely. After only two rehearsals, things are not going well, and there is no guarantee that our performance at the garden party will result in a mad rush for bookings over the festive period.

But, if I don't take the bet he's won a grudging admission from me that he is right; another defeat in the history of Stephens-Hayes conflicts. I have not had many successes. There was the 7-0 drubbing at Subbuteo when his head was streaming with a bad cold, his fingertips sticking to his players, hindering his trademark flicks and boomerang shots. That, and his penalty saved when I was in goal for the 2nd X1, playing against the first team, are my only victories in recent memory.

'I only have five shillings at the moment.'

It's my only hope of an honourable retreat.

Joe slides the note back into his pocket uttering a derisory laugh. John offers a sympathetic smile.

I try a bit of one-upmanship.

'Tupp's back in town with Ibex. Got tickets to go to The Sink on Monday.'

Like a poker player presenting his final hand, Joe slides two Sink Club tickets and two rail tickets out of the inside pocket of his coat and slaps them on the table. 'For me and Alison. Then we're heading down to London next month to stay with Tupp in Shepherds Bush.'

Alison is Joe's girlfriend. She is a friend of Jean and, like her, she is a rock girl, arty, attractive and confident, with the same masses of wavy hair and Afghan coat which seem to define the image, in Widnes and Warrington at least. I wonder what she sees in Joe.

'Be great to see a real group,' says Joe nonchalantly. I'm not quite sure he exaggerates the word 'real' but, in my head, it has a resonance. 'Let you know how we get on. See you for a Subbuteo thrashing when we get back.'

63

I don't respond with an affirmative which would hand him a psychological victory before I even set foot in his plushy house and his plushy spare bedroom with the pitch raised to eye level on a table giving him an instant advantage while I have to re-adjust myself spatially from playing in a cramped position on my bedroom floor. I finish my coffee, nod to Al, and we head off to the Music Shop.

Inside we meet Ralph, with Jimmy Mason, who lives up his way in Hunts Cross. This is the first weekend he has spent without Anne for five years. He has the look of a man who has just been freed from prison but is out with his minder having difficulty coming to terms with the bright new world into which he's been released.

After sifting through the LPs, the four of us head for The Black Cat Snooker Club by the market. It's an old furniture store which has been laid out with twenty full-size tables and is an alternative meeting place when the pubs are shut. Sitting on the pavement outside, wrapped in a poncho, is Silent Moon. He's really a Scouser called Eddie Gannon who believes he's an American Indian and makes a living begging and reading fortunes.

'Spare us a few bob for a cup of tea, lads.'

If Eddie has any pretensions of becoming the real thing it's strange he should consider drinking tea. I mean I've never heard Tonto ask The Lone Ranger to brew up or Little Plum suggest to Chiefy that they share a pot of Earl Grey and a scone.

Ralph is not in charitable mood, 'Fuck off, Eddie. Try the Chinese restaurant down the road. They've got hundreds of reservations in there.' For a second the old Ralph surfaces, almost breaking into a laugh, before reality closes in on him and he shoulders open the door of The Black Cat.

The ceiling is low and a cloud of smoke hovers above the table as Ralph cues off. He takes his pent-up anger out on the first break and the white hurtles down the table into the mist, collides violently with the reds, leaps into the air, and bounces away on the concrete and out of the front door.

'Fuck!' Ralph slumps onto the table knocking all the colours off their spots. He lies for a moment, like a beached whale giving up on life, before lumbering reluctantly out into the fresh air in pursuit of the ball.

We need to cheer him up but it's harder for lads. If we were girls we'd be sat in a bedroom with a pile of photos spread out on the bedspread ready to be ripped to pieces. We'd have a poignant record playing in the background while we all pulled together agreeing that we'd all been here before, the opposite sex is worthless, not to be trusted, and that we are all better off without them. Then we'd go for a girls' night out, glued together by female camaraderie making sure that, before we headed home for the evening, the lost love had been replaced with a suitable free spirit; a much better looking and nicer person than the worthless bastard who had propelled us all into this situation.

It's different for lads. We don't like being finished with, it fractures our masculinity and makes us want to creep into a deep hole for a week or so to avoid the unwanted sympathy from other lads. Not that lads do sympathy much. In fact, they don't do it at all really. They just invite you to fill the empty space with an intensive course of male bonding. Since my break with Lesley, Al's made me play more football, drink more beer, hone my Subbuteo skills and insist I go to all United's home and away games. It's the lads' way of helping their mates through a bad time.

Ralph heads back through the door. 'How do you get tar off a fuckin' snooker ball?'

I've decided Ralph's not the only one in need of some sort of guidance. I've got to talk to someone about my dilemma about returning to The Sink Club and reawakening the ghosts of my soulful summer. It's not easy being an only child; it's a pretty solitary existence, really. I mean you get everything you want from your parents without having all that sibling rivalry stuff but it can be pretty lonely sitting in your bedroom when you just want to talk about something that's on your mind. Still, tonight I'm off to a family do where I'll meet up with my cousin, Babs, who tells it like it is. It'll be no holds barred. She's younger than me and in the same year as Lesley and Judith. I want her advice about moving on. Babs will know. She's good at that sort of thing.

NINE

A Way Of Life
The Family Dogg. Single Release. Bell Records.

Usually, on a Saturday, I head straight home, hoping that my Dad will have checked the Pools and that he'll be waiting to tell me that we're millionaires and that I can escape to anywhere with enough money to last me the rest of my life. It's a good dream, even if it only lasts for the length of the bus journey home, but today it'll have to wait. On my way to the family do I've decided to call for my cousin Geoff. I don't want to be the lone target for the new Conservatives who populate that side of the family.

Geoff is more of a target than me. He's a member of the Labour Party with his beliefs fired by growing up in the same streets as me in West Bank. Church Street was sandwiched between the railway viaduct, the Mersey, and a metropolis of chemical factories which belched toxic fumes into the air around the clock. Life was tough, but the families were forged together into a community which stood fast against the noise and pollution, taking pride in their clean steps, scrubbed children and Sunday outings to New Brighton and Walton Hall. There, for a few hours, dressed in their Sunday best, they could at least enjoy freedom and fresh air, returning for a Sunday tea of pink salmon sandwiches, cakes and tinned fruit. Then there would be a brief period of rest before they retired into their freshly laundered sheets to gather strength for the next day when they would be summoned to their shifts in the iron foundry, bleaching plant or alkaline works.

Geoff and I are bonded to our side of the family. The other side doesn't like Labour and Liberalism. Harold Wilson has definitely wound them up. For a start he's abolished capital punishment, which in their eyes has been a license for murderers to roam unchecked around Widnes, committing gruesome deeds, and spending the rest of their days in luxury cells with colour televisions. He's relaxed the laws governing homosexuality, but that won't be mentioned tonight. It's something that goes on in dark alleys behind the town centre when all ordinary people are safe at home with their doors bolted, occasionally peering out of the curtains, phone in hand, ready to dial 999. They're critical of him sending the troops into Ireland but only because his approach is too soft and he should be clearing out the IRA with force and establishing a checkpoint at the Pier Head to turn back every Irish person attempting to disembark onto the English mainland. The thing that worries them most though is Harold's determination to establish more equality for women. This threatens the very status quo of life at the golf club and fear that the day will come when a group of bra-burning Amazons storms through the door, heads for the men-only bar, and drinks the place out of Greenhalls Bitter.

I hop off the bus at the end of Deacon Road and head up past the Plaza where there are a few people queuing for the early showing of *True Grit*. The last time I was there was when I went to see *Far From The Madding Crowd* when I was doing my O levels. I suppose if Hardy is right, then there's always a remote chance of people getting back together. You just need the twists and turns of fate to bounce randomly around and come down in your favour. It took six years for Bathsheba and Gabriel to get it together. Perhaps I'll be heading down a highway to California one day, bump into Lesley at the airport, and realise that it was all worked out on Al's tapestry of life and our destiny is complete.

I can always warm to Hardy with his tangle of seemingly unconnected events craftily weaving themselves into hopes, dreams, and memories, and maybe I've met my girl. A few days ago Judith and I were living, breathing, unaware that our lives were on an inexorable collision course and that we were powerless to do anything to stop it.

Geoff has collided with his girl. His is a small tapestry about the size of the Widnes Weekly News and it's all sewn up around the edges. His girlfriend, Jackie, opens the door. She has a sunshine smile, and maybe Ronnie Hurst and Hardy are not separated by such an intellectual chasm, both wanting a simple, uncomplicated life. Whoever put together Geoff and Jackie's tapestry must have been one of the better Fates, peering down through the chemical cloud-haze and believing that some people in Widnes deserve everlasting happiness.

Geoff and I head for the station. It's not worth rehearsing detailed ripostes as we've done it all before and they don't take any notice. They'll look at us beatifically as if they're tolerating a phase we're just passing through, safe in their belief that, before we're twenty-one, we'll have grown out of it, our Wrangler jackets and jeans will be in the bin, and we'll morph into tonight's young role model.

The do is round at Uncle Reg's and Aunty Joan's house. It's Young Reg's 21st party. Geoff and I have promised our Mums we'll make an appearance. We're good like that.

We approach the row of neat, three-bedroomed bungalows, just off Ash Lane. There's an almost semi-rural feel as the road meanders down towards open fields and the Mersey flood plain. Unusually, as we reach Uncle Reg's house, the street is full of parked cars. The golf club crowd is here and the roofs of a couple of Rover 2000s shine in the late afternoon sun.

The door is opened by Uncle Reg. 'Eh up, it's Chairman Mao and Che Guevara. Suppose we'd better let you in then.'

Aunty Joan is more accommodating, giving us both a hug and directing us to the kitchen where the hostess trolley is packed with slices of beef, roast potatoes, peas, gravy and cocktail sausages.

Trying to find any points of comparison between me and Reg is a challenge. He left school at fifteen, has short hair, wears a suit, is engaged to a girl who works in the Social Security Offices, has his own car and a job working for the Recreation and Leisure Department at Liverpool Council. He's a step up from Ronnie Hurst. He's management, the sort who'd make Ronnie's life a misery. In Action Comics

Superman's doppelganger, Bizarro lived in a world where everything was the complete opposite of life back on Earth. Young Reg is my Bizarro. I'm convinced he's slipped into Widnes via a time fissure from another dimension and is in cahoots with Lex Luthor waiting to drag me into Uncle Reg's garage. There he'd strap me in front of a huge glass and metal machine and flick the switch, letting loose it's mind-changing properties in a flash of cobalt-blue sparks. Every last ounce of individuality would be extracted from my shaking body so that a few minutes later we'd emerge in Aunty Joan's kitchen sharing the same vision of Widnes' brave new world.

My Mum had given me two pounds with which to buy him a birthday present and alleviate the need for her to suffer acute embarrassment should I turn up without one. With the money I've bought myself Free's new album and with the change, 7s 6d, I've bought him a copy of this week's chart topper, 'In The Year 2525' by Zager and Evans. I couldn't really be bothered looking for anything else and it's where I'd like to send him should I ever invent a time machine.

The scene is all too familiar and, as usual, the guests have spread out into pre-defined areas according to age and mobility. In the living room, occupying the comfy chairs, are the grandparents and older aunts moulded into their seats for the duration and waited on hand and foot by sons, daughters and grandchildren. In the kitchen men stand around, talking about business, golf, or rugby league, with the women perched at the breakfast bar sucking Babycham-soaked cherries on the end of cocktail sticks. The majority of the younger generation, including Young Reg, are indulging in polite chit-chat in the dining room where the lavish buffet has been laid out. There's music playing but it's barely audible above the conversations which seem to be mostly about savings and investments.

Geoff's gone straight onto the offensive and is pinning cousin George against the wall. He's just back from South Africa impressing the guests with his stories of a lavish lifestyle, a houseful of black servants and a bank balance bulging beyond the dreams of the assembled entrepreneurs.

I look around trying to find a point of reference, something or someone I can latch onto. There's no sign of Babs and I do a mental calculation of what time I can leave without offending anyone. If I stay a couple of hours I can still make last orders at The Tavern or go home and think through my strategy to cope with The Sink Club.

I take a glass of beer from the kitchen and make my way into the dining room. Nobody seems to notice me so I grab a sandwich and amble back into the kitchen. My Mum is here with the Babycham crowd although she's knocking back a gin and tonic and talking in an affected accent to some guy in a lounge suit who looks like Tom Jones.

'Hi, Mum!' I interrupt her conversation. Even though I've not seen her for about a week, she looks at me disapprovingly.

'Philip, when are you going to smarten yourself up?'

I've not even thought about what I'm wearing and even if I had I'd have dressed the same. I don't have many clothes and what money I have is spent on jeans, jumpers, and t-shirts. Well, at least I'm wearing a shirt even if it's a faded, blue Wrangler.

'This is Jim, he's the captain of the golf club.' The waver in her voice is embarrassing.

He holds out his hand and I shake it, feeling mine disappear inside his substantial fist.

'And what are you doing, son?'

'I'm in the sixth form at Wade Deacon.'

'Oh, studying, are you? Well. I never had much in the way of brain power. Didn't do any exams or anything like that. No bloody good at them.' He leans forward as if he's about to impart some long-hidden secret. 'But I tell you what, I've worked bloody hard and I've made a few bob. That's why I'm where I am today, aren't I Evelyn?'

He looks at my mother. I want her to say, 'Oh, but we've always supported Philip to do his studies and go on to

72

university. We're really proud of him.' I look at her, naively waiting for motherly encouragement.

'That's right. You want to take a lesson from Jim. Boys of your age shouldn't still be in school. You're always happy when you're doing nothing.' She turns back to Jim, whose red face is glowing with the sweat of drinking too much whisky. 'He needs to get out in the world and do something with his life. He'll be studying until he's fifty.' She laughs a pathetic little laugh. 'Won't you love?'

Jim reaches into the pocket of his expensive suit and pulls out a card. 'Here son, if you ever fancy some graft give us a ring. I'll take him on for you, Evelyn. He'd be on seven quid a week for starters.'

I look at the card. 'Jim Morrison and Son. Contract Cleaning Services. Halewood Industrial Estate'.

'What do you say, Philip?'

I look at Jim and his beaming, ruddy face. He's a dead ringer for one of Hardy's characters after a night at The Pure Drop Inn but, if he was transported to nineteenth century Dorchester, he'd be dealing in reapers, binders and combine harvesters sending modernist shockwaves through the tranquil Dorset countryside.

'Thanks, but no thanks. I'm doing my A-levels and then I'm off to college.'

My mother tuts. 'He never knows when anyone's doing their best for him.'

I smile and move on. The trouble with being here is that I just wander from one similar conversation to the next. I've had enough.

I'm almost through the door when I realise I've not given Young Reg his present. I retrieve it from the window ledge in the kitchen, saying a quick goodbye to my mother, who is still fawning around with Jim, and nip back into the hallway where he's entangled with his girlfriend, Sheila.

'Reg, sorry! Happy birthday!' I hand him the record.

'Thanks, Philip! Cheers!' He passes it to Sheila who unwraps it for him.

'Aw, Reg, you've got this one already.' There's a look of disappointment on her face. 'Never mind we can always swap it for 'A Boy Named Sue'. Your Dad likes that.'

I turn to go, 'Hey, I've got something for you.' Reg disentangles himself and starts rummaging in his jacket. 'Some freebies!' He hands me a buff-coloured envelope with my name written on the front. 'For you! Your sort of music. Drug-crazed hippies and all that!' He seems to find some amusement in his description and sits back with a patronising grin on his face.

I take the envelope and back off towards the door. 'Well, thanks, Reg. Enjoy the rest of your do.'

I'm just about to leave when I'm stopped by Babs 'Hey, stranger, don't leave without saying, hello.'

Babs was amused when I'd suddenly turned to soul. For her birthday I'd bought her *United*, by Marvin Gaye and Tammi Terrell. She'd laughed at the thought of me creeping into Dawsons undercover to buy it but she was pleased I was going out with a nice girl. She knew Lesley, passingly, and joked that maybe I'd change my image and smarten up. The important thing about Babs is she knew I never would and she suggested it jokingly and with affection and tolerance. She'd talked to me when Lesley and I had split. She told me Lesley was really upset but I couldn't understand that.

We both grab a drink and head into the quiet of the garden past Geoff, who is still battering George into submission.

'So you've formed a band then?'

'Yeh, it's therapy. I'm back in the real world. I feel good!'

Babs looks at me knowingly.

'Not quite, I think.'

I attempt to explain that I'm getting there and that being in the band is a pretty good distraction. I feel a bit stupid when I tell her about not wanting to go back to The Sink but she knows all this and I can guess what's coming.

'Phil, I can tell you now Lesley will not be thinking about you. There's nothing to stop you from moving on. Breaking up was inevitable but letting go is optional. You've just left a good place and want to go back. Don't we all?'

She downs her gin and tonic in one and looks as if she's about to reverse the roles, but she carries on.

'Look, you were happy before Lesley. You just need to find yourself again. Don't try to change too much; I liked you as you were before. Anyway, I've not seen you for ages and I missed your birthday. Hold on, I've got you a present.'

She rummages deep inside her bag and hands me a small square packet which feels like it contains a couple of singles.

'For both your musical tastes,' she laughs and gives me a peck on the cheek and a hug. Keep in touch. She says it as if I'm leaving on some faraway journey.

'Thanks. I'll go to the Sink tomorrow. But you know that already.'

'I knew it yesterday,' she smiles.

Out into the cool September air and I'm free. The night is clear with a red tinge, and there's a peaceful feeling in the calm streets as I head home. Back in my bedroom, I put the unopened present from Babs on the shelf next to my bed and place the envelope from Young Reg on top of a pile of LPs. I settle down and pick up *Tess*, with images of ancient woodlands, forgotten country lanes and miles of empty spaces, taking me away from the thought of stirring any embers of a lost relationship which may lie waiting to be re-kindled in the dark recesses of the Sink Club.

TEN

I'm A Mover
Free. Tons of Sobs. Island Records.

It's Tuesday evening and we're in the Philharmonic, just down the road from The Sink, and the members of Ibex make an entrance. Not an entrance like The Beatles at Speke Airport or Shea Stadium; just an entrance. They look like a rock group but they've seen loads of groups in here so nobody takes much notice of them. There's Mike Bersin with his outrageous afro-electric hair, Miffer the Milkman looking like he's just finished an all night shift, and Tupp with his golden locks, wearing a black, floppy, hat straight from the cover of *Hendrix's Greatest Hits*. He looks the accomplished rock star, putting my ambition to bridge from dreamy schoolboy into rock musician into harsh perspective.

There's a lot of backslapping and comments from us about how the three of them have changed but no comments back to us because we haven't changed and I feel boring and naïve. These guys left for London just a few months ago and, while I've been studying Hardy and grappling with metaphysical poetry, they've been playing in pubs and clubs and meeting other rock bands. It all seems a million miles away from school and Widnes and my cosy bedroom and Bush record player. Although they've only been gone a short time, they seem years older.

Miffer is the doubtful one. He's a bit older than us and has given up his steady job as a milkman after a bit of persuading from the others. He's a Widnes lad and he's the one who still looks the same while London has chipped away at Tupp's and Mike's northern roots. Then Freddie makes an entrance. This is a different entrance because he's different and people turn to look at him because everybody's wearing jeans and t-shirts and he's in a fur coat, multi-coloured shirt, and tight, crushed velvet trousers with a chiffon scarf. Ralph gets in the pints but it's one too many because Freddie only drinks port and lemon and Ralph has to head back to the bar and sheepishly order something that isn't beer, Guinness or whisky for the first time in his life.

Freddie stands around absorbing the gazes and fragments of conversation which scatter in his direction. He's a product of some culture far removed from the jigsaw of stereotypes which have shaped our characters.

I lean across to Tupp. 'Where did you meet him, Man?'

'Ken's girlfriend and her mates took us down to meet a band in the Kensington Pub. Turns out they were called Smile. They've supported Yes and Family and got a recording contract. We had a few pints, got talking music and noticed this guy hanging around on the fringes, obviously not in their band but looking pretty sharp in a short fur jacket. Turned out to be Freddie. Afterwards, we all went back to the flat and their guitarist, Brian picked up Mike's guitar and blew us away playing some original stuff. Freddie knew all the words and put on a show. They didn't need a frontman, we did, so he was in. No more soloing endlessly until half the audience fucks off to the bar. You should see him on stage. Hey Freddie, come and meet my mates from school: Al, Phil, Ralph.'

Freddie shakes our hands like he's known us for years. He has a huge smile which is all teeth. Al's fascinated. 'So are you from London, Man?'

'Bit further from there, my friend, Zanzibar. John's brought me up here. I have no idea where I am.'

He tells us of his life in Zanzibar and that he's a Zoroastrian, which really impresses Al because it sounds psychedelic. He says he's from a land of peace, tranquillity and beauty, wild beasts and spiritual calm. At least it was until his family was run out of the country by an Arab dictatorship and he's been at college in London since then.

It's like listening to Electric Ladyland but this time it's all real, and we're hooked. He tells us about his school and the productions and singing in the choir, and we realise he's the same as us except we've been trapped all our lives in a small northern town and the world out there is different and weird and exciting. After we're released from Freddie's spell, I feel grey and flat and sad that I've only escaped my world through a transistor radio, TV and books without setting foot outside the greyness and discovering the reality beyond.

'So what's Widnes like?'

It's a good question. I mean I never say to Al or Ralph, 'What's Widnes like?', because they'd just say 'shit', and that would be the end of the discussion. So I tell him it's got a decent record store called The Music Shop, and there's the Wilton Coffee Lounge if you like Espresso and listening to top twenty stuff and Calverts does a good range of chiffon scarves (which makes him smile). But it's a town of scrap metal merchants, welders, wood turners, sheet metal fabricators and haulage contractors. It has nothing to connect it with Zanzibar except maybe at the Queens Hall when they dig out the plastic palm trees for the Caribbean Night. Deep down though I want to say it's my home and I'm proud of it and I like the rugby league team and I pay 3s 6d now and again to watch them slug it out with Saints, Wires or Wigan, but I don't think he'll be interested. So I just say it's ok and leave it at that.

Tupp says they played the Bolton Octagon and Bluesology sessions in Queens Park last weekend and they're ending with the Sink Club gig before they trek back. They're hopeful of some breaks and have a few connections down south. The scene is brilliant, and they go to the same pubs as Eric Clapton, John Mayall and The Stones.

They have a picture of Freddie from the Bolton Evening News. It's taken from a low angle down below the bandstand and Freddie is on tiptoe looking like he's reaching for the sky. The cutting doesn't mention him or the band, it just says, 'One of the singers enjoys himself.', and leaves it at that. But Freddie's pleased because he looks the part, and it's his first appearance in the press.

There's more from Tupp and Mike about life in London and Widnes gets smaller and greyer and I know I have to leave but their life is failing to draw me in. It's a long twisted journey but I see the determination in Freddie's eyes and he's travelling the road, heading towards the last leg. I look at the others and I'm not sure, but Freddie's come thousands of miles. It's a long way to head back.

8pm. I'm outside the Sink Club with Al and Ralph and I don't feel so bad because I'm with my mates and the place is different. The front door's dirty and there's rubbish collecting outside the cafe between the electrician's and the beer shop. The queue to get in is grubby too with plenty of students in grubby t-shirts and grubby jeans and psychedelic sounds are drifting up from the cellar where a weak, blue light beckons you down the stairs into the claustrophobic underworld. I get talking to someone in the queue who tells me that soul is dead in Liverpool and Neil English, the owner who started it all, is selling up.

I feel sorry for him. The club's gone, sliding away on a one-way journey to dereliction. A few months of seedy rock gigs, a reputation for excessive alcohol and drug-dealing, with the police turning up every night, equals closure.

My nights with Lesley had been spent in a safe place. Neil didn't allow drink and anyone found with drugs was reported to the police straight away. Even if the boys upset any of the girls he'd chuck them out and the black guys danced the night away to the sounds of Stax, Atlantic and Motown, welcomed into the soul family; refugees from the clubs like Ugly's where steel-faced bouncers barred them entry because of their colour. I survived an all-nighter with Lesley, topped up with coffee, lemonade, and sweets from the Rumblin' Tum Café on the upper floor. You didn't need the alcohol, the atmosphere was intoxicating, but now James Brown, Marvin Gaye and

Sam Cooke are just ghosts drifting back across the Atlantic, and Hardman Street feels empty, threatening and cold.

Tupp's stamped our tickets, 'Guest', and we flash them at the bouncer on the door. He stares us straight in the eyes, tears our tickets in two without looking at them, and we're in.

Down in the smoky, ultra-violet world the band is setting up and Geoff Higgins wrestles with a large Grundig Tape deck which he's balancing on a couple of beer crates underneath Tupp's bass amp. It's a stupid place to put it if he wants a balanced sound but he can't get to the middle because the place is so small that Freddie's mike has been placed in front of the stage to make room for the musicians behind him.

The place is filling up, and it's a predictable audience. There are lots of freshers from the University and the Poly, more interested in making friends than concentrating on the band, but there are a few friends from school and Tupp's out at the front with them swigging from a bottle of Johnny Walker's Red.

There's no entrance, the rest of the band sort of wander on and there's a lot of talking and fiddling with guitar leads and amp settings. It's Tupp who does the introduction. Geoff starts his tape machine running and, even though he's restricted for space, Freddie's pretty animated at the front. Tupp's bass intro causes Geoff to hold onto his tape recorder and Mike's guitar drives out the first chords of 'Communication Breakdown' as the light show sends multi-coloured bubbles bursting behind the stage.

Freddie has a style of his own and seems theatrically distant from the jeans and T-shirted trio who lapse into the shadows rooted in their own space. It's not the menace of Robert Plant, it's a more tuneful controlled vocal, and he seems in a world of his own, parading extravagantly in a small island of light which forces back the suffocating darkness of the cellar. He's driving the performance, and the band is trying to keep pace, but the audience is with him. The place gets hotter with steam rising off people's heads as they pack towards the front. I can't talk to Al and Ralph, the noise is too great, so we gaze and watch as the set runs through.

There are plenty of highlights. Freddie's certainly going for the high falsettos and he gets smatterings of applause and yells from the audience. Mike's guitar sound on 'Rock Me Baby' is glittering, the notes played with ice-clear precision, and Miffer drums away keeping perfect time and looking every bit as competent and arrogant as Ginger Baker.

They're halfway through and Geoff's struggling with his tape recorder now. The right-hand reel is spinning wildly as the tape comes to an end and the tension between the two reels is released. Tupp's perfect bass continues to pound out of the speaker as Geoff recovers the microphone from its rusty hook and there's decent applause at the end with calls for an encore but it looks like the band has run out of songs.

As the applause fades, Freddie nods to a couple of guys at the front of the stage. One has long, frizzy hair and is holding tightly onto a guitar case while the other's carrying a pair of fancy drumsticks. After a few hurried discussions, Miffer leaves his drum kit for the blond guy who's looking pretty in his fur jacket and velvet jeans. The tall, gaunt-looking guy plugs in his guitar ready to jam. Miffer's covered in sweat and is ready for the pint Ralph offers him.

'Who are those two, Man?'

'They're mates of Freddie's out of Smile, up here gigging. Brian's the lead guitarist. See what you think. The drummer's Roger, he's almost as good as me.'

They start a number and it's different to Ibex. The guitar has a sound. Not a Clapton, BB King, Jeff Beck, blues feel. It's a strident, clawing, pitch, teasing the fretboard with sharp sustained notes mixed in with some tricky riffs. It's different enough to make the audience stop talking and listen. Freddie's become noticeably more animated, more outrageous, as if the chords are breathing new life into him, making his body rise and fall with the notes from each sustained sequence. He

81

seems to be picked, held and released by some invisible, electrical impulse connecting him with the guitar.

It goes down well. The audience doesn't know the songs but it's no matter. The gig's ending with a theatrical show and the music's almost irrelevant, just a vehicle for Freddie to connect with the masses and draw them into his space.

The last chords of the song bounce around the walls of the club fading into the applause, the mist, and the clatter of glasses and beer bottles. We make our way out of The Sink collecting our thoughts as we head back towards the station.

'Des would friggin' hate that,' says Ralph, as we board the train back from Lime Street. 'Dickhead like him poncing about the stage. He'd find it bloody immoral.'

Al doesn't share Ralph's view.

'Can't you see it? The omens are all there. He could have stepped out of a parallel universe. We're at a point of intersection and decisions we make now could influence our lives forever. It's obvious he's got the rock star charisma but at the end of the day, he's just like us.'

'How is he friggin' like us?' says Ralph, 'He talks posh, is from a bleedin' island thousands of miles away and he drinks port and friggin' lemon.'

The train is heading at a pace towards Hunts Cross so Al hasn't got much time to argue. I'm not sure if Ralph's listening anyway as he's stretched out across the whole of one side of the carriage with his feet resting on the half open window.

'Look, it's like some cosmic collision of fate. Things like this don't happen by chance. He's been to the same sort of school as us. I know it's private and all that, but he's played sport, like us, sang in the school choir, like we had to, formed a pop group with his mates and played at functions and fetes.'

Al exaggerates the word 'fetes' as if it's the ultimate connection; as if we should start rifling through old copies of *NMEs* to find out at which fetes Clapton, Kossoff and Beck played their first dates. 'He's listened to English and American

82

music like us and the area he's from, Stone Town, it could almost be a pseudonym for Widnes.'

'More like friggin' stink town,' says Ralph. 'Bet there are loads of chemical works and iron foundries in Zanzibar. And his school was posh, not like our friggin' dump. You can tell that 'cos he sings in a posh voice. He hasn't got a chance of being a bluesman.'

'He likes the same music as us. He loves Hendrix, Little Richard and Fats Domino, and he likes Cliff. What about that for a connection? What more do you want?'

Ralph swings out of the carriage door and thuds onto the platform. 'See you for the rehearsal tomorrow, Men, and Morefield, don't start trying to sing and jump about like that weirdo. Remember, we sing blues and we drink friggin' Guinness.' The train starts to move away but Ralph continues to shout through the window in between the gasps of steam. 'And we wear proper friggin' clothes, not bloody velvet and silk like your gran, Phil.'

ELEVEN

Man Of The World
Fleetwood Mac. Single Release. Immediate Records.

Al won't let go and has decided he wants to know more about Freddie's home country. It's Wednesday afternoon, school's finished, and most of the staff have headed home. We wander into Badger Brocklehurst's Geography room which is full of old, cloth maps, a giant globe and chalk dust. There are layers of it everywhere. Works of art once drawn meticulously on his blackboard have been swept away by his board duster. Rivers, mountains, contour lines and oceans are lying in microscopic fragments across the desks, cupboards and windowsills of his room. We rotate Badger's globe looking for Zanzibar. We know it's in the Indian Ocean but we can't find it. There's a dent near Sumatra where Mugga head-butted it in a fit of temper after coming bottom in the exam five years running, adding fathoms to the Sundra Trench and removing bits of plastic from the surface leaving large, rusty land masses which don't exist. Al thinks he's spotted it but it's Madagascar, and it's miles too big.

There's a pile of *Phillips Intermediate School Atlases* on Badger's desk. The top one is Mugga's, and it's been lavishly illustrated with pencil drawings including a couple having sex across the whole of France. There's a missionary being boiled in a pot by natives in the Amazon with a speech bubble coming from the mouth of the unfortunate minister pleading, 'Kin 'ell. It's puckin' hot in Brazil.'

We flick to page 56. There are no drawings and we find Zanzibar nestling off the coast of Tanzania. It's minute and looks isolated, alien, one of those places never brought to life in Geography lessons. The small green smudge on the map, surrounded by the bright blue of the Indian Ocean tells you nothing. I mean Widnes looks ok on a map and the Mersey's the same bright blue as the ocean. The difference being that the Mersey is often really that colour, or red, or yellow or orange, depending upon which chemicals the factories on Spike Island pump into it on any one day.

There are a few places marked on the map with strange African sounding names like Chukwani, Mkunguni and Banda Kuu, and there's Zanzibar City near where Freddie grew up. The whole place is marked mostly in green, so it's pretty lush with lots of hidden creeks and smaller islands dotted around its coast.

Al's got a piece of string and in five minutes he's worked out the distance from Zanzibar to Widnes. He's pretty good at this sort of thing and he reckons it's around 7,200 miles if you drive through Africa and up the Trans-African Highway.

Badger ambles into the room and eyes us suspiciously. He knows neither of us is studying Geography A-Level.

'What can I do for you, gentleman?'

'We're trying to find out about Zanzibar, Sir'. There's a genuine interest in Al's voice and for a moment it throws Badger who was not expecting a geographical response.

'Zanzibar? What do you want to know about that for?'

'Oh just interested in the people and what it might have to offer the World?'

'Morefield, the only thing you need to know about Zanzibar is that once you're inside you'll never get out. It is a dangerous un-Westernised place full of drug dealers, armed robbers and corrupt policemen who you have to bribe to get you out of trouble. Malaria or yellow fever can kill you in twenty-four hours as can the Zanzibar Leopard and the Zanzibar Giant Rat if you are unlucky enough to encounter them. Being bitten by mosquitos, snakes and spiders can make your life miserable and, if you don't die from some horrible infection procured through their bites, you'll most likely fall victim to coconuts falling out of the palm trees.'

85

Badger rambles on unaware that he is elevating Zanzibar to legendary status in Al's eyes. He's painting the ideal picture to compliment Freddie's romantic description. It is seemingly the country that has it all.

'Have you ever been on holiday to Zanzibar, Sir?'

Badger glowers at us as if we've just suggested something beyond the realms of reality.

'Gentlemen, I take my holidays in Lyme Regis and you would be well-advised to do the same. Journey abroad only in your imaginations. Stay within the confines of the English counties or, failing that, the United Kingdom.'

'We've met someone from Zanzibar, Sir.'

'Oh really, Morefield and who might that be?'

'He's a singer, Sir. Freddie Bulsara. He sings in a band with John Taylor and Michael Bersin.'

'Well, he was lucky to escape the country but extremely unlucky to fall in with those two. Both of them could have had an academic career. Bersin was very gifted at Geography until he discovered the guitar.'

'They're doing alright, Sir. They're living in London. Going to make it big.'

'The only things big in London,' snaps Badger, 'are big egos, big prices and big ideas which come to nothing. You need to stay here in the real world, boys. Study hard, work hard, and in the future you'll have a good job and a three-bedroom semi in Upton Lane like me and Mrs Brocklehurst. Visiting Zanzibar is a figment of your imaginations, the stuff of *Boys' Own Annual*. Now go. I'm locking up for the evening.'

'Fate is the master of all our destinies,' says Al, as we head to the pub. 'Events are irresistible. When Freddie was born what odds would you have got that on September 9th, 1969 we would be sat with him in an old pub in Liverpool mere tangents on his life's journey to fame and fortune? Think of all the thousands of happenings which could have prevented it.

Our lives could have been completely different, but Fate has decreed, at a point in time we should all meet in the Philharmonic thousands of miles from Freddie's home. Muse on that.'

Muse is obviously a new word in Al's vocabulary. He likes to think of himself as a creative thinker, someone who can strip away the layers of basic meaning and explore the depths of even the simplest of theories. He drives Herbie mad in English lessons going round in circles about what if this and that had, or had not, happened.

'So what's the difference between fate and coincidence?' I shouldn't really have bothered asking the question as it sets Al off on one of his philosophical expositions.

'Easy! Fate is the result of action or inaction in a person's past life and has some direct relation to that life. So, Freddie is here because he made conscious decisions to take up singing, travel to London, and look for a rock band. All those things are propelling him towards his fate or destiny which is already written in the stars. Conversely, coincidence has nothing to do with fate. He could bump into someone from Zanzibar on Oxford Street, they could have a chat and a bit of a reminisce about giant rats, recovering from malaria, that sort of thing and then just move on, fate and destiny unaffected. Lots of coincidences happen to you every day but they don't affect your life's journey. It's coincidence when Angel Clare sees Tess dancing in the field at the start of the novel but it doesn't affect her fate or destiny. It's events later on that determine that. If he'd been so taken with her and leapt into the field, swept her up in his arms, and asked her to marry him, that would have been a different matter. They'd have lived happily ever after and you'd have nobody to be so bloody obsessed about. I'm hoping to get an 'A' in Literature.'

'So making conscious decisions can drive fate even if you can't change the outcome?'

'That's it. We need to make a conscious decision to ignore Hayes and drive ourselves forward to rock stardom, so our fate can just take its course.'

I'm not sure about rock stardom but on Friday evening Steve has arranged an extended first rehearsal of *Hound* and I just hope we don't get to page 22 before I've had a chance to manipulate my destiny to the point where I can actually ask Judith out. Even though we haven't had time to explore our characters, I want to be fast forwarded to the closing curtain so that Simon Gascoigne and Lady Cynthia Muldoon can be banished back to their fictional world, wedged tightly on my bookshelf between a giant *Oxford English Dictionary* and *The Complete Works of Shakespeare*.

I've carried my copy of *The Real Inspector Hound* around in the hope I might have bumped into Judith at The Dell, with Stoppard providing the perfect bridge to hurry things along. But now I'm in the pub, looking at the script, searching for a way to rescue a love which has not yet come to pass.

'You've got to delay the event, Man!' says Al. 'Pretend to have tonsillitis, glandular fever or some other contagion which is transmitted by kissing for more than five seconds.'

I look at the lines spoken by Cynthia before the second kiss.

The stage directions make things worse. How am I supposed to kiss her 'ruthlessly'? What does it mean? Do I have to grab her and kiss her hard while she flails around helplessly like Olive Oyl in the arms of Bluto? Cynthia obviously doesn't enjoy what's going on. She's just submitting to this cad, this bounder, this character who is becoming my nemesis. It isn't going to be a pleasurable experience. I suddenly decide I don't want the part. The dead body seems an infinitely better bet. At least I could lie on the floor, taken away from all the complications of having to sort out a relationship involving four people.

'Look,' says Al, 'Judith will be arriving alone on the train. She's the only member of the cast travelling down the line from Padgate. Arrive a few seconds earlier, meet her by chance, and ask her out. It will be your own personal brief encounter but this time with a happy ending.'

TWELVE

I'm Gonna Make You Mine
Lou Christie. Single Release. Buddah Records.

Friday. Seven o'clock. Widnes station. The amber light on the signal indicates that the 6.40 from Padgate is a whistle away down the line. I've decided I'll wait on the bridge and then catch Judith up before she gets to The Dell. All I need is the first line. It has to be something that gives a good impression but not something over-familiar or too nonchalant. I have to come over properly. Cool, approachable, friendly, homely, macho? I have no idea. I know nothing about Judith or her taste in boys or even whether she is dating someone outside school. For all I know she could be in the middle of a long-standing relationship and I'm just another admirer who needs to be wafted away.

She is definitely a Paul Rodgers type of girl. I can see her standing at the side of the stage, staring out from the wings, swaying gently to the intro to 'I'm A Mover'. Paul's girl would be just like her. The sort of girl who caught your eye while you were watching a band. The sort who would throw your mates into fits of envy if you turned up to the pub with her. Ralph had described her as untouchable. Well, in seconds, I'll be within touching distance.

The slim, green, two-car diesel slides smoothly under the bridge and into the station. I sense a terrible sinking feeling in my stomach and an overwhelming desire to rush down onto the platform, jump into the first coach, and travel on down the line to Hough Green and sanctuary away from Simon and Cynthia. A few passengers alight and there's Judith, her thick blonde hair mingling with the fleecy top of her coat. The script she's obviously been reading is clasped tightly in her left hand.

I feel reassured. She's been thinking about me throughout the journey. Well, Simon really, but it is me. I mean her vision of Simon will physically be me. She'd have seen the kiss as me and her, imagined it and lived it. The trouble is I don't know what emotions this has conjured up. Maybe, just maybe, she's thinking the same as me and she envisages our first kiss in the way I've dreamt it. In which case, she'll be looking for a way forward too and we can sort out the problem before it's started.

As she disappears into the ticket office, I shoot down off the bridge and stumble after her. She's a little way up the station approach when I catch her up.

'Judith! Hiya!'

'Oh, hi, Phil!' She smiles and we keep on walking.

'Have you read through the script?' This is not the line of my dreams. Of course she's read the script. This is the first major rehearsal. She wouldn't come to it without reading the script.

'Yes, good isn't it?'

'Brilliant! Yeh! Brilliant!'

'Which is your favourite bit?' We stop outside The Dell.

'Well,' I pick my script out of my pocket and sit down on the wall, 'I suppose........' I scramble through the pages. What is my favourite bit? I've been so preoccupied with the events of page 22 that I haven't really read the rest of it in any detail. Judith sits down beside me.

'My favourite scene,' her eyes sparkle as she turns the pages, 'is the bit where Lord Muldoon crashes down the stairs on page 23 just after Cynthia and Simon kiss.' She laughs, 'Have you got a girlfriend?'

'No, why?'

'Well, it might be a bit embarrassing if they're in the audience. I wouldn't want my boyfriend kissing another girl, even if it was acting.'

'So won't he mind Cynthia kissing Simon?' I can't say, 'You kissing me'. I haven't accepted that this kiss on stage has anything to do with real life. Simon could be played by anyone.

'Oh, I haven't got a boyfriend, yet.'

91

'Right!' I smile at her, hoping I don't look too stupid.

'You don't smoke, do you?' The smile is suddenly gone, replaced by a quizzical frown.

'No, I've never even tried one.' It's almost a truth. I've never really touched cigarettes except on a few occasions when Al, Ralph and I rode on the back of Mick's milk float, down to the Mersey near Fiddlers Ferry Power Station at sunset. We'd park up off the lonely back road from Warrington to Widnes, Mick would pass around a joint or two, and the four of us would sit watching the huge, brick, cooling towers belch out steam, pretending they were rockets about to propel Earth off into some distant star system. Mick would link his record player up to the battery on the milk float and we'd puff away into the night listening to *Electric Ladyland*.

'I just hate kissing boys who smoke.' The furrows have disappeared. I feel guilty that a simple untruth has made things alright but this is definitely the chance to move things along.

'Erm, seeing as we're going to be seeing a lot of each other during the play, I was wondering if you'd like to come out one night.'

'You mean on a date?' There's a moment of hesitation. She looks me up and down as if she's in a shop thinking about buying something but not sure whether to bother.

'Well, yes, I mean we could go for a drink and talk about the play, or maybe a concert if you fancy that.'

'Ok! Why don't you come over to Warrington tomorrow? I usually go out on Saturday.'

'Great, where to?'

'Young Farmers. We meet in the Grey Horse near the river.'

Well, it isn't exactly what I'd envisaged, but I can hardly say no. I've never met any young farmers. Al will tell me to put it down to experience and, anyway, I have a date with Judith. I can finally begin to forget the pain of Lesley. Now all I have to do is avoid page 22 today and hope that Young Farmers ends early enough to get the last bus back to Long Barn Lane and pray for fine weather and moonlight.

'You remind me of someone.' Judith touches my arm but a few alarm bells start ringing. I mean she could pull any name out of the hat here and it could give me an awful insight into what she thinks of me. I just pray it won't mean a complete image-changing exercise again. I've had enough with the Rock-Motown-Rock identity crisis. I'd need a regeneration of Dr Who proportions to turn me into a young farmer. Better to pre-empt the whole thing and even put someone into her head who maybe she's never thought of.

'Not Paul Rodgers, by any chance?' I say it as if everybody says it. As if I am fed up of people coming up to me in the street and asking me for my autograph.

She pauses for a moment. 'Who's he?' My heart drops into my baseball boots. She's never heard of Free.

'Oh, he's just the lead singer of a band I like. They're pretty good really. I'll lend you some of their records.'

'George Harrison! Definitely George Harrison!'

This is slightly worrying because I don't know which George Harrison she means. Is it the quiet, innocent, half-smiling stooge, who was occasionally allowed to step forward and sing a few phrases with Paul and John, or is it the mysterious follower of the Maharishi Yogi who has cloaked himself in a cloud of spirituality and started writing some decent songs. More worrying is that his Dad was a bus conductor like Ronnie. George even auditioned for a part in the Quarrymen on top of a double-decker. If he hadn't managed to convince Lennon he could play he might have drifted into familial obscurity, with a ticket to ride the bus routes of Liverpool, instead of his spiritual journey to the Himalayan foothills.

A couple of hours later I'm in my bedroom flicking through my Beatles albums trying to pinpoint where the point of comparison lies.

I can take some heart in Harrison's appearance since his encounter with the Maharishi Yogi. At least he's ditched that big, floppy fringe which masked half of his eyes. At least on

93

Abbey Road, he has a passing resemblance to Paul. The hair is about the same length and the tight, flared blue jeans are similar to the two pairs I own, but he just lacks any sort of charisma.

I pick up *Tons of Sobs.* Inside the gatefold sleeve, the four members of Free are sitting in what looks like the bedroom of a dilapidated, old flat. There are just bare floorboards, a bed and a refreshing decadence about the whole picture. This is me! Nothing is exciting or different about George Harrison. He's too clean cut, too nice. I want to be nice to Judith but not in a George Harrison kind of way. I want us to end up somewhere like that, to take a grainy black and white picture of us both, so we can show it to our children in years hence and say, 'That was us back in the Sixties, weren't we cool?'

THIRTEEN

You Ain't Livin' 'til You're Lovin'
Marvin Gaye and Tammi Terrell. Single Release. Tamla Motown.

My father loves trains. At home, we have a large bookcase next to the fireplace and it's full of train books and magazines. There are things like, *Great Railway Wonders of the World*, a collection of magazines full of black and white pictures of enormous engines hauling freight across the Canadian Rockies and the wastelands of Siberia. There's a complete railway timetable for the Steam Navigation Lines of America, Canada, Mexico and Cuba, full of journeys across the continents which are perfectly navigable if you have the time and financial means to put them into practice. After driving his lorry all day, my Dad settles down to read his books well into the night steaming, in his imagination, across the continents of the World, away from his drab, monotonous journeys to distant crisp factories in Corby or Broxburn.

When I was younger our holidays always included some railway experience. We'd often have a week in a camping coach at Hest Bank in Blackpool, parked up just outside the station, with the waves breaking in from the Irish Sea on one side and the express trains thundering towards Glasgow or London on the other. There were journeys on The Cambrian Railway across Wales, through picturesque backwaters, to the coastal stations of Barmouth and Aberdovey. Most excitingly, we'd travel on a sleeper from Warrington to Edinburgh and then on into the Highlands to Inverness. All this happened before my Mum left home after which the journeys stopped, and Dad settled back into his books and the occasional trip alone up to Scotland to see a friend I've never met.

Still, if all this has resulted in one thing, it's given me an overwhelming belief that a journey on a train is taking me somewhere special and I'm standing on Hough Green Station waiting for the 8.05. to Warrington, with those feelings from my childhood giving me the same hope and anticipation that I'm about to begin a journey which will take me off to better things.

We don't get many steam trains on this line anymore. They are mostly drab, green, diesel multiple units that leave the station with an unpleasant rasping sound and an abusive honk. When I see the steam from the ageing tank engine drawing down the bank from Hunts Cross it has to be a good omen from those seaside days. It's pulling some old compartment coaches and I settle down alone gazing out of the window pretending the clouds gathering across the Mersey Estuary are really the mountains of North Wales and, in a few minutes, I'll be arriving at Portmadoc Station and Judith will be there waving from the end of the platform.

I've dressed carefully for the occasion. I don't really know what to expect. I know the Grey Horse is a popular folk venue and I've supposed it's the sort of music young farmers are into. I wonder if the guys will be dressed in check shirts with their girls in long, flared dresses. Well, it isn't going to be as bad as trying to adapt from rock to soul and I do like some folky stuff. Joni Mitchell is ok, and Fairport Convention almost bridges the gap into Al's progressive world. In fact, in my beige Wrangler jacket, white t-shirt and blue jeans, I bear a passing resemblance to a photograph I've seen of their bassist, Ashley Hutchings, in the *New Musical Express*.

Warrington Central doesn't fit into any of my images from childhood. It's dark, cold and draughty with the echoes of slamming doors and porters shouting, reverberating around the green, steel canopy above its platforms. I've arranged to meet Judith here but after five minutes the train and its passengers have departed and I'm left alone in the silence with the wind whipping inside my jacket and bits of paper blowing down the platform.

97

I button up my Wrangler, feel it looks stupid, and unbutton it. I walk on down the platform into the buffet thinking about a cup of tea but I grab a Coke in case Judith appears in the next few minutes.

The room is empty except for the assistant who sits behind the tea urn, half masked by a shroud of warm steam which occasionally generates enough pressure to lift the lid. There's a sort of half-light giving the impression of the end of the day, a time for clearing up and putting away. All the anticipation of the train journey is beginning to ebb and I think of all the unmet lovers who must have sat here, one eye on the door and the other on the clock which sits ticking unrelentingly above a large poster of the Yorkshire Dales.

It's half an hour after our scheduled meeting time when I hear footsteps hurrying along the platform. Through the steamy windows, I catch a glimpse of Judith as she heads past in the direction of the waiting room. Suddenly, I don't want to meet her like this. Paul Rodgers wouldn't have stayed. After a few minutes, he'd have left the station and gone and found some bar. He'd have picked up another chick by now and it would have been tough luck on Judith.

I poke my head out of the door. There's no sign of her and I nip into the gents' toilet which is just next door After a few anxious moments there are some more pattering footsteps, a couple of banged doors, and then silence.

I give it a few seconds and then make my way to the top of the station approach. Judith is disappearing in the direction of The Grey Horse but she'll sensibly keep to the well-lit streets which take her around by Bridge Street and the bus station. I know a short cut across the back of the railway yards and some waste ground near the Persil factory. In a few of minutes I'm there, leaning on the bar drinking a Whisky Mac with my eyes glued firmly on the door.

Judith arrives. She's wearing a three-quarter length fur coat, a tight, beige, woollen jumper, grey mini skirt and black boots. Her blonde hair has blown back over her shoulders and she

98

has a reddish complexion from the cold outside. She looks every inch Paul's girl.

'Judith, I thought you weren't coming, I was just about to go.'

She looks puzzled.

'I thought we'd arranged to meet at the station.'

'Oh, you weren't there, so I thought we must have agreed to meet here.'

'Sorry, I got delayed at home. I had a last-minute row with my dad. He doesn't like me coming out on my own. I missed the bus and had to hitch it.'

I feel a sudden overwhelming protectiveness towards her, a feeling I've not encountered since Angel Clare dumped Tess on their wedding night. She's hitched a lift to meet me, against her father's wishes, in the dark. This is serious stuff and I want to give her something of the same back, but at this moment I don't know how.

'You want to take care out there. You never know who you'll meet.' I don't know whether I sound over-protective. The remark could have been made by Paul or Jimi who would have said it pulling her close. More likely it sounds like my Dad would have said it, or probably her Dad. It sounds like a telling off.

'Come on, let's go!' She beckons towards the stairs which lead to the upstairs room. I can hear the dull thud of a bassline from the room above but can't make out what kind of music it is. I down my drink and follow Judith who is already part way up the stairs.

The room is pretty full and noisy. I'm expecting to see some kind of band but in the far corner of the room is a guy with some battered, old disco equipment and a couple of spotlights which provide most of the light in the place. Lots of young farmers about my age are standing around drinking pints. They are dressed mostly in t-shirts and denims and there's a sort of after work atmosphere as if they've just come in from the fields and are quenching gigantic thirsts born out of working for hours on the land.

'Pretty Woman' ends and the DJ swaps the records without talking. Judith walks across the dance floor to the opening bars of 'Friday On My Mind'. It seems to grab the attention of some of the guys and they start applauding and singing loudly. Two lads and a girl are sitting in the corner near the bar.

'Steve, Lenny, Janice, this is Phil, he's a friend.'

Janice raises her eyebrows at me and smiles. The lads carry on drinking and I begin to feel a little uncomfortable. The atmosphere is getting loud and people are shouting above the music.

Judith leans forward and whispers something in Janice's ear. I'm just about to offer to buy some drinks when Judith takes me by the arm and guides me back towards the door.

'What's happening?' I look back at Janice, Lenny and Steve who are re-immersed in conversation.

'We're going. I don't want us to spend the evening here? I was just telling Janice I'd see her in the week. Come on!' She draws me down the stairs, through the bar, and suddenly we are out into the cold, clear night away from the smoke and the singing and the Easybeats.

'Young Farmers is fine once in a while but it's not where you'd want to spend a first date.'

I laugh, trying to hide my relief. 'Right, so where is a good place?'

'Well,' she smiles, 'I thought perhaps we could go for a walk first. I've never been one for sitting in smoky pubs and talking above loads of noise. Then, if it's ok, there's The Mersey View down across the river. Not many people go in there and it's near my bus stop.'

It sounds brilliant. The night is cold but even the Mersey can look romantic in the moon-reflected light. We walk away from the town centre and down to the riverside walk with its quaint metal lamp posts and red sandstone. There are recesses every few yards and we sit on one of the cold, metal seats

100

claiming some protection from the wind which is stronger down by the river. We sit next to each other, almost touching.

I've never had a first date like this before. Mostly you meet someone and go somewhere which fills up a large part of the evening, like a film or a concert, so that you don't have to worry much about conversation because it only needs to happen in bits and you get through to the kissing bit at the end without too much mental exertion. Now there's no film, no concert and no alcohol to steady the nerves. Does she want us to talk or should I just lean across, slide my hands inside the fleecy coat, and draw her close? It's an attractive thought. I'm starting to freeze and the coat looks easily big enough for two. Across the river, I can see the lights of the Mersey View and the orange glow coming from the lounge window.

I get up from the seat. 'I think I'd rather walk, it's getting a bit chilly here.'

'Ok, you can tell you don't live on a farm. You get not to notice the cold, especially when you're up at six in the morning milking the cows.'

'Just like Tess.'

'Oh, you're doing that for A-level as well. Don't you feel for her, the way she battles against fate and the injustice of it all?'

'I think Angel treats her really badly.'

'Worse than that. He destroys her because he just doesn't understand her. He has this idealised vision of her; all that genuine daughter of nature rubbish which he comes out with. As soon as he learns of her real mistakes, he just can't cope. He just hypocritically rejects her for the exact same things he's done himself. I'd hate someone to have an idealised version of me, not bothering to find out what I'm really like.'

I take a deep breath and make a mental note not to call her Tess if my concentration lapses.

'I just want to jump into the book and tell him what I think of him.'

'I feel exactly like that.'

101

I think back to my first date with Lesley where she'd talked about the lyrics to 'My Girl' and how they were her favourite. After she'd finished we'd kissed and that had been the start of it all. Smokey Robinson had built the bridge between us and now Judith is talking with the same sort of passion about Thomas Hardy. I take hold of her hand, pull her around and kiss her. We never get to The Mersey Tavern. An hour later we are still under the sky looking across the river at the stars which shine above the dark, industrial outline of the Persil factory. The fur coat is gathered around us and we're wrapped up in ourselves, warm and alone, every bit as wonderful as I'd imagined it to be. At next week's rehearsal, Simon and Cynthia will be banished back to the level of fictional characters with no more substance than the lines from the script.

On the train home, I watch the moon unshifting in the sky knowing that Judith will be lit by the same glow as she walks home down Long Barn Lane. I sink back in my seat and stare out of the window giving a mental nod to Clotho as I gaze up at the stars.

FOURTEEN

Do What You Gotta Do
The Four Tops. Single Release. Tamla Motown.

I run the mile from Hough Green Station to home. I want to talk to someone, tell them about how I feel. As I pass Al's house, I want to knock him up even though the lights are out and there are no sounds drifting through his half-open bedroom window. I think better of it, carry on running to Regal Crescent, jump the garden wall, and in a few seconds I'm lying flat out on my bed, staring at the plain, white ceiling listening to Jimi coolly singing the opening lines to 'Angel' which wash over me like breaking waves.

This has to be our song, even if Judith doesn't know it. I open my drawer and find a picture of Lesley. It was taken the previous summer when she was on holiday in Weston Super Mare, leaning against the promenade railing on a gloriously hot day. Her dark hair and complexion contrast with the blue of the sea and sky and she looks beautiful and happy and content. She'd told me that I made every day feel like that day and that I had to keep the picture forever and promise never to part with it. Tonight is the first time I've been able to bring myself to look at it since we finished. The feelings have finally been replaced and it can be consigned to the file under my bed which contains oddments of memorabilia from other important parts of my life.

The track finishes and I lie on the bed for a few minutes just contemplating, drifting off into a half-sleep of contentment and warm feelings. The picture of Lesley slips from my hand and slides onto the floor next to my Subbuteo pitch.

I'm dragged back to full consciousness by the sound of my Dad making a late night trip to the toilet. As I wait for him to finish, I reach for Babs' present. Inside are two singles and a small card which reads,

Not sure what you're into but don't forget
Motown. Babs. XXX

The first single is a second-hand copy of 'Hey Joe' on the white 'Track' label with the name of the previous owner scribbled out in biro. The second single is new, in a chocolate brown, starry Motown sleeve. 'Do What You Gotta Do', by The Four Tops, is in the charts but I have no recollection of actually hearing it.

Judging that it's rather late to subject my Dad to the heavy metal of one of Jimi's finest, I slip the Motown disc out of its sleeve and drop it onto the turntable. It will be my first Motown track since the break with Lesley. Sentimentally, I pick up her picture and sit back.

The intro is pleasant enough with a few whimsical horns playing over a slow melodic beat. It's typical Motown, and I'm just about to flick off the needle when the opening lyrics fracture the atmosphere, sending me spiralling backwards, the excitement of the last few hours suddenly crumbling into sharp fragments of depression and pain. I try to shut out the vocals but I'm being held by a song about a guy letting his girl go because it's for the best, knowing it's the most painful and devastating decision of his life. There's empty hope that maybe one day she'll come back but the message that she's gone repeats through the chorus before the tone of the singer drops. Suddenly, Levi Stubbs is in my bedroom talking to me, whispering, drawing together all the emotions which have been buried and I'm trying to smother the explosion of feelings but I don't have the strength. The final click from the record player switches on the silence. I sit holding the picture of Lesley, the tears trickling down from my face waterlogging the goalmouth of the Subbuteo pitch which sticks out from the end of the bed.

After a sleepless night, I've headed to The Tavern for a lunchtime drink with Jimmy. We are having a quiet pint; a sort of pub etiquette we've developed over the last couple of years. It works well. You find a table away from friends who are in a more positive state of mind. You drink your beer at half the usual speed, pausing significantly between sups to consider issues. You agree on strategies and meet again for more quiet pints later in the week to review progress, reverting to a normal consumption rate depending on the amount of mental unravelling which has taken place.

I unload the events of the last twenty-four hours to Jimmy and sit back. He takes a sip and thinks. He takes two more sips, downs his pint in one, savours the moment, and places the empty glass carefully on the table. He motions to me to do the same and seconds later my empty glass joins his without a word passing between us.

'So?'

'I can tell you're an atheist.'

'What?'

'Well, you believe that there's no life after death. Soul's dead. Your thing with Lesley's dead and you're just sitting in a black void instead of resurrecting yourself. Get over it! Forget her! Can we talk about football, now?'

I pick up the empty glasses and amble over to the bar. Bernice is her usual laconic self. If she is a body snatcher, one of her key powers will be the ability to completely wipe the minds of Earthlings, so I decide to give her the chance to make contact.

'Hi, Bernice. Two pints of Guinness. Do you have the power to make people forget?'

'Course I do, love.' She reaches under the bar and pulls out a bottle of Johnny Walker's Red. 'Few shots of this in your beer and you won't remember anything. Works wonders for the blokes in the bar, most of them can't remember their wives after about twenty minutes. Shall I?'

She holds the bottle high above the Guinness as if poised to dispense some magic elixir which will banish the World's evils.

'No thanks, Bernice. Just thought you might have had the power, if you'd done it before, that is?'

'Don't be bloody stupid. And, anyway, I thought you were all into books and remembering things. Isn't that what you do up at the Wade? Too bloody intelligent for your own good if you ask me. What have you got to forget, anyway?'

'Oh, just the summer of '69, that's all.'

'Bloody easy, that! I went to Skegness and it pissed down. Forgotten it already.'

FIFTEEN

Race With The Devil
Gun. Single Release. CBS Records.

I am seeing a new side to Mugga. His elevation into acting circles has brought out a hidden side to his character. He's got the part of the dead body and he's taking it seriously. Apart from being given this comatose acting role, Steve's made him props manager and we need a wheelchair.

Ralph's part demands that he's pushed around the stage as the crippled Lord and Tommy has done his best to give him a Stanislavskian insight into the role by practically breaking his leg in a First XV training session. Ralph has decided that the time has come to incorporate the wheelchair into rehearsals, thus protecting his leg in preparation for the forthcoming encounter with some Argentinean schoolboys who are to play the school as part of their European tour.

The problem of where the wheelchair might be acquired has been solved by Mugga who has suggested we 'borrow' one from Farnworth House, an old folk's home, situated at the end of a long slope, a quarter of a mile from the school.

Each Thursday the occupants of Farnworth House are taken by bus to Widnes Community Centre. Some residents are pushed to the gate and then helped, or carried, by two carers onto the bus. The driver has the responsibility of loading up the wheelchairs and, as he can only complete this task one wheelchair at a time, a cluster of a dozen or so are always left unguarded. Mugga has a plan to distract the driver and snaffle a wheelchair from under his nose providing us with a first class realistic prop and some unsuspecting pensioner with a two-hour sit on the coach instead of an afternoon of tea and bingo.

He's also got permission for us to skip General Studies; an unsurprisingly simple task as any request to masters for him to miss their lessons is greeted with an affirmative almost before the reason is half explained. Our names have been mumbled as part of the package and we are freed into that strange afternoon world you don't see very often unless you are wagging it or out on a cross country run.

It's an empty world free from the hustle and bustle of children, and there's a feeling of anticipation as we throw off the shackles of school and make our way past The Tuck Shop and up the slope along Birchfield Road. The only people around are two women who are waiting for a bus opposite the school gate. They wear the light-blue uniforms of the dinner ladies from Farnworth House, a sign that the mass movement of metal is about to get underway. The air is crisp and clear with the low, September sunshine throwing long shadows across the empty road.

The bus has just arrived as we approach the brow of the hill. Two residents of Farnworth House have reached the coach early and have already been loaded onto the bus. The driver sits in his cab smoking a Woodbine and two wheelchairs stand invitingly out of sight at the rear of the bus. Mugga seizes the opportunity and deploys Ralph to engage the driver in conversation.

'Don't you drive the bus to Hunts Cross?' Ralph has the knack of talking to people as if he's known them forever and the driver is soon chatting about his life and classic bus journeys to be found in this year's Yates' Excursion Brochure.

The two residents on the bus have also been drawn into the conversation as Mugga sweeps one of the wheelchairs behind a nearby bush. The single remaining chair is joined by a dozen others as the remaining residents arrive and the party is soon on its way leaving Mugga to wheel out his prize to ripples of applause from the rest of us.

'Do you know,' says Ralph, 'that if you're going to Llangollen on a day out you never take the A542 through the Horseshoe Pass you come off at Mold and take the diversion down the A494 through Ruthin and Corwen?'

'This wheelchair knows no diversions,' boasts Mugga. He opens out the wheels and jumps onto the canvas seat. 'Give us a puckin' push.'

In a flash, Ralph has launched all his body weight against the chair. The wheels skid on the gravel drive before straining to gain traction on the tarmac. Slowly the chair increases its momentum like a Gresley Pacific leaving Kings Cross on a long run.

The rest of us run behind Ralph. I'd watched the 1968 Winter Olympics from Innsbruck and fleeting images of the bobsleigh events flash back into my mind. At any moment, I envisage Ralph, as the brakeman, leaping onto the back of the chair and disappearing with Mugga in a shower of dust down Widnes' re-creation of the Cresta Run.

The chair has reached a fair speed at the brow of the hill when disaster strikes. The brakeman loses his footing and sprawls onto the floor. His desperate attempt to save himself serves only to give the chair one final push and Mugga is adrift, hurtling down the hill with his cry of, 'You stupid bastard, Clayton!' fading into the wind.

At the bottom of the hill, the two dinner ladies are still waiting. As they gaze impatiently up the rise looking for the town centre bus, which is already late, a flash of silver on the empty road catches their eyes. They strain their heads forward, simultaneously reaching into their handbags to retrieve their glasses to give them a better chance of identifying the object.

We run after Mugga, but it's no use. While we've reached our maximum velocity, Mugga is speeding away from us getting faster by the second, the theory of acceleration due to gravity being wonderfully illustrated before our eyes.

At one point we think Mugga might brave the pain of burning flesh on rubber to grab the tyres and arrest the speed enough for him to jump off but it is not to be as he sits paralysed with fear. There are no cars on the road but, just past the school gates, is the beginning of the steep decent down Kingsway into the town centre. If Mugga reaches this point the acceleration will send him hurtling towards the town hall at time-travelling speed and the discovery of his skeleton clinging rigidly to a piece of unidentifiable machinery will become one of the great mysteries of the 31st century. I think of the irony of Mugga's remark, 'This wheelchair knows no diversions.', and mentally begin to prepare his obituary for the school magazine.

Up to now the speed of the object has made it too difficult for the dinner ladies to make out, even with the aid of their glasses. However, as it races into view, the full horror of the situation dawns on them. One of their inmates is adrift and out of control in a runaway wheelchair. They are going to be first-hand witnesses to its terrifying journey as it hurtles past them leaving them trembling and traumatised in its wake.

Mugga is desperate now. His hair is swept back and his face contorted by pressure. The wind whistles a terrifying tune through the heavy spoked wheels and the point of no return is approaching at an alarming speed. In panic and desperation, Mugga leans all his weight to one side of the chair. The effect is dramatic. As he draws level with the bus stop, the chair lifts onto one wheel and takes a 90-degree turn across the road and through the school gates. There is a squeal of rubber and a distinct smell of burning as the free wheel makes contact with the ground, but without any discernible drop in speed the chair carries on towards the staff car park.

The two dinner ladies gallop across the road in pursuit of the chair which is hurtling towards Headmistress Thakara's Morris Minor. Mugga tries in vain to exact another deviation from the chair but his strength and determination have been sapped with fear. There is the terrible rending of metal on metal as the wheel of the chair makes contact with the back wing. The retaining bolts snap under the strain and the force of the impact removes the wing from the bodywork sending it spiralling into the air before coming to rest in the middle of the school drive.

Amazingly, the chair carries on, finally impacting with a grass verge and sending Mugga sprawling gratefully onto the soft surface unscathed from his ordeal. The two dinner ladies are almost upon the scene when they witness a wondrous event. The cripple leaps from the ground and, without a backwards glance or a hallelujah, runs for his life leaving the women with an empty wheelchair as the sole evidence of the miracle which has just materialised in the grounds of Wade Deacon over three thousand miles from Capernaum.

We carry on running, arriving at the front gates breathless and bent double as we try to stifle the pain of the laughter welling up inside us. Composed, but not entirely under control, we saunter nonchalantly down the main drive, but images of the consequences are already forming, with the humour of the events replaced by a rising fear of an inevitable appearance in the WAB's office.

The next time we see Mugga is at the specially convened assembly later that afternoon. The knees of his trousers are torn through, and a pocket flaps freely from the side of his old blazer.

These special assemblies are almost gladiatorial. If you are innocent then you wait eagerly for punishment to be heaped ceremonially upon the villain, especially if it's someone you don't like or a bully getting his comeuppance. The frightening thing is that this time, it's us and the traditions of the school require you to own up and die with honour.

Eric Huntingfield, the Deputy Head, stands lookout at the front of the stage, scanning the hall for boys who might be moving or speaking. We all stand up. This is part of the WAB's strategy. The longer it goes without the offender owning up, the weaker we all become and exhaustion or peer group pressure forces a capitulation. There is silence.

I stare at the stage. Behind Huntingfield is the WAB's table with three empty chairs. On either side are two small rostra.

On one is a slightly damaged wheelchair and on the other a grey, nearside wing from a Morris Minor. The two dinner ladies sit behind the gathered piles of metal.

'Be prepared for the Headmaster!' Huntingfield's voice cuts the heavy atmosphere.

Somewhere back along the corridor a door slams and there is the muted noise of heavy footsteps approaching the hall. The double doors are swept open by the senior prefects and the WAB pounds in followed by Miss Thackara and the warden from Farnworth House. The WAB is at the midpoint of the aisle when somebody coughs. He stops dead, frozen in an exaggerated tableau, listens intently to the silence for what seems an age, turns on his heels, and marches with the platform party back out of the hall.

We wait, wondering how we can improve on the silence. Moments later there is the same heavy tread and the same dramatic entrance. The stillness is painful. Every bit of noise has been squeezed out of the hall save for that generated by the WAB and I swear the walls are pulling in from the sides compressing the space into a vacuum of fear. The emptiness is unnerving, worrying. Somewhere at the front a first-year faints and is carried out silently.

This time, the platform party reaches the stage. Huntingfield edges backwards without taking his eyes from us. Everyone on stage, except the WAB, sits down. He motions to two prefects to come forward. They pick up the wing from the Morris Minor and, like two assistants at a Sotheby's auction, bear it to the edge of the stage. The WAB speaks.

'Gentlemen, I would like to test your powers of lateral thinking. Two dinner ladies from Farnworth House, a stray wheelchair and the wing from a 1967 Morris Minor have arrived at this point in time on our stage. I would like every boy in this hall to think this perplexity through and put up their hands if they think they have a plausible explanation.'

If anybody has an answer they don't dare announce it to the rest of the school. This is no place for humour and answers such as Farnworth House are melting down Morris Minors to make their own wheelchairs or dinner ladies, wheelchairs and Morris Minors all have a top speed of 5 m.p.h. would not have graced the atmosphere which is now approaching oppression.

'We will all stand here until I have an explanation!' This is no surprise. It is the WAB's usual tactic. In 1967 the whole school had been detained until early evening waiting for Eric Ecclestone to confess that he was the one who had locked a supply teacher in a Science Department cupboard overnight.

This time, the wait is mercifully short. Gallantly, Mugga puts up his hand and without any exchange of words between himself and the WAB turns and leaves the hall for the Head's office.

I glance at Al and Ralph and seconds later the four of us are lined up outside the heavy, oak door, the first years filing silently past us back to the safety of lessons.

I've only ever been in the WAB's office once before. That was to get my O-Level results. I'd stood outside anxious and nervous, more worried about letting him and the school down if I hadn't passed. I did just enough to get into the sixth form. I came out with five passes and he'd made me feel like a king.

The WAB sweeps past us into his room carrying the Morris Minor wing under his arm. He slams the door shut, waits approximately ten seconds and reopens it quietly. 'Come in gentleman.' It is as if he is welcoming us to his club.

'Fellows,' he says gently, 'You have let the side down.'

I feel bad. We explain the events of the afternoon and wait for the WAB's judgement.

'You, McKenzie have let the side down continually over the past six years and you will be suspended for one week. Before you return make sure you have this repaired and returned to its position on the rear, nearside of Miss Thakara's car. Now, you may leave.'

Mugga takes the chunk of metal and stumbles through the door without a backwards glance.

'Sit down.' He indicates the three green, leather chairs to one side of his desk. We hesitate. 'Sit down fellows.' We seat ourselves on the edges of the chairs and wait for the WAB to continue.

It is the naivety of youth that's led me to believe that if you keep out of somebody's way they never bother to find out anything about you. I've assumed that, because I haven't actually spoken to the WAB since that August day in 1966, he knows nothing about me. I'm wrong. I should have known I was wrong. He knows the name of every First Year after two weeks of the new term. This is my seventh year.

'Old Stephens,' the potted history of my life begins. 'This is only the second time you have been in this room. You have five O-levels and are studying English Literature, Economics and Art in the sixth form. You captain the Second X1 and are a member of the school Drama society. You are playing the part of Simon Gascoigne in *The Real Inspector Hound.* You live with your father and grandmother and are not a bad sort. You are more interested in popular music than work but should just do enough to get through your A-levels. Am I right?'

'Yes, Sir!' I have no option but to agree with his assessment. The statements are all true. What else does he know? Does he know about Judith and Lesley? Does he know about my desire to turn into Paul Rodgers and my collection of Superman comics?

The biographies are completed in similar detail for Al and Ralph. I don't know what the WAB is trying to achieve. Maybe they are our school obituaries to be completed with the final detail, '.....and you were expelled in September 1969 for your part in the theft of a wheelchair and subsequent damage to a headmistress's Morris Minor.'

The WAB's tone softens. 'Chaps, you have got in with a bad sort. Old McKenzie is one of the types we have to take on board but he does not belong here.'

115

I know at this point we are not going to be expelled. The guilt inside is instantly halved. I've let the WAB down, which is bad, but to have to go home to explain to my Dad that I'd been an accomplice to the theft of a wheelchair would have meant a major shattering of the trust between us.

'You will go over to Miss Thackara and carry the apologies of the school with you and then you will go to Farnworth House and assure them that an incident of this sort will never happen again. You will arrange, with the warden, to do two hours community service on Saturday morning thus, Stephens and Morefield, missing the First X1 and Second X1 matches against Bluecoat, and, Clayton, the prestigious encounter with the Argentinian touring team.' The WAB rises from his chair and strides over to his bookshelf. He smartly removes three copies of The New Testament and hands us each a book. 'In addition,' he continues, 'you will copy out the whole of *Corinthians 2,* paying particular attention to 'Forgiveness For The Sinner'.'

He detects the puzzled look on our faces and reads from his copy of the Bible. 'I have forgiven in the sight of Christ for your sake, in order that Satan may not outwit us. For we are not unaware of his schemes. Tread carefully gentlemen, Satan himself masquerades as an angel of light. I will receive the copies at 9.00.a.m. on Wednesday morning.'

He opens the study door and we leave, thanking him on the way out.

SIXTEEN

Something
The Beatles. Abbey Road. Apple Records.

.

Farnworth House is an old vicarage standing in leafy grounds next to Widnes Cemetery. We push through the iron gates breaking the early Saturday silence with the crunch of our shoes on the gravel drive. There's silence too as the warden beckons us in. There's no need for explanations and we're ushered briskly into a small side room. There are smells of creams, ointments, antiseptic, old books, papers and clothes but they're overwhelmed by the odour of grease as the remains of breakfast are trolleyed away into the kitchen.

'Ralph will be helping to clean the ovens this morning.' I glance through the window which looks out over the cemetery and hope she's not referring to the crematorium. 'Alan will be helping clear the leaves and moss from the pathways around the gardens and Philip will be indulging in some social intercourse with two of our oldest residents.'

Ralph almost breaks into a snigger but manages to disguise it as a cough. They're led away and I'm taken by one of the care staff into a large, empty lounge which is stiflingly warm with a thick, Axminster carpet which sticks to my feet. In the corner of the bay window, sitting bolt upright in solid wing-back chairs, are two old ladies. They are both wide awake and their eyes cast an almost demonic glint as if years of waiting for someone to appear are finally over. Halfway across the room the carer stops and drops her voice.

'Those two over there are Minnie and Mabel. They're both eighty seven, sharp as splinters, and they talk the staff to the point of exhaustion. You can chat with them for a couple of hours. I'll bring some tea halfway through.' With that, she exits towards the staff lounge unbuttoning her plastic apron and slinging it onto an empty chair.

'Hello, love. Sit down and take your coat off.' Minnie is the slightly larger of the two, looks better fed, and smells as if she's just climbed out of a vat of Eau-de-Cologne. Mabel is thin and wiry and looks as if she's spent a lifetime running marathons, squeezing every ounce of fat from her fragile body. She rattles her false teeth into position, leans over and touches my arm with her bony fingers.

'Will you be coming every Saturday, love? We like having a chat, don't we, Minnie?'

'We do, Mabel, we do,' croaks Minnie. She pushes a packet of Old English Spangles into my hand.

'Unwrap two for us, love? And have one yourself.'

'Are you from round here, love?' says Mabel.

'Well I live in Hough Green but I grew up in West Bank.'

Minnie's eyes shine as if a golden light has been switched on inside her head.

'Spent all our lives there, didn't we Mabel. Both born in Hurst Street in 1882, right next to the river. Settle down, love, we'll tell you all about it.'

Two hours later I'm on Widnes station. It's my second date with Judith and I've run up and down the platform a dozen times to try and disperse the cocktail of smells lingering in the folds and threads of my clothes.

Second dates are always tricky. The temptation's usually to play safe and go for more of the same from the first date, but today's the opposite. We're off to Liverpool in broad daylight, with no comforting darkness to mellow the sharp edges of life, heading for a few hours in the Central Reference Library to research Hardy and poetry for the mocks. Usually, the first few dates are all a bit shallow and heavily dependent on drinking, dancing and physical attraction. It's as if we've bypassed all that and gone straight to the deeper, meaningful stuff. I've gone over and over things to say to her but they now lie in the outposts of my memory replaced by Minnie and Mabel's tales of love, life and laughter before the coming of the chemical industry to West Bank.

Judith's leaning out of the carriage window as the train pulls in and I'm grateful for the smell of oil and coal and the flakes of ash which swirl around the carriages, heavily overpowering the offensive odours from Farnworth House. We share a quick hug and kiss before settling down for the twenty-minute journey to Lime Street.

Judith holds my hand and leans her head on my shoulder. 'I can tell you've been in Farnworth House all morning?'

'How do you know that?'

'You smell like my Gran,' she laughs, grabbing my waist and pinching it hard. 'Eau-de-Cologne can be a real turn on. Know what to get you for Christmas now.'

We laugh and kiss and hug a bit more and the train rattles on. It's September 20th, and we're talking about Christmas.

'So tell me how you got on.'

'Well, I had an interesting history lesson on Victorian and Edwardian life on the shores of the Mersey.'

'Go on.'

By the time we're settled into the Central Library, Judith has drawn a parallel with West Bank and Wessex. Minnie and Mabel's peaceful world had been plundered by the Industrial Revolution and the arrival of John Hutchinson's factory in 1847. They just about had time to enjoy an idyllic childhood playing along the sandstone promenade, building sandcastles on the wide stretches of golden sand and watching the small, white fishing boats trawl in their catches of salmon from the sparkling, bright waters of a river whose days were numbered.

By the time they were teenagers the clouds had literally gathered in, cloaking the town in a suffocating fog and turning life into several shades of grey. The salmon disappeared along with the sand which was replaced with mudflats and, although life continued heroically, it was set against a background of relentless industrial strife. Hardy's world creaked, groaned and splintered under the pressure of modernisation, but Widnes

120

folk just built an arsenal of Woodbines, brown ale, cod liver oil tablets and vapour rub then met the revolution head on. Minnie and Mabel's life continued. The walks in Victoria Gardens, the choir in St Mary's Church, the summer evenings listening to the sounds of a brass band drifting across the estuary, the crowning of the rose queens and the trips to the Century Cinema were the green shoots of life which grew determinedly out of the darkness.

'Hardy's worst nightmare,' says Judith turning the images over in her mind. 'The bit in Tess where he describes that steam threshing machine at Flintcomb Ash. He says it's like a deity, a monster which has to be fed and tended. It strips away the identity of the workers who can't communicate because of its incessant noise. Just like your families in West Bank, I suppose. Heading for the factories each day must have cast them into a miserable plight.'

I've never been out with a girl who drops words like 'deity' and 'plight' into conversations. Lesley and I didn't talk like this. We talked about song lyrics and people we knew, and what they might be doing, and what we thought about what they might be doing and how good the Sink Club was. Then there would be more talk about people we knew and the circle continued on and on. This is all new and different and an awakening telling me that there's something more than physical attraction and the trivia of everyday life. I sit back in the old, wooden chair and look at Judith. She's half hidden behind a pile of literary crit books searching for evidence that Tess is a 'pure woman' battling against the hostile forces of fate as the omens stack against her.

We're on a second date in a cold, dusty library, a stone's throw from the Sink Club, wrapped together in unbroken silence. It's as if the world has shut us in and swept away the clutter of our lives. For two hours I'm with Hardy and my girl, the muddle of modernism swirling outside the impenetrable walls of the old Victorian building. As we leave, I'm almost expecting to step into the stillness of a late Wessex morning with the sun burning away the mist and allowing the muted calls of redstarts and tree pipits to break through the warm haze of a new day.

Disappointingly, it's pouring down and we pull each other through the puddles, tucking Tess under our coats to shelter her from the northern rain.

On the way home we plan our third date. I'm going to Judith's for tea and a look round the farm. I'm in a different world; no hanging around the streets and no clubs, with music and alcohol synthesising my emotions into the shallow lyrics of pop songs.

SEVENTEEN

Rainbow Chaser
Nirvana. You Can All Join In. Island Records.

It's been nearly two weeks since the last rehearsal and Ralph's breakup with Anne. He's sat in the window of the school library gazing in the direction of the girls' school, looking as if he's turning over several life events in his head and trying to establish some kind of symmetry between his love for Anne and his need to check out his desirability with Lisa Wilcox. The library's buzzing with activity. Three first years are copying out *Corinthians 2.* Ralph has had a word with Tommy who has agreed to help. It's cost us ten shillings. The first years get a shilling each, and blistered, ink-stained fingers, and Tommy pockets the rest by way of an arrangement fee.

Paul Wareing and his team are organising material for *The Griffin,* Wade Deacon's annual magazine, consisting of self-congratulatory reviews of the school's achievements. Features are submitted randomly by boys from all years and assorted advertisements from local businesses cover the costs. Paul is arranging some lunchtime interviews with prospective contributors. Al and I sit behind him looking at his list.

12.30 Tomlinson. 3 Gamma. U-12 Chess Champion 1968.
12.40 Lawrenson. 2 Alpha. Junior Conker Champion.
12.50 Boardman. Lower 6th. Arrested by Spanish Police for stealing a lilo on the school trip to Lloret-de-Mar.

The small, plump Tomlinson is dead on time. He wears national health specs, with a cheery face liberally scattered with freckles. Al and I listen in on the interview. Ralph lurks in the background.

'So, Tomlinson,' says Paul, 'what's your first name: Brains? Professor? Maestro?'

'Michael.'

'And you won the chess championship last year?'

'Yes.'

'And what are your ambitions?'

Tomlinson's face lights up. 'I'm going to practise hard and enter the county championships after Christmas and then, if things go well, try for the England Schoolboys' Competition in May. Mr Crewe thinks I have a good chance.'

Al leans across Paul's shoulder and peers into Tomlinson's eyes. 'Chance,' says Al, 'is something beyond your control. Remember, when you set foot out of that door, you are just a pawn, an insignificant speck on the chessboard of life. Your destiny has already been mapped out, every move shaped and preordained by the whim of the Fates.'

Tomlinson gives a toothy grin and laughs. 'You're mad.'

'Ralph jumps off the table and grabs him by the ear. 'Listen, squirt, respect your elders, and remember, someone out there is checkmating the end of your miserable existence even as we speak. Take care with your next move; it could be your last.'

Tears tumble from Tomlinson's eyes, zig-zagging a path through the maze of freckles. He squirms free of Ralph's grip and escapes through the door.

'Thanks,' says Paul. He scribbles out Tomlinson's response. 'I had him down for half a page.'

'No need to take things out on him,' says Al. 'It's not his fault Anne's ditched you.'

'Bollocks! It's all part of the character building process,' says Ralph, 'and, anyway, we need to re-group. Rehearsal, Wednesday night. I've sent a message to Shuttleworth.'

By the time we meet at YPF there's been a discernible change in Ralph. He's standing up straight and is more Zebedee than Eeyore. Something has changed to lift his spirits and catapulted him from the dark gloom of his breakup with Anne back to optimistic bass player. It appears that he's seen

Dave and come to an 'arrangement' which seems to suggest that a fragile truce has been struck between them, in the interests of keeping the band together, and he has the air of someone detached from the events of the past few weeks. Al and I are suspicious. His emergence from his post-relationship abyss has been swift and unexpected and marked by a determination to head back to his chosen image of guitar-toting, highway bluesman.

We assume the panacea has to be Lisa. She's here in the hall, chatting with Carol and Jean, and occasionally casting half-glances in our direction as we set up the gear. She looks stunning, as usual, but I wonder what's floating around in her head and what her points of contact are with Jean and Carol. They look like they've just returned from Woodstock, whereas Lisa looks like something from Littlewoods autumn and winter collection. However, the effect of her presence on Ralph is marked; he's become busy, accommodating and polite, even if his re-discovered social etiquette doesn't extend to Dave. Not a word has passed between them since we arrived.

He calls across in the direction of the three girls. 'Hey, Lisa! Listen to this.' He plays out the intro to 'Summer Holiday' on his bass.

Lisa responds with a disparaging shake of the head and shoots off into the kitchen.

'You are desperate,' says Al. 'You'll be asking Ronnie to get you Cliff's second-hand, double-decker next.'

Jean beckons me over. 'Had a call from John earlier. Told him about your group. He said if you ever make it to London to look him up.'

'And how is it for him?'

Jean smiles. 'Well, you know John, he never exactly tells it like it is but he says Freddie's fitting in ok and they're thinking about writing some original stuff. Covers don't really get you anywhere.'

She says it with a shake of her head as if she's said it to countless pub bands who have then drifted off into obscurity leaving the closing bars of 'Stairway To Heaven' frothing in the bubbles of a dying light show.

We spend an hour going through the songs and they're ok to the point where Ralph thinks we can do the first full run-through. The girls have drifted in and out of the hall but are now assembled and eagerly anticipating what we have to offer. The exception is Lisa who has sat at the rear of the hall as far away as possible from the instruments. Ralph looks slightly disappointed. She's a long way back to make eye contact with, as he sways coolly with his bass, and there's worse to come. Halfway through 'I'm So Glad' she picks up her bag, motions to Jean and the others, and disappears out of the hall.

Ralph's bubble has suddenly deflated and the train journey home has that familiar post-rehearsal feel. Instead of the effervescence and excitement of a set well-played, we are back on the edges of the phantom zone, Ralph descending into a ghost-like existence from which he can observe but not interact with the regular universe.

'Look, Man,' says Al. 'Your problem is that you haven't asked a girl out for five years; that's most of your teenage life when the rest of us have been learning how to read potential girlfriends and working out how we can connect with them. At the moment, Lisa's not interested in your world. She's got her own space and she's pretty happy with it. You've got to get in there somehow and connect. Then you can start bringing her over to your side.'

The phantom is unmoved. Most phantoms, when they were released from the Zone, went off to live in Kandor, a city in a bottle, which Superman kept in his Fortress of Solitude. Ralph's been in his bottle for the last five years, safe and secure, oblivious to the explosion of teenage relationships orbiting outside his universe. Now he's been released into a world of alien parameters and he can't see around the next corner.

The train is nearing Hough Green. 'Look, Man, just think how you can connect and ask her out. Ok, she's refused

127

everyone who's ever tried but if you can find a connection, some small thread of common ground, you might just stand a chance.'

The phantom is still unmoved and is left in silence on the train as we head off home.

EIGHTEEN

Living In The Past
Jethro Tull. Single Release. Island Records.

We are at the back of Herbie Gravitt's English lesson. He's just returned from his cigarette break. It's a sort of unwritten rule between us and the staff. We both get to relax and re-group, and it gives the masters time to steady their nerves before coming back to struggle through the last dregs of the lesson.

Herbie likes our class because we engage in conjecture and debate, even if our contributions are several intellectual levels below his Oxbridge degree. Being from a different generation, Herbie's view of Tess' predicament is a bit different to mine. He goes down the route that she was the inevitable victim of industrial change and the disappearance of the old country ways. I'm positive she could have been saved and that it was just a matter of her meeting someone like me instead of the insufferable Angel Clare.

Herbie has the look of a weary, Dickensian scrivener as if living the triumphs and tragedies of the great works of English Literature has brought him to the point of exhaustion as he struggles towards his final chapter of retirement.

He lives near the station in Hough Green and, when you look into the window of his front room, it's filled with books. There are stacks of them on shelves, filling up the space that would usually house a TV or a radiogram or several pictures of English watercolour scenes; at least that's what I imagine most teachers have in their living rooms. I once sat on his garden wall and tried to count them. I reckon there were at least five hundred and I perched there for ages wondering if Herbie had read them all and, if he had, could he remember the plot, structure and characters of every single one? He puts my knowledge of Literature into perspective and I envy all the places he can escape to in his mind.

At the moment, I'm drifting around Talbothays and The Blackmoor Vale, but Herbie can go anywhere, roaming the wild expanses of Middle Earth, frozen wastes of Narnia, or even the lost horizons of Shangri-La. I wonder if he's found his Tess and whether Mrs Gravitt is his very own Lizzie Bennet or Jo March. Most likely he's more Betjeman than Bradbury, preferring the genteel reality of Clevedon and Malmesbury to the fictional silent towns and wildernesses of the red planet. He has a Morris Traveller in his drive with a series of triangular, plastic stickers combining to create the circle of his life: Anglesey, Bridlington, Stratford-Upon-Avon, Windermere and Great Yarmouth.

'Sir, do you think Hardy's characters are always thwarted by fate and a consequential failure to control their own destiny?'

Herbie looks at me suspiciously as if I am trying to test his knowledge with a phrase I've dragged up from the back of *Coles Notes*.

'Any student of Literature, Stephens, will understand that our own philosophies and the forces which drive fate are constantly in conflict. Character is fate! Remember that! The demise of Tess is inevitable because she submits to fate at every turn in the story. She has a lack of resolve to confront the inauspicious happenings in her life.'

'So, Sir, are you saying that if she had been a bit stronger she could have changed things?'

Herbie suddenly becomes animated as if a mixture of existential theory has been stirred and risen from the depths of his intellect.

'Fate is a hostile force, Stephens! It can stack coincidences up against you to the point where you actually believe a malevolent force is out to destroy you. Be prepared! Keep watch for the omens which forewarn us of the attack of that pernicious beast. Action and inaction! Are we willing to take on the Gods or bow down without resistance? He pauses, and his voice drops to a sigh. 'Such is the tragedy of Tess. Such is life.'

He sits at his desk possibly contemplating why fate has planted him in the draughty corners of Wade Deacon when, if his resolve had been greater, he could be sitting on the leafy banks of the Cherwell watching academics wave to him in gratitude, floating by in their punts eating salmon sandwiches and sipping champagne.

He closes his book thoughtfully and places it in his briefcase, consigning Tess and her troubles to a state of limbo until the following afternoon. I wonder how many troubles he carries around inside his old, battered bag and whether the weight of those tragedies is finally seeping deep into his soul. He's about to wind up the lesson when a breathless first year enters the door clutching a note. Herbie regathers his glasses from his jacket, lifting them from the breast pocket as if they've suddenly increased in weight to the point where he barely has the strength to put them back on.

'Stephens! Morefield! Mr Rothwell wants to see you in your form room after the lesson. I imagine it's something to do with that intolerable play you're acting in.'

He returns his glasses to their resting place, mops the day's sweat from his forehead with a large, white handkerchief, gathers his bagful of misfortunes, and heads for the staffroom.

Ralph's in conversation with Steve as we enter the form room. We're about to take a seat but he rises, swinging his smart, cream, cotton jacket from the back of the chair.

'It's excellent of you to volunteer to run a discussion group at the Christian Education Movement Conference next Saturday. Big plus point for me too, having a presence from my form group.' He picks up his briefcase. 'Thanks, lads. See you at *Hound* rehearsals on Friday.' With that he exits, leaving me and Al staring blankly at Ralph.

'What?' says Ralph. 'You told me to make a connection with her.'

'What!' says Al. 'We're up to our eyes in two lots of rehearsals and mocks revision and you drag us into a bloody Christian conference?' He grabs the leaflet from Ralph's hand.

'The theme of this year's conference will be 'Do Morals Matter?' Bloody Hell, Man, you've got the answer to this already. You're a living, breathing example that the moral fabric of society is on the verge of collapse.'

'Not from today,' says Ralph. 'This is the start of a new me. I've been bogged down in one image far too long. I'll still be the cool rock star, but with a softer side, all the edges knocked off, a bit like George Harrison. He found religion and that's when he started writing all his best stuff.'

'You can't be George Harrison. Judith thinks I look like him. We can't have two clones in the group.'

'You don't look like friggin' Harrison,' says Ralph. I don't wait for the punchline.

'Look, do me a favour and tell me I look like Paul Rodgers.'

Ralph looks me up and down. 'Yeh, a bit, but you need to grow a beard. Girls love it. Adds a bit of menace and mystery. They want to know the man behind the beard. It's like Clark Kent. They all want to know who's underneath the disguise.'

'He didn't have a beard, just a pair of glasses. How could people not tell he was Superman?'

'Because he was meek, mild and well-mannered,' says Ralph. 'This is going to be my new disguise, a sure fire way of luring Lisa into my world. I could tell she was interested at the rehearsal. She's just playing hard to get. It's what girls do when they really like someone.' He pauses and looks at me. 'So Judith said ok to you straight away?'

NINETEEN

Going Up The Country
Canned Heat. Single Release. Liberty Records.

I'm mulling over Herbie's theory of action and inaction shaping your destiny. I mean, obviously, there's a lot about life that's beyond my control. If I'd have been born into a posh family somewhere in the Home Counties in the Thirties, I'd be immersed in the world of Noel Coward, playing croquet and tennis, and sipping Pimms in a country estate with any number of young socialites hanging around to snare one of the most eligible bachelors in Teddington. Still, fate has landed me in Widnes in 1950, so I'm mulling over my Karma and how my own thoughts and actions have plonked me on the train to Padgate, on the 27th September 1969.

Was it already up there on my tapestry, a nicely woven little steam train chugging through fields of cross-stitches, or have I caused Clotho to throw a tantrum and unpick a picture of me sitting despondently in my bedroom with a team of neatly embroidered Subbuteo players? When I stood on the station bridge a couple of weeks ago, Clotho would have been poised with her needle, but maybe she'd had a good day up there in the clouds. Now the train to Padgate is carrying me off to Long Barn for tea with Judith's family and my tapestry is all bright colours with the edges sharp and neatly stitched.

Out of the carriage window I can only see flat, green fields unless I lift my head and gaze south to where the smoke and dust from the chemical works and the power station cast an untidy smudge along the horizon. Once the train's through Warrington though we're into the real countryside and, as it pulls into Padgate Station, the small cluster of old, red-brick houses, sitting in the stillness of the early afternoon, give a feeling that the train has journeyed through years as well as miles.

As I step out of the carriage I'm wrapped in the still September air. Padgate seems asleep, with just an old, chocolate Labrador lazily settling down between the bright, red fire buckets and the station's parcel trolley. I stroke the dog for luck, and head off on the twenty-minute walk down Long Barn Lane. Can the Fates travel in time, take my tapestry and start again unpicking Widnes 1950 from the front panel and re-stitching Marlott, Wessex, 1891 in perfectly woven copperplate? I glance across the landscape but there's no John Durbeyfield tottering back from Rollivers Inn, and it's not quite the green and rolling countryside of Dorset. Still, there are cows, sheep and those country smells which tell me that, even though I'm just a few miles from Widnes, I've travelled into a different world. I can see the farmhouse in the distance with smoke rising vertically from the chimney and Judith's at the gate waving to me wrapped in her Afghan coat with a friendly-looking sheepdog for company.

'I love the play, Phil.' Mrs Adamson is a larger-than-life farmer's wife with a fireside glow in her cheeks. 'We go through all the lines with Judith but we can't practise the kiss. Only me and her dad here now; brothers have left home. Not that she'd have practised on them,' she laughs, heartily, 'but you know what I mean.'

The house is timeless, spacious and warm with a crackling log fire in the kitchen and loaves of fresh bread cooling by the oven. It's the first girlfriend's house I've ever been to but, if I'd been to a hundred before, this would be a world apart from the rest; a haven of real country life away from the shadows of the urban sprawl.

Judith takes me on a tour of the farm. The animals all have names, but there are some special ones. There's Maisy the cow, Fluff the donkey, and Jess the carthorse, who was born in the same week as Judith. By the end of the afternoon, I feel like I'm part of one big family and I don't want to leave. Judith talks about Christmas and I get a picture of rural celebrations and the traditions which tie her family together. I don't like to ask if their animals make it onto the menu. There are a couple of worried-looking turkeys scratching around the yard, and they have names.

After tea, Judith walks me back to the farm gate. It's getting cold now and there's a hard, red glow in the sky. I wonder if this is the moment where I lift her onto the gate and kiss her goodnight but I'm scared I'll hurt her, or me, and the whole idea is probably ridiculous, so I just hold her close and we kiss. It's a different kiss. It's warm and strong. A kiss that tells you that the other person feels the same as you, that asking her out was the best thing that you've ever done, and that Lesley is a speck disappearing towards the end of time.

When I get home I gather up *Tess* from the small pile of novels on my bookshelf and head over to Al's. He's lying on his bed listening to the Moody Blues new album through his headphones, cramming his mind with images of journeys to multi-coloured worlds and undiscovered civilisations. I lower the volume on his record player, his eyes open, and I swear he almost levitates from the bed.

'Have you heard this yet, Man?'

'Yeh, a couple of tracks on *Night Ride*, but I'm changing. I mean I can't go with all the progressive stuff, or even the blues. I don't think I want to escape anymore. I've sort of found what I'm looking for.'

'In music?'

'No, that's the strange thing, Judith and I aren't bonded by music, it's more literature. I feel like all my empathy has been sucked from music and crammed between the covers of *Tess*. I mean, have you ever been so connected with a story that it's as if you're experiencing it in real life?'

'You can't be living *Tess*, Man, it ends in disaster. Just look what happened when Fate got hold of her. Look, you've just spent the day on a farm, big deal. You can't just pretend all the emotional clutter of the real world's evaporated. Take it easy, step back. Do you want the headphones?'

'No thanks.'

136

'Just enjoy what you've got. Judith wouldn't be best pleased if she thought you were harbouring feelings for another girl. You can't exist in two different worlds at the same time.'

He puts the headphones back on and drifts away.

TWENTY

That's The Way God Planned It
Billy Preston. Single Release. Apple Records.

About forty of us have assembled in the girls' hall for the Morality debate. Everyone is in school uniform, even though it's a Saturday. Al and I are in denims. Ralph has squeezed into his Dad's old wedding suit.

There's an overwhelming sense of formality; the complete opposite of the *Hound* rehearsals with their laughter, jokes and swearing which all contribute to an atmosphere of collective spirit.

This is different, it's serious, and there's a feeling we've been propelled into the world of adulthood before our time. I look around trying to find any point of contact, a friendly face to nod and wink at, sending a message that once we've muddled through all this, we can escape to the Tavern for an early evening pint.

I can't see how Ralph is going to connect with Lisa. From what I can pick up from snatches of conversation, we're going to be split into seven groups of eight and given various rooms around the building to debate our given topic before returning for a light lunch with more of the same in the afternoon. Odds of 7/1 are not good and I have a sense of time slipping away when I could have grabbed it to use for more important things.

The WAB and Miss Thackara lead the platform party onto the stage for the opening formalities and the babble of polite conversation subsides.

'Gentlemen, and ladies, I should very much like to thank you for giving up part of your weekend to engage in what I am sure you will find a challenging and stimulating debate. May I introduce the following good men who have been instrumental yet again in organising one of the highlights of our school calendar. On my left, the Reverend C. E. Corbett,

Vicar of Farnworth Church. To my right, the Very Reverend E. H. Patey, Dean of Liverpool.'

The WAB outlines how the day will unfold. As predicted, there will be seven groups with one discussion topic in the morning, lunch, a second topic in the afternoon, and a final coming together where we all throw around our philosophical viewpoints. Each group will have its own chair, responsible for organising the debate, gathering ideas, and feeding back. The topics will be unseen and given to the group leader in a plain envelope. The Reverend Corbett hands out the lists. Ralph is the leader of Group C and it doesn't include Lisa.

There's general movement as the group leaders call out names. The other lad in our group is Johnny Starmer but I don't even recognise him. I think I've seen one of the girls coming out of the knitting shop on Widnes Road next to The Music Shop.

'Bollocks to this,' says Ralph, looking at his list. He carefully folds it in half and tears it down the middle detaching the boys from the girls. He bundles his way through the bodies in the direction of the other group leaders. Seconds later he's back with another half of girls and he's calling out their names: Jenny Parsons, Tina Dawson, Wendy Jenkins, Lisa Wilcox.

A few minutes later we're sat around a table with the first unopened envelope clasped in Ralph's hand. He sits up straight trying to look like someone who's in control of his body and mind. Lisa looks like she's ready for the afternoon, with a headful of theological knowledge drip-fed from her parents over the last eighteen years, and Jenny and Wendy look similarly keen to plunge into the debate. Tina Dawson is the odd girl out and the only one I've regularly seen around school, usually snogging a different lad each week on a remote area of the playing fields. She's leaning back in her chair and chewing gum looking the four of us up and down as if wondering who to invite down to the outskirts of the golf course in the lunch break. Catching my eye, she looks across.

'You the one who's kissing Judith Adamson in that play?'

139

I roll my eyes and nod at her.

'Poor her. Bet she wishes she had a different part. Can we get started? I'm meeting my boyfriend at Cronton chippy for lunch.'

'Shut up, Tina,' chips in Al. 'It's a debate and you can only speak with the chair's permission.'

Her brow furrows. 'Don't be stupid, it's made of wood.' The other three girls are too polite to giggle and Ralph exerts his control.

'Right!' He tears open the envelope. 'Our topic for this morning, gentlemen and ladies,' he takes in everyone in a sweeping glance slowing momentarily to smile directly at Lisa, 'is: Why are we restoring York Minster when there are millions starving in Biafra?'

Lisa and Wendy are about to enter the debate but Ralph gets in first.

'Ok, I'd like to give my view first to sort of start things rolling. A very small percent of the population build churches and it's that tiny percent who collect money to feed those starving abroad through collections in churches and holding money raising events like Lisa's dad down at St Mary's, where our group's playing in a couple of weeks' time by the way. Furthermore, too many of us spend our money unwisely on the fripperies of modern living. We should give up spending money on records, overpriced fashion goods and especially alcohol, and give more money to aid the relief of famine and world poverty.'

Al and I wait for the lightning bolt to obliterate the classroom but before it can arrive Lisa jumps straight into the debate.

'Ralph's right. My Dad and the church raise their own money for repairs and at the same time donate hundreds of pounds to charities like Oxfam. If we are all prepared to go without some of our luxuries, world hunger and poverty would be wiped out.' She nods empathetically in Ralph's direction and the debate proceeds while Tina looks out of the window filing her nails.

By lunchtime Ralph and Lisa are inseparable, wrapped in their own world of morals, considered judgements and acceptable codes of behaviour. Ralph has catapulted himself into Lisa's world arriving with the force of Jor-El's rocket propelling the infant Superman to exciting new beginnings in an alien culture.

Al and I hang around on the fringes of the debate, drinking tea and resisting the urge to head across the road to the Tuck Shop and abandon the salmon and cucumber sandwiches in favour of a steaming hot, Holland's meat and potato pie. Tina has returned from the chip shop chewing gum and drinking what looks like a clear liquid out of a Coke bottle. She stares across at us and meanders over.'

'Bloody boring, this.' She takes another swig from her bottle and I catch the smell of vodka as she gulps it down.

'Why are you here, Tina?'

'Thackara, the bitch, made me come. I've run out of detention time so she said I could make it up by coming here. Don't ask me to say anything this afternoon, I'm just sitting in the corner and having a kip. I feel so sorry for Adamson. Best looking girl in the sixth form and she ends up with you.'

True to her promises, Tina has dozed off at the back of the classroom as we all enter for the afternoon session. Ralph and Lisa are not quite arm in arm but they're very close together, smiling and whispering to each other as we settle around the table. Ralph sums up the salient points from the morning's debate and opens the envelope containing the topic for the afternoon.

There's a slight hesitancy before he reads it out and I swear there's a discernible reddening of his cheeks. He coughs loudly as if to jolt himself into collecting his thoughts.

'This afternoon's debate is an interesting one: What are the group's views on sex before marriage?'

I turn round and check on Tina. I'm sure one of her eyes momentarily flashed open but has been clamped back shut before I can double-check.

'I'll start,' says Lisa, who seems to be twice as animated after the break for lunch.

'I believe sex is not the casual, transitory and totally physical thing it is for animals. It is a highly personal encounter between two people who are in love.' She looks sideways at Ralph, reddening slightly. 'If you accept this view then casual sexual relationships should never be indulged in before marriage.'

'Why not if the couple genuinely love each other?' says Al.

'It's obvious, Man,' says Ralph. 'Even if they intend to marry the marriage might not happen; unforeseen circumstances and all that. Also, sex before marriage might not cement a relationship; it could have the opposite effect. I agree with Lisa. Couples should think twice before they indulge.'

'Oh, yeh, is that why you've been screwing Anne Woodley since you were fifteen?' Tina is awake, chewing furiously, and staring directly into Ralph's eyes.

The rest of the group stare at her, turn back, and look at Ralph.

'Is this true?' There's a slight waver in Lisa's voice which I can't distinguish between anger or disappointment.

'No!' blurts out Ralph. 'Well, yes and no. We were sixteen, not fifteen, we waited until Anne's birthday.'

'Bloody Hell!' Tina is looking directly at Lisa. 'Bet you never had a birthday present like that.'

'No, because I'm not a slag like you.'

'Oooh, lovely language coming from a vicar's daughter. Not what I'd expect from the queen of the fuckin' virgins.'

'Well, you can just..!'

'Enough!' The voice of Miss Thackara brings the room to silence. She is standing in the doorway with the Reverend Corbett. 'What on earth is going on here?'

'They couldn't find any common ground on the topic,' says Al. 'It's a sort of stand-off, the moral equivalent of a penalty shoot-out.'

'Ladies, proceed to my office now. The rest of you may continue with reasoned and controlled debate.'

Lisa pushes her desk away angrily. 'Charlatan!' She barges past Ralph and exits without a backwards glance.

'Plan B?' says Al, as we sit supping early evening pints in The Tavern.

'Already got one.' Ralph has the arrogant air of a man who is on a blinkered course to failure as the rest of us look on at the inevitable.

'At the moment, it's a love-hate relationship. Lisa's struggling with the emotional ambivalence of her early childhood, being brought up to value reliable, Christian, squeaky-clean guys whereas her inner self is really coveting someone like me. She'll be wrestling with the positive and negative aspects of becoming my girl but, two weeks today, I'm going to burst into her psyche and tip the balance. When she sees me up there on stage her emotions will be set free and she'll realise Cliff Richard is just a dickhead. She'll see blues as a way of life; an irresistible alternative.'

'She won't want to live the blues, Man.' She's younger than us and comes from a quiet, middle-class home,' says Al.

'That's irrelevant! Blues is linked to the Church, Man. It grew out of gospel music and the spiritual experience of slaves. All those people Lisa was saying we should help in Biafra are going through the same experience which gave birth to the blues: pain, alienation, separation. When she twigs that's what we're about the connection will click into place. Ok, I might not be the stereotypical guy she imagines ending up

143

with, but when she realises we're feeling the same pain about the World's moral dilemmas, she'll understand Jesus was a bluesman, just like me.'

'And how do you square the sex before marriage thing now she realises you're lost to that one?'

'Repentance, Man. Christians believe that you can turn away from sin and make a new start. Look, we need to add another song to the set. I'll introduce it and do a Christian intro sort of thing. Des will love it and Lisa will think I've been saved. 'Turn Turn Turn' by The Byrds. We don't even need to involve Shuttleworth, just me with you on the guitars and Al doing some harmonies, just before 'Toad'. Look, it's a song about replacing the World's evils with healing, peace and laughter. It's perfect to follow 'Eve of Destruction' and the lyrics are taken straight from the Bible; *Book of Ecclesiastes* Chapter 3. It's blues for peace and reconciliation. When she hears us sing it she'll just melt away and realise she's been mistaken about me. I've decided she's got to connect with my world. Me going to hers was never going to work but her coming into the world of blues is a natural progression for her beliefs. It just can't fail.'

.

TWENTY ONE

Fault Line
Deep Purple. Deep Purple 111. Harvest Records.

Joe and Alison have returned from their weekend in London. Alison has the look of a girl who has been rescued by Dr Who from a nightmarish world light years from Widnes. She is asleep on the settee in Joe's front room wrapped in enough towels to suggest she has spent some time in the shower after their return.

We head up to Joe's bedroom for a game of Subbuteo. Irrespective of the teams we choose the match is always Hough Green versus Farnworth, the working-class upstarts from the council estate versus the middle-class homeowners from the leafy suburb. It's the latest in a series of David v Goliath clashes with the big boys from Farnworth usually getting the better of the plucky underdogs away from their home turf. Joe lines up against Al, with me as referee, but this time the commentary is not about fouls, flicks and front men but of Joe and Alison's immersion in the world of almost penniless rock musicians living on beer, dope and hope and struggling to find gigs.

He begins to paint a picture of life in West London with the air of a lecture being delivered to a naive audience who are about to have their romantic vision of the rock music industry obliterated.

'They needed a bloody time machine to travel to London in. They've arrived two years too late. They're stuck in 1967; blues ruled the place then. Hendrix had just arrived, Cream were massive, Ten Years After and Fleetwood Mac were about to break through. They'd have been welcomed into that scene. Now it's all draining away, the old culture's gone, and something different's about to explode.'

He looks at me and Al and shakes his head. 'Just getting a Coke before we start.'

He squeezes through his bedroom door letting in Alison who's wrapped in a fluffy, fleece blanket. She's cool, creative and good at spotting trends and fashions.

'I think the trouble for Ibex is they're like you lot; all jeans, T-shirts, long hair and simple dreams. Nothing wrong with that but you can feel a change down there. Look at The Stones in Hyde Park, even Mick Jagger was wearing eyeshadow and lipstick and an effeminate white dress. Can you see Mike, Tupp and Miffer dressing like that? I can't, but I can see Freddie doing it. He's looking forward; he's got a foot in the future and wants the big theatrical stage. Everything's too fast and new for Ibex; they're just northern lads struggling to come to terms with changing direction and identity.'

'So what was it like down there?'

'Joe won't admit it but we were pretty nervous going down to London on our own. We had directions but it took us a while to work out where their place was. Think we got the Tube to Warwick Avenue and then we wandered around for ages trying to find the house. The area was pretty run down; a warren of bedsits and flats crammed into big, old Georgian houses. When we got there the garden was totally overgrown with loads of rubbish scattered around everywhere. Tupp came out to meet us but he seemed a bit distant and tired like he hadn't had any sleep for a couple of days. He took us in through this really dark hallway which was freezing and damp. The flat was chaotic, it didn't have a good feeling. It was as if troubles were lurking in the shadows. I just wanted to get out before they did.'

'Sounds pretty grim.'

'It upset me a bit. The last time I'd seen Tupp was round at his house with Jean and all our friends over summer. It seemed a long way from home.'

'So, did you stay there?'

147

'No, thank God. Miffer turned up and took us to another place over in Shepherds Bush where he was crashing with two girls. It was cleaner but really small. We ended up sleeping across two beds pushed together. Miffer ended up sleeping in the bath.'

Joe returns and the game commences. By half time it's 2-0 to Al with Joe blaming the distractions of London and my biased refereeing for his poor performance. The four of us sit on Joe's plushy carpet with his central heating beating back the cold from the rain which sweeps in from the west across the sports ground.

'Miffer's not happy, is he?' says Alison.

'Loves Widnes, never wanted to break the ties, never should have left. Plus, he's older than Tupp and Mike; he's not looking through their eyes. They're dreaming of rock stardom but he can see the reality.'

'They just seem so out of place,' says Alison. 'You've got Freddie who's all chiffon, velvet and fur. He's the complete opposite of Miffer, but it's not just that. Those other guys from Smile who played at the end of the Sink gig are part of Freddie's scene. They've got a recording contract and they've been supporting some decent bands around London. I'm sure Freddie's got an eye on joining them and is just using Ibex as a stepping stone.'

The second half starts and there are more details but no early goals.

'That Morefield is a bloody shove. You moved that player half the length of the pitch without spinning. Referee!'

'Sorry. Wasn't looking. What were you saying, Alison?'

'It doesn't feel right for them. Mike's not there all the time. He promised his parents he'd start his art degree if they didn't start getting regular gigs, so he's hitching back and to from Liverpool to rehearse and play what gigs they've got. I think Tupp's ok, he's always been the optimist, but it feels like they're travelling down a dead end.'

Al tries an elaborate defensive flick in the penalty area, misses the ball, and collides with an attacker just inside the box.'

'Sorry, Al, that's a penalty.'

'What do you mean, 'sorry'?' You're the bloody referee. You're supposed to be impartial.'

Joe places the ball on the penalty spot and lines up the shot. Al goes into commentary mode.

'With time running out can Hayes hold his nerve or will he fail miserably and be on the brink of an unbearable home defeat?'

'Will you bloody well shut him up, ref? Or book him for ungentlemanly conduct.'

Joe unleashes a well-executed flip chipping the ball onto the underside of the bar and into the net.

'2-1. How long left?'

'Two minutes. So what's actually happening down there now?'

'They need something spectacular to happen for them before Christmas. Mike says Freddie's opened his eyes to different musical styles, and he's interested in exploring those, but whether or not they can become a bit less bluesy, I'm not so sure. I think they hit London at the wrong time. When they got down there the students weren't back and the college circuit was dead. Think Tupp said they've got one gig booked at Ealing College at the end of October. They'd have been better staying around here.'

Joe's brow is furrowed with concentration, his head bowed almost to ground level, focusing on the plastic players, willing them to move with the power of telekinesis.

Al continues his commentary. 'And can the tiring Hayes summon up enough energy for one last assault on Morefield's defence? What a shock this result will be if he fails to find an equaliser? The news will inevitably reverberate around Hough Green and....'

'Oh, just fuck off!' Joe flicks his attacker viciously and randomly in the direction of Al's goal. It connects with the ball which heads wildly out towards the corner flag, bouncing off a ring on Alison's hand which is resting just inside the touchline, before looping dramatically over Al's keeper and nestling in the net.

'Wow, have I scored?' says Alison.

'You've just saved the weekend for Joe,' I say. '2-2. Full time.'

Al is not impressed but we can find nothing in the rules about deflections made from objects to be found randomly on the pitch. Alison's hand was within the field of play, so the result stands, and we head back down to the front room for the final assassination of Ibex's decision to leave.

There's more coffee, Coke and biscuits and Joe is in the ascendancy following his late comeback. There's a stack of LPs in the corner of the room. He takes two out of the pile and places them next to the fireplace. There's *Unicorn* by Tyrannosaurus Rex and *In The Court Of The Crimson King* by King Crimson.

'Carry on with playing blues and your future's at the Labour Club on Sunday night supporting Johnny Rocco or some other crooner. Ibex have missed the boat, everything's moving and changing. It's a bit subtle at the moment but you can see it happening.' He grabs the copy of *Unicorn* and waves it in our direction. Marc Bolan's pretty face stares out from the cover looking slightly effeminate with his mass of curls and skimpy yellow vest. The contrast with Steve Peregrine Took, the other member of Tyrannosaurus Rex, is marked, He has the standard long hair, moustache and beard of any number of blues musicians and they look worlds apart. Joe flips the cover over and reads the titles of a few of the tracks; 'Stones For Avalon', 'She Was Born To Be My Unicorn', 'Evenings of Damask', 'The Misty Coast of Albany', are not the titles of blues tracks.

'The other guy still looks bluesy to me,' says Al.

'He probably still is, but Bolan's just ditched him. He's not gonna carry that image forward into his next album, and surely you can see it. Al, how many blues records have you bought lately? You just spout out the lyrics of King Crimson and the Moody Blues. Everyone's escaping to other worlds. Blues has been left behind on a back street somewhere and Freddie's already working on Mike. But it's all image! It's not enough to write good songs and play the guitar, there's got to be a performance on stage, so you guys need to think seriously about that. What are people gonna see when they're pressed against the stage peering up at you? They'll expect you to be outrageous, flamboyant and theatrical; just strumming away isn't the business.' Joe looks me up and down. 'You won't get away with having the onstage presence of Hank Marvin.'

Joe's comment is not unexpected as he rarely misses an opportunity to put me and Al down, particularly when buoyed by what he perceives is a Subbuteo result against the odds. He's never seen me on stage but in his eyes I'm Hank, and I don't have the raging, wild, Biblical, persona of Paul Kossoff, writhing like a chained bull in front of his Marshall stack. Hank stands on stage like a waiter who's inexplicably had a guitar placed in his hands by some passing customer but continues to maintain his cheesy grin, welcoming diners to their tables with the notes of 'Wonderful Land' spilling around him like the repetitive chink of cheap wine glasses.

Joe lounges smugly on the sofa and takes on Al's third person, football commentary tone. 'You're lucky Hayes' experience of life in London, and his superior knowledge of the traps and pitfalls of the music business, have been brought back to home to Widnes. This early warning, to the would-be bluesmen, means they must lower their ambitions and concentrate on Subbuteo in an attempt to rise to the top in one thing before they mistakenly head for the impossible dream of another. Right, Alison?'

Alison is her own person and refuses to be drawn.

Joe returns to Subbuteo. 'After an astonishing comeback, Hayes' position as number one flicker is secured.'

'No 1 fucker,' mutters Al under his breath.

TWENTY TWO

Listen To The Band
The Monkees. The Monkees Present. Colgems Records.

Al and I are heading to St Mary's, excitement building inside
at the prospect of a live audience. We've managed the final
rehearsal with no mention of Anne, Lisa or musical differences
and Dave says he doesn't give a toss about 'Turn Turn Turn'
as it'll give him a chance to get backstage and have a couple of
cans before we launch into 'Toad'.

We can hear the music as we approach the field at the back
of the church. The amplification is of such poor quality that,
with every gust of wind, the sound fades then rises back
leaving snatches of music abandoned in the trees and in the
crevices of the old, sandstone building.

Des has just escaped from a funeral and is dressed in his full,
flowing smock, looking every inch the jovial country parson.
He's trying to test the P.A. which is a separate entity to the
record player and speaker. This is proving a real challenge, as
he has to scream for the music to be turned down before he
can deliver his announcements. Even then the competition
with the atmospheric conditions is testing his outward calm.

'Testing, test .... to St Mary's Church Autumn .... lots of ....
opportunities to .... prize draw .... Oh, Christ Almighty!'

Thirty watts of power relay his blasphemous outpourings
around every stall on the field. Fifteen lady parishioners
pretend not to hear and carry on industriously with their
preparations. The sun ominously disappears and a few drops
of rain begin to fall. I wonder what my chances are of being
electrocuted on stage and if I unplug my guitar will anybody
notice anyway. Dave has already been here for a couple of
hours. His equipment had been loaded up and accompanied

him on his early morning round. He sits on stage tapping rhythmically on two empty milk bottles.

There's a distance between us socially, as well as musically. He knows we're on Ralph's side; disapproving of him for stealing our mate's girlfriend. To himself, he's a martyr, the misunderstood drummer who would die on his drum kit rather than consider himself a complete prat for trying his luck with Anne in the first place.

We sit in a tent next to the stage, listening to Des as he outlines the plan for the afternoon. We are to play our five songs consecutively, sandwiched in between the judging for the Best Home-Made Cake Competition and the draw for the raffle. All other musical entertainment for the afternoon is being provided by Julian Smith who runs Doubting Thomas Discos which specialises in playing pop songs that have a Christian message.

Although the fair is beginning to fill up the only other person in the tent is Julian. He has his singles case with him and is methodically planning out his playlist for the afternoon, sliding his fingers through his black, greasy hair, cut to one length just below his considerable ears, which poke out through the strands like the two tops of a fairy bun. He wears straight, corduroy trousers and open-toed sandals with no socks and an orange t-shirt with 'Doubting Thomas Discos' on the front and 'Jesus. The Original Pop Idol' on the back. On the floor beside his chair is a multicoloured, embroidered, cotton bag with a dirty shoulder strap. A handful of LPs tests its stitching to the limit.

With thirty minutes to go, Ralph walks in carrying his bass. He looks like a man who has bitten a hard bullet but has finally concluded that the Wheel of Fortune, having tossed him into the depths, could have something better in store for him.

The something better has to be Lisa who drifts in behind him. However, she flounces past us all and focuses her attention on Julian.

155

The self-defence mechanisms snap into place. She can't fancy Julian. There must be some other reason why she's gone over to him. Maybe she's after a rare Cliff Richard single in his record collection, or she's secretly his sister. Perhaps she's too shy to come over to us first, or she wants to tell him what a prat he looks and how he shouldn't be in the same tent as us.

Suddenly she puts her arms around him and gives him an enormous hug. I feel disgusted, the same sort of revulsion as watching your parents, or anybody's parents, indulge in physical contact. I mean we've taken all this time to develop some sort of image that seems to be relevant to teenage culture and this thing, which in my opinion can't even be relied upon to have a bath more than once a month, has managed to attract the affections of the local vicar's daughter just because he has some tenuous link with God. I can only suppose that because hardly any normal teenagers believe in God or get any sort of turn-on listening to the Joystrings or the Edwin Hawkins Singers, Lisa's choice of potential male friends has been drastically reduced. Still, if Julian is the best that's on offer, then I'm glad I'm an atheist.

Ralph remains unfazed by all this. With calm assurance, he picks up his bass and leaves for the stage.

Dave is already seated at his drum kit as we arrive. I've dreamt of this scene a thousand times. The roadies have left, apart from some sound guy who is desperately scrabbling about on all fours making last-minute adjustments to the jack leads. The auditorium hums with anticipation as the lights dim. Cheers cut the air with the fans yelling out our names in uncontrollable anticipation. The whole of the stage is spot-lit and a nerve-rending cacophony of noise rises from the audience. We shout 'Hello' out to the fans, 'One! Two! Three!' and the heavy opening bars of our anthem burn out into the darkness.

Back in reality, Des is addressing the audience as four twelve-year-old girls with Monkees badges, two mums and

156

Julian and Lisa, gaze judgementally up at us from below the stage.

'We'd like to thank David, Raymond, Alan, Ralph and Philip for giving up their time to play for us this afternoon. Young people today are often tarred as the black sheep, but it is so gratifying to see we have such a united flock this afternoon with so many youngsters here to enjoy themselves and take God and the church.....'

Des doesn't reach the end of the sentence. Dave hits his drums with a vengeance and we are away. I strike the first chord of 'Roll Over Beethoven' and it sounds good. Al grabs the microphone and growls out the opening lyrics.

The four Monkees fans stick out their tongues, turn on their heels and leave in the direction of the pop stall, so we play on to the two mums and Julian and Lisa who stand at the front of the stage. They are showing no signs of the affection which had driven us out of the tea tent and have actually moved apart. Lisa sways from side to side enjoying the music and smiling invitingly, at who it's hard to judge, but Ralph smiles back from behind his bass, and his notes became sharper and more defined, as we bash our way through the first three numbers.

By this time, about a dozen or so teenagers have joined the mums and a bit of an atmosphere is starting to develop. The sun has come out, and from the stage I can see the hills in the distance. The chill of autumn adds freshness to the air and my spirits lift. The three songs have gone well, we are pretty tight, and I know this isn't the Fillmore East, but it's a start. We are on our way.

'Ok!' Ralph stares down at the audience and into the eyes of Lisa who is gazing up seemingly enthralled by the atmosphere we're building on stage. 'Dave and Ray are going to take a break now and I'm going to do an acoustic version of a song with Phil and Al which means a lot to me. This song can mean different things to different people, but for me, it's a song about the importance of reconciliation and replacing evil and

157

sin with spiritual peace. It's about going through troubled times, making mistakes, and realising the path you've been treading has been the wrong road.' He looks down at Lisa who is still gazing up at the stage, but I swear she's looking straight through him. Ralph leans forward over the edge of the stage and looks directly at her. 'I hope the song connects with you too. It's called 'Turn, Turn, Turn'. The Lord's words set to music.'

There's significant applause, and Des leaves the cake stall to come across to stand with Lisa. The song goes well and a few of the audience know it and sing along, swaying to the lyrics. The volume of appreciation rises at the end. Ralph half bows and says nothing, standing in an over-exaggerated, reflective pose before bursting back into life.

'That one was from me to all you believers out there. We're all one family on the same path. Let's hear it for Jesus.' Ralph claps forcefully into the mike sending crackling shockwaves across the field. He mumbles something which sounds like, 'Thanks for coming', and smiles down at Lisa who turns her head away shyly. Julian has disappeared.

The rest of the band return and we head off into 'Toad'. Al, who doesn't have to sing, whacks the old tambourine against his thigh and the audience starts to clap. We build it up to the middle and then, with one last strident riff from Ray, we leave Dave centre stage for his agreed ten-minute drum solo.

The crowd cheers as we exit and then turns its attention back to Dave whose eyes are fixed in demonic concentration, his arms flailing the drumsticks in a wild thrashing motion.

We gather at the back of the stage. I am really looking forward to the re-entry, picking up my guitar and hitting that first chord to bring the whole thing back together and welcome a massive thunder of applause for the mighty, sweat-stained hero behind the drum kit.

'Right!' says Ralph. 'Off to the pub!'

'Don't be stupid, Man, we've only got ten minutes.' Al's voice can barely rise above Dave's thundering onslaught but

Ralph is already on his way and he carries in his hand the three jack leads which link our guitars to the amps. His intentions are obvious; to leave Dave drumming away until either he hammers his drumsticks into matchwood or drops dead with exhaustion.

We follow Ralph in the direction of The Chapel House Hotel opposite the Church grounds. It's one of those traditional, Victorian, two-roomed pubs which has managed to retain most of its character despite the ravages of Sixties' pub conversions. The interior is in stark contrast to the brightness of the day, full of dark wood panelling, thick carpet, and a roaring log fire. There's a long glass cabinet in the lounge which is stocked with sandwiches and cakes and a smell of tomato soup wafts across the bar.

'Five pints of bitter,' orders Ralph. The barmaid flicks the electric pumps and the frothy mixture squirts out into the measured pint pots. Ralph drinks a pint in one and we retire to the beer garden.

The steady thud of Dave's drums echoes across the road. I look at my watch. We've been off stage for ten minutes, the time we'd all agreed for the solo. We sit in silence at a cold, damp picnic table. After a further few minutes, Ray speaks, 'When are we going back?'

'Let the bastard sweat,' replies Ralph. He swings his legs up onto the bench, almost kicking Ray off in the process.

'Come on, Ralph, we can't do this to a mate,' pleads Ray. His fingers are moving forming the shapes of the first chords of the intro.

Ralph turns philosophical. 'Mates,' he stresses, 'do not snog with your girlfriend behind your back. Mates,' he continues, 'are people you like and admire and', glancing at me and Al, 'can be trusted to stand by you in troubled times.'

There are almost tears in Ray's eyes. He finishes his pint, gets up and tries to wrestle the lead from Ralph's iron grip. It's no contest. Ralph pushes Ray down onto the grass, takes his guitar lead and rips the jack plug from the end leaving a few bits of wire and traces of solder hanging on the end. Ray dusts himself down and leaves, trying not to run but moving with the pace of an Olympic walker.

The drumming continues. It's now been twenty minutes. I wonder about the next move. Is it back to the fete to witness the last throes of the drum solo and the taunts from the audience? If there still is an audience. Presumably, they've been beaten back by the wall of sound, down into the embroidery tent to buy up surplus packets of cotton wool to stuff into their ears. Or are we just to go home, get the bus, and leave Dave to drift on in a sea of drumming like some musical manifestation of the Flying Dutchman?

'Your round!' Ralph nods in the direction of the bar. By the time I return with three Double Diamonds, Dave has been going for thirty minutes.

After a further five minutes, Ralph has finished off his pint. He slams his glass down on the table. It's time for us to return. The drumbeat has slowed to a steady four-four time. 'Toad' is dying and Ralph wants to be there.

We enter the gate as the last drumbeat signals the end of Dave's marathon stint. However, peace is restored for only a few seconds until the throng of adults, children, stallholders and assorted helpers, practically everybody involved in the planning and running of the fete, break into rapturous applause. Dave has united and transfixed the whole bloody lot of them. He leaps down like a victorious gladiator, punching the air alongside two elderly women from the church committee who are doing the same.

We're speechless, but not as aghast as Ralph, who watches in horror as Dave and Lisa hug each other and walk off with some urgency towards his milk float.

TWENTY THREE

Sleepers Awake

The Incredible String Band. Changing Horses. Electra/WEA Records.

Moonshine has died and, in a way, I'm pretty relaxed about it. I can clear my head of any notions I had of becoming a rock star, and there's a sort of comfort in watching Ronnie flitting around in his own world untroubled by the pressure and pretension we've brought upon ourselves over the past few weeks.

'All right lads?' He takes a crumpled piece of paper out of his bag and stuffs it into my hand. 'You fancy this? Back in a mo, I've got something to ask you.' He regains his balance and shuffles off down the aisle to collect more fares.

It's a rough outline of a flyer for the Bus Corporation's Christmas Social at the Queens Hall. The leaflet advertises an evening of music, dancing, refreshments and raffle prizes. At the bottom it says 'Fancy Dress Optional', but it doesn't give any details.

Ronnie sways back up the aisle. 'I've been talking to Len who's organising things, and he was asking if I knew anyone in a band who could do a few numbers for us?'

'We've split up,' says Al, 'and to be honest a fancy dress evening wouldn't have been our thing. What's the theme?'

'Clippies and Conductors.'

'Bloody Hell, Ronnie,' snaps Ralph. 'How can you go to a fancy dress evening in your work stuff? It's not fancy dress, is it? It's just like heading off for a few pints after you've done your last shift. That's just friggin' stupid.'

Ronnie looks suitably unfazed. 'Len likes the idea, and the best part is that those who don't come as clippies or conductors can be passengers.'

'Ronnie you are a friggin' wasted on the buses.' Ralph glances across to me and Al and winks. 'Listen we might be reforming. How much would we get paid?'

'Not sure about that. I'd have to ask Len. It's just three or four songs in the interval while people go to the buffet and have a break.'

'A break from what?'

'The turns,' says Ronnie. 'It's an open mike thing. We're going to provide our own entertainment. Clippies and Conductors Night featuring Busking With The Buses. We've got some real talent down at the garage, and there's a prize for the best act.'

'Oh, yeh, like a meal for two in the bus depot canteen?'

'Better than that, lads. One of our drivers has connections at Radio Merseyside. There's going to be a feature about the bus service in Widnes. It's a local history special about how the buses connect with all the interesting and historical places around the town but, better still, the programme's going to play out with a song from the winning act. They're gonna be asked to go into the studio and sing it live. It'll go out across Merseyside.'

Sparks of the old Ralph suddenly seem to crackle and bite.

'What kind of song are they looking for?'

'Something to go with the theme of the programme. It's got to be a song inspired by Widnes: the town, its people, its history, its buses, that sort of thing. Len says it's got to be modern and appeal to teenagers but has to draw older folk in as well. Should be easy. Great place, Widnes! Great people! Nice places to live! Great social life!'

Ralph slaps Ronnie heartily on the back almost dislodging his ticket machine. 'We'll probably be interested, but there's a condition. If we do the songs in the interval, we get to be part of the competition with a chance of winning the prize.'

'Not sure, there,' says Ronnie. 'I'll have to check with Len.'

'Tell him,' says Ralph, 'we are frigging professionals and most of the acts will be shit. How would that reflect on the bus company if the programme played out with a crappy performance? We are rising stars, Man, with the talent to reach out to a massive audience around Widnes and Liverpool, especially with the new stuff we're getting together.'

'What kind of stuff do you do?'

'New direction, Man. We're gonna re-invent ourselves and head out with something completely fresh. We're moving with the music scene and Len will love it. Check it out with him when you get back to the depot and we'll see you on the 3.30 to confirm.'

We leave the bus at the top of Leigh Avenue and head towards school.

'New direction? What are you talkin' about, Man?' says Al. 'We thought it was all over.'

'This is a friggin' brilliant opportunity,' says Ralph. 'I've got some great ideas. We'll meet up at Anne's on Saturday to discuss.'

'At Anne's? I thought Dave Shuttleworth had driven an immovable wedge between you.'

'No chance,' says, Ralph. 'He's welcome to Lisa, friggin, Wilcox. Anyway, nothing happened on the milk float, she was too streetwise to be taken in by his advances and he ended up taking her home, dropping her off with the milk, and picking up the empties. Exciting times, Men! I can feel our music careers are about to be reinvented here in Widnes. No travelling down to friggin' London, sleeping in crappy flats and putting up with a load of pretentious prats. Our new sound is gonna take off right here on the banks of the Mersey. We'll become celebrities. People will flock to see where it all began. There'll be coach trips to the Tavern and guided tours around Wade Deacon. The WAB'll be raking it in.'

164

TWENTY FOUR

Everybody Knows This Is Nowhere
Neil Young. Debut Album. Reprise Records.

It's Halloween, the start of October half term, and the ghosts and demons of my rock career are far from being laid to rest. Len has confirmed that we can be honorary entrants in the competition as long as we play the interval for free. So, I'm on my way to Anne's house, a long hop from the cricket ground, down leafy, green streets with manicured grass verges and Ford Prefects and Austin 1100s tucked on the drives behind the privet hedges and fancy wrought iron gates.

The pace of life in plushyville has slowed almost to a standstill. Farnworth's not like our estate where posses of kids on bikes round up the packs of dogs which have been roaming the streets all day, lassoing them with bits of old rope and charging a shilling to return them to their owners. There's always at least two football matches going on at the same time in our road with the balls and players getting mixed up in a frenzy of mistaken identities. I almost feel like I'm crossing a border without disguise and that, in a moment, a group of men closely resembling John Steed, sporting expensive suits, black trilbies and carrying umbrellas, will materialise out of the front drives and escort me back to Birchfield Road. There they'll bundle me onto Ronnie's bus, slipping him money for a one-way ticket back to Hough Green. Mr Woodley already has his defences up. There's a hosepipe spread neatly across the front of his drive, and he keeps lookout from the top of his stepladders which just about elevate his head above the parapet of his leylandii hedge.

'Pass friend. They're inside.' He motions with his rattling electric hedge trimmer towards the side of the house and I follow the smell of coffee and cakes round into the kitchen.

The house is pristine with the kitchen full of gadgetry, whirling noises and wires. All the labour saving devices are here: washing machine, hoover, electric oven with timer and electric food mixer. It's a generation removed from our house. My clothes are still hand-washed by my Gran and rung out through an old mangle before being transferred to the washing line. Anne's Mum has been freed from this labour-intensive world of drudgery and has time to organise coffee mornings and 'Bring and Buy' sales at St Luke's Church around the corner. This morning there's the smell of home-baking drifting through the light and airy semi. Anne's Mum runs the house like clockwork, and the cakes have to be finished by 10.30 and boxed up ready for the vicar to collect at 11.00.

I'd love to come home to a house like this every night, snug and cosy with thick carpets, colour television, tea on the table and warm smiles. Mrs Woodley brings a plate of cakes into the living room, 'Overbaked again,' she says comically, reprimanding herself. 'Tuck in children they can't go to waste.'

I smile at the use of the word 'children' not sure whether she's being sarcastic or papering over the images of Ralph and her daughter which no doubt drift into her mind in quiet moments between leafing through *Good Housekeeping* and listening to *Woman's Hour*. Ralph scoops three fairy buns up in one hand and, deftly flicking off the paper cases, stuffs the lot into his mouth.

'Listen, Men,' mumbles Ralph, 'We've got to move on. I've got some ideas about where we go and how we win this friggin' competition. The rules say we need to appeal to a modern audience.' He sweeps an album up from the side of the settee. 'Anyone heard of James Taylor?'

The guy on the front of the album, which is just called *James Taylor*, doesn't look like my kind of rock star. He's sitting on the grass against a stone wall, has a neat haircut, and is wearing a light brown suit with the trousers supported by braces over a yellow shirt. If anything he looks like Ronnie

Hurst, smartly dressed for an evening down at the golf club. He looks how my Mum sees me in her dreams.

'Never heard of him!'

'Listen to this track.' Ralph slides the vinyl out of the sleeve and carefully places it on the Woodley's stereogram. 'It's called 'Carolina In My Mind'. Listen to the friggin' lyrics.'

The needle crackles away and the song kicks in. It starts off pleasantly enough with some crisp, jangly guitar, followed by some softly-sung lyrics about Carolina and sunshine and the sky being on fire. It reminds me a bit of a couple of Country and Western songs my Mum has in her collection but the guitar's different, picked sharply with the notes ringing clearly to complement the lyrics. The song fades at the end but with the title repeated over and over; a clear statement of the theme of the song, just in case the listener's concentration had drifted and they hadn't quite taken it in.

I look at Ralph and wonder where this has all come from. Anne sits whimsically gazing out of the window. We listen to rest of the album and the images of wind-blown leaves and sunshine rising to chase the cold. Smiles, tears and warm relationships presented softly through James' mesmeric vocals. It's a world away from the aggressive, worrying sounds of blues and a similar distance between Ralph's world and the one James is softly drawing us into. The thing with Lisa didn't happen but it seems he's paying the price. Anne has mapped out her world and Ralph is being woven back into it without resistance.

The last bars of the album fade away and the needle clicks, leaving a few seconds of reflective silence.

Ralph carefully lifts the album from the turntable and holds it aloft as if he's celebrating some sort of musical triumph.

'Look at the label, Men, it's on Apple. He wrote it about Carolina while he was over here in London last year. He was friggin' homesick. He's written about the place he left behind, all the sunshine and warmth, wishing he was back there.'

'So?' says Al.

'It's exactly what the judges will want, and it's the future of friggin' music, Man. All that heavy blues stuff about stealin' away and treatin' your girl bad is dead, guys. Girls,' he pauses, looking across at Anne, 'don't want all that crap now. They want the music of candles in the bedroom and rain falling on the window panes. Songs about things they know and love. Real feelings about where they belong. Open your eyes and go into The Music Shop. They're all creeping out of the shadows ready to take over the scene: Elton John, Cat Stevens, John Martyn, Leonard Cohen. Our music's got to come from us, not some fucked-up rockers who don't live in our world and don't connect with people's real lives. Surely we can each write a song which makes James Taylor's effort seem like a New Seekers b-side. Simple lyrics about everyone's Carolina; love, happiness and home.'

'There's just a bit of difference. Carolina is full of wide open spaces, the Blue Ridge Mountains and golden beaches which stretch for miles. Widnes is grey, dark and squashed between Warrington and Liverpool.'

You're missing the point, Man. Music history is littered with songs about people leaving home and wanting to get back, it doesn't matter where it is. This is our big chance. Look what's happening down in London. Tupp and Mike are blowing it because they don't see the future. Freddie whatshisname is right. Blues is dying and we need to re-invent ourselves. If we're gonna have any chance of winning the competition we don't want to make the same mistake as them; we have to embrace new directions and stay one step ahead of the game. Ok, we're not going to share his vision, play fancy stuff, and prance around the stage like some outrageous show-off, but there's more than one scene developing and we can be there before anyone else around here. We've got a couple of weeks to come up with some ideas then we'll put the songs together and perform them back at YPF before we take them out to the people.'

'I'm not sure about another gig; I mean I'm sort of relieved the pressure of the band thing is over. I've got exams and other stuff to do.'

'Phil, this is your town, it's your chance, your opportunity to elevate Widnes to the stuff of legends. You've walked the streets, lived with its hopes and fears, loved its people, breathed its air and survived, even though it's full of crap. Al and I will get another two songs together so we've got the beginnings of a set. He hails from the lands of the north, the lonely roads, big horizons, legends, mysteries and stories told by generations who will never leave. I've got a great idea for a song about Liverpool. Why would people want to listen to songs about Carolina when they can have stuff which goes straight to their own hearts and pulls at the ties of home?'

He sees the doubtful look on my face.

'Look, we've got a month before the competition and I'm not thinking of another gig. When we're ready we'll go out busking, fine-tuning our image on the streets, so when the night comes, we're the professionals who blow away the judges. We start outside Widnes Market and then head up to Lime Street so we get a good range of listeners. We need to make sure we're making that connection the judges will be looking for, so they have no choice but to propel us to stardom on the radio. Right! See you at school on Monday to check progress. Next YPF is the 19th November so we've plenty of time to try things out before then and, if all goes well, we can fit in the busking before the competition and earn some money for Christmas.'

'Are we still Moonshine?'

'No, I've got us a new name. We're gonna be Western Highway because it's the bus route on my way home.'

'Never heard of it.'

'Yeh, well, it's Speke Road, the A562, but it heads west out of Widnes, so it'll be a statement that we're heading off towards new musical frontiers.'

With that, he stuffs another three fairy buns into his mouth, kisses Anne, spraying her with crumbs, and leaves us to head off in his new direction.

TWENTY FIVE

Who Knows Where The Time Goes
Fairport Convention. Unhalfbricking. Island Records.

Heading in a new musical direction is a big decision, but my need to be Paul Rodgers or whatever manifestation of him is possible, has moderated since I've met Judith. She appears to like me just as I am and doesn't really seem into rock identity and the image thing. I don't feel I have anything to live up to, which has taken the pressure off a bit, but I'm still worried. Judith is different. With previous girlfriends, it was just a matter of asking them out, going for a few bops, or a film, talking about trivia, and the usual endgame of snogging and things. I mean the kissing's great, and she smiles a lot. She clearly enjoys my company, and I'm sure she's attracted to me physically. But now I have a girl who wants to talk and discuss, and is obviously keen on intellectual attraction, and I'm worried about being out of my depth.

So, I've been swatting like mad, reading *Tess*, Shakespeare and the poetry anthology, and even taking a real interest in Herbie Gravitt's tutorials. She also likes the idea of songwriting and busking; there seems to be an arty Bohemian side to her too. In fact, I've found the perfect girl which is exciting, frightening and also sad. A few months from now it could all be over, and we'll probably be heading away from Hough Green and Long Barn, woven out of each other's tapestries.

She says we make her laugh and that we're all heroic, in the literary sense of course. Ralph has grand intentions of setting out on a musical odyssey but she thinks Al and I need a push to pick up the momentum.

Today we're spending a whole Sunday together and I've asked her to help me find material for my song. She's really enthusiastic about helping me out so I'm taking her down to West Bank to see if I gain some inspiration from what's left of

172

the quaint little terraces, winding promenade and the expanse of the Mersey, as it flows out into the wide estuary and around towards Hale Lighthouse.

It's a crisp, November morning with warm sunshine fighting to clear the damp haze. The Victorian station looks glorious in the winter light. It's plucked straight out of a Frank Henry Mason railway poster, with the gabled roofs of its Cheshire Line buildings pointing proudly into a cloudless sky, and mirroring those images which promised an escape into a slower, more undemanding world. There are flowers in tubs all along the platform, the stonework's painted in gleaming, bright, whitewash, and the stationmaster and his dog have appeared out of the booking hall ready to collect tickets. The air feels momentarily fresh and, as I glimpse the smoke of the engine some way down the line, I have the urge to write a song that's the opposite of 'Homeward Bound' based on journeys and meetings and happiness.

The train heaves into the station and Judith's there, the slight worry that she might think our relationship's developing too quickly and decided to stay at home, dissipated in the clouds of steam from the engine as it fires up ready to head off to Liverpool.

It's warm. Her coat's stuffed inside a sizeable shoulder bag, and she's dressed in denims and a short-sleeved, woolly top. She smiles, waves, and seconds later we're sharing a quick hug on the platform before heading out up the slope and into Victoria Park to take the short walk to the town centre. Everywhere is browns and golds and we pull each other through piles of fallen leaves laughing like kids. We wind through the narrow paths down towards the cenotaph, which is losing its early morning frost, as the thin rays of the sun fall respectfully across its white, stone face. The aviary is full of the sounds of birds chattering madly and two old guys call to each other as they prepare for an early morning bowl on one of the immaculately prepared greens.

'Widnes is nice.'

'Bet I can count on one hand the number of people in the whole of history who've said that.'

'You're too hard on your town,' says Judith. 'It's home and that's important. You might leave it one day but your memories won't, and you'll always come back even if it's just in your mind. Come on, let's look for some ideas, songs about parks won't be very inspiring.' She grabs my hand and we walk down Peel House Lane where we jump onto the West Bank bus and head south to start our day.

After leaving the town centre, the road gets narrower as we move towards Spike Island. The plumes of smoke from the chemical plants drift vertically into the cloudless sky above the spit of land between the Mersey and the Sankey Canal. The bus speeds down Mersey Road, inches from a long stone wall, jogging memories of Mum telling me to hold on tight until we reached our the stop opposite Church Street.

I want to get off here today. I've not been back since we moved to Hough Green some years ago and maybe there's a song here somewhere. At the head of the street, the old, Victorian terraces, with polished red steps and window sills, take me back but I know our house will be gone, flattened and swept away to make space for the approach road to the Jubilee Road Bridge. It dominates the skyline, dwarfing the houses which shelter under the green metal of its criss-cross of girders. There's the noise too. When I lived here it was the distant sounds of foghorns on the river or the clanking of trains steaming their way through the iron lattice of the Ethelfleda Bridge. Now it's the constant whine and hum of traffic and the smell of exhaust smoke which filters down from the sky into the backyards and through the open windows of the terraces below.

Gone too are my Uncle Nuck's corner shop, my Uncle George's and Aunty Vi's pub, The Bridge Hotel, and the houses of friends and neighbours. The roar of heavy vehicles drowns out the whispers of any ghosts who might who might have stayed on in the hope that the clutter and sprawl of 20th-century life might one day disappear allowing the old ways to return.

'Whereabouts was your house?' Judith gazes around almost bumping into a young woman who is pushing a set of twins purposefully along the old, flagged pavement.

'Just where the middle of the approach road is, and the pub was opposite.'

I glance back to a house on the corner of West Street. It's been clumsily converted from my Uncle's shop with UPVC frames, and orange, nylon curtains, banishing to memory the dark, timbered windows advertising Bisto, Vimto, Tizer and Capstans.

'My Uncle Nuck used to tell me that people didn't just come in to buy things. He reckoned he knew the darkest secrets of half the people in West Bank; every single story, rumour, and conversation was like feeling the pulse of the place. The chat and banter went on till shutting up time and continued when the pubs re-opened. Apparently, you could stand outside the window of The Bridge and hear the fragments of conversation picked out between the laughter and the clink of beer glasses: football, the Chemics, pigeons, politics, tales from work and the docks. It was non-stop. He said it only ended at chuckin' out time with the shouts of 'Goodnight!' and the slam of the front doors.'

Judith listens and smiles. She looks out of place standing amongst the noise and the dust which cling to the senses as we gaze at the drab streets. Suddenly my childhood seems a long time ago swept away in the name of progress and development. There are no women proudly scrubbing their front steps, or neighbours gathering for a quick chat on the street corners, or the sounds of children running and laughing. There are no thuds of a football smacking into a goal drawn in chalk on the pub gates and no men striding down the streets, betting slips in hand, arguing the merits of Nicolaus Silver or Team Spirit. The place is dying, and the former site of the houses in Viaduct Street is marked by a line of ugly, grey, concrete tombstones which supports the approach road.

'This is a sad place,' says Judith. 'It's lost something. What you're looking for isn't here any longer.'

It's a depressing scene, so we turn away and head down West Street towards the river. Most of the shops which served the community have vanished but the Century Cinema's still open for an early morning showing of *Jason and the Argonauts* and there are a few scruffy-looking kids and a dog hanging around outside looking at the film-stills inside a scratched glass case. As we reach the junction with St Mary's Road we're at the end of the prom looking across the mud flats to the river which twists sluggishly between islands of wading birds. We stand in the thin morning sunlight which bounces grey sparkles off the flat surface.

Judith grabs my hand and leads me down the sandstone promenade towards the site of the old transporter bridge. Mersey Road is different now, the former route to the river crossing cleared of the lines of cars and lorries that waited to be ferried across the divide on the Transporter's rattling, metal platform. It's empty and quiet and there's a lot of boarded up shops and splashes of graffiti across the flaking paint of their doors. We climb some steps up towards St Mary's Church, where I was christened, and sit on the grass in a warm patch of sunlight. Across towards Runcorn, a large tanker moves silently along the Manchester Ship Canal and under the bridge.

I stare out at the industrial landscape on the southern side of the river and the reflections of metal and flame dancing on the water. 'How do you immortalise this in song? I can't imagine people wanting to flock back here in a hurry.'

'You wouldn't want to come back now but don't think you have to write about the actual place. It's an emotional thing: sentiments, relationships, snatches of half-remembered stories which drift in and out of your head. It's about getting back to those warm feelings it once gave you: safety, security, family, a

176

place to drift back to when life is not exactly as you want it to be. Literature is full of people who dream of journeying back. You need to talk to people living in Widnes who believe they belong here. They may not realise it but the feelings will be buried away. Tess doesn't think about going back to Marlott to have her child, it's her natural instinct because it's the place for her to go to when life tries to knock her down. You need to think about people who love the town, why they stay here, and what would bring them on a journey back.'

'Do you worry about leaving Long Barn?' It's the closest I can get to asking Judith about the future.

'Not really. It'll always be there. Farming folk don't tend to flit around from place to place. The farm's doing pretty well and Mum and Dad are still young enough to manage it.'

I have an irrational panic that time's passing too quickly and that Clotho has gone into overdrive weaving our tapestries at the speed of light when she could spin out our story a little more slowly. I can't ask Judith anything about what'll happen after Christmas. I can't contemplate a response which will eat into the present and spoil things.

'What about you?'

I have no idea if this is Judith thinking in parallel with me or whether it's just a question that anyone might ask me about my plans.

'I'll be leaving Widnes but probably not too far.'

'That's good. I wouldn't want us to lose touch.'

'That won't happen.'

Judith squeezes my hand and smiles, and there's no need to say anymore.

TWENTY SIX

Only A Northern Song
The Beatles. Yellow Submarine. Apple Records.

The inspiration for my song is going to come from Geoff and Jackie. I figure that seeing as they love the town and have been together since they were fourteen, their heads must be full of stuff I can blend into the message I'm looking for. They're usually in The Ring O'Bells on a Sunday night, and I'm hoping the meeting might spark some ideas from their stories, memories and half-remembered moments.

The Ring O'Bells is not the Philharmonic. Its identity is in question and it's been trying to resist the pressure to move from genteel, suburban hostelry to 'traditional', Sixties boozer. Geoff and Jackie's estate has crept within staggering distance of the pub and tonight the mild and bitter mob is holding sway. The pub is packed, and the chords of Pinball Wizard rip through the shouted conversations turning the bar into a cauldron of unintelligible noise. I struggle through the smoky haze of the lounge and manage to find them tucked in a quiet corner under a yellowing picture of Widnes rugby legend Frank Myler.

Frank wouldn't need a song to fire his love of Widnes. Even though he's moved on to play for St Helens he still lives in the town; a local hero with the grey-flannelled, betting shop, Brylcreamed men of his generation. His song would be one of a career living with the ferocity of professional sport cheered on by hard, lean-faced supporters escaping from the toil and monotony of their grim lives. I need Geoff and Jackie to give me ideas for a softer sound. Poignancy and affection are not feelings associated with rugby league.

I brave the scrum around the bar, return with three pints of bitter, and explain what I'm looking for.

Geoff looks thoughtfully into his drink. 'You can't be over-romantic about a place and try to conjure up an evocative song about pubs, factories and mudflats.'

'Yes, but it's as Judith said, I might go and never come back but do I ever abandon all that I leave behind? I mean look at James Taylor's lyrics. He sings about the callings from another place and restless ghosts from his past. He describes being away from home as the dark side of the moon. I need to tap into those sorts of feelings. Every place in the world must be held in someone's hearts, even Widnes.'

Jackie's halfway through her pint and is listening to us thoughtfully.

'I don't think people are bothered about the muck and the grime.'

'Go on.'

'Well, home's a place where you can be free and be yourself. It doesn't just have to be how the place looks; it's the people around you and whether your heart is there.'

She finishes her drink and heads over to the jukebox. Seconds later she's back and 'Reach Out I'll Be There' is a welcome relief from 'Pinball Wizard'.

'Home's all here inside. If I ever think about music it takes me to a time and place and, apart from a couple of holidays, those places are here. Widnes is in a thousand songs inside my head. Listening to this, I'm not in Detroit.'

'So where are you?'

Jackie smiles and grabs Geoff's hand.

'Probably that summer night when we climbed up to the top of Pex Hill and looked out over the town. It was one of those moments when I really felt like I belonged.'

'So, go on, what did you see?'

'Well, you sort of look at things differently when you're up there. You can see all the life below. The good things about growing up are almost there in your hand. You just want to reach out, grab them, bottle them up and keep them safe. We were just alone on the edge of the world, and we didn't need to be anywhere else because we had everything we ever wanted. I was wishing for time to stop. I always think about that night when I want cheering up.'

'Go on.'

'Well, I don't want to sound mad, but the memories will always stay with me wherever I go. I know that if I ever left the ties would never break. If things went wrong I would always be pulled back and the town would gather me in and make everything all right. Those feelings of belonging will always connect with home. Can you write a song about them?'

'Well, I can try. I could call it 'Edge of the World' or something like that. I can see it, first track, side one, on the album. We open the set with it and draw everyone into your world. The whole crowd sways as one at the front of the stage singing the chorus. Widnes becomes the new Galveston and you get a credit on the album sleeve.'

'Really!' Jackie looks like she's won the Pools.

Geoff heads back from the bar and she starts on her second pint. By the time we've finished our third, it's nearing closing time and we've thrown a few more ideas around, but I have a feeling that I need something deeper. I don't want to end up with the simplicity of a Motown song and see Jackie's chart-topper from a couple of hours ago slipping down the Top Twenty.

Geoff and Jackie wrap up in scarves and gloves and we head for the door. We're going different ways and they walk off down Upton Lane, the wind whipping the leaves around their ankles. The world is silent with the damp, November air muting even the light pad of their shoes on the path of mud-trodden leaves. They seem to stop, the yellow grain of the streetlights freeze-framing them in a sepia-toned study; ghosts of couples who have trodden the path for years. The deeper ideas are here somewhere, but I can't bring them into my thoughts, and the songwriting is filling a disproportionate amount of space in my head. I have to make some notes for

Herbie's tutorial tomorrow, so I leave them both to drift off into the mist and head for home.

'Valediction; Forbidding Mourning' by John Donne. 1612. The title was scribbled into my exercise book a week ago but the pages are empty, except for the word 'Metaphysics' sitting on the second line. I've listened to enough of Herbie's theoretical meanderings to know it's a movement involving sophisticated thinking about identity, time and space and, in the case of the poets I'm studying, mainly love and religion. It's about a husband leaving his wife for a journey to France. He's trying to convince her not to be sad because their love is transcendent, heavenly, and has a spiritual level as well as a physical dimension. It's filled with the usual philosophical ruminations about how their minds will remain united even if their bodies are separated.

I yawn and lay back on the bed. I could try and persuade Herbie that all this existential analysis of life, love and the inner soul is alive and rumbling through the speakers of Joe's stereo and that Al drifts around on a metaphysical plane most of the time except when the demands of everyday life tip him back into reality.

I scribble a few things into my jotter, and I'm about to jump under the sheets when I realise the poem continues onto the next page. I turn over and discover another three stanzas.

Donne's comparing their relationship to the movements of a mathematical compass. The wife sits fixed at the anchor point while her husband is the adjustable point moving off on its journey. He proposes that although they're apart, they're actually inseparable, irrespective of how far the outer point travels because the compass is one unit and when it closes the two points will always end up back together again.

It's Jackie's feelings. She's summed up the metaphysical nature of life in Widnes. Identity, time and space; she's sat on the top of Pex Hill and touched them all. I grab a pen and start jotting down some of her ideas. Tomorrow I can hurtle into Herbie's lesson and engage him with my theory that Jackie has been floating around the edges of the metaphysical up on Pex Hill and that her observations about love and life are actually worthy of deep, literary consideration. I scribble a title for a song in my jotter and imagine someone like John Martyn doing his intro on stage, charming the audience with metaphysical tales before pausing slightly. He'd check the tuning of his guitar with a single strum and whisper huskily into the mike, 'Ok, this one's inspired by a girl I once knew in Widnes. It's about the attachment and feelings I have for my hometown. Hope you enjoy it. It's called 'Compass Point'.'

TWENTY SEVEN

It's Getting Better
Mama Cass Elliot. Bubblegum, Lemonade and Something For Mama. Dunhill Records.

The sound of Ronnie's ticket machine rattles into my ear as the bus jumps erratically along Liverpool Road.

'Had a good weekend, lads?'

'Better than you,' says Al.' How did the round of golf, shopping with Sandra and her Mum and the dog walking go?'

'Ronnie looks curiously at Al. 'We didn't do the dog walk. It's not too good.'

'Really!' says Al. 'What's wrong with it?'

'It's dead. We gave it some new food which didn't agree with it.'

'Jesus, Ronnie,' says Al. 'Is there space in your garden to bury any more animals? I bet when you and Sandra hit the pet shop all the creatures crap themselves.'

Herbie's had a better weekend than Ronnie. He's got our latest set of essay marks and they're good.

'B+, Stephens. You seem to have developed an intense understanding of Hardy's tragic heroine.'

'That's because he's going out with her,' says Ralph. 'She's moved from Dorset to Padgate.'

Al and I are at The Dell. Ralph has stayed with Herbie, writing out two hundred lines for being flippant.

My slight worry that Al might have decided Ralph's new ideas are too far removed from his musical roots is unfounded. In fact, he believes that once our reputation as innovative singer-songwriters spills out across the clubs, pubs, and suburbs there'll be any number of girls wanting to be seen hanging onto his arm. He's already got the idea for his song based on looking back at his life in Bishop Auckland which is full of images of Northumberland and the romance of its wild open spaces, windswept coastland, mystical saints and ancient ways.

'It's about being drawn back. How those primordial feelings are embedded into you at birth; inseverable ties, connecting you with the dawn of your existence.'

I guess there was no chance of Al completely cutting his own primordial ties with prog-rock but at least he's kept to the theme and it'll suit the acoustic platform pretty well.

Ralph ambles down the drive ripping up his lines and tossing them nonchalantly into a flower bed. He's also come up with a song over the weekend but it's predictably dark and menacing. It's called 'Dead Man's Ghost' and it's about an old guy who moved away from Hunts Cross but never got to come back, so he returns as a restless spirit. The suggestion is that one day all our ghosts will walk the highways and byways of our youth searching for the things we left behind. The lyrics seem pretty good and it's an upbeat number, even if the subject matter is depressing. Still, we have three different songs built around a similar theme and Al reckons they reflect the diversity which all good bands have. Suddenly we're full of enthusiasm, talking through ideas for the songs and throwing in some of the rhyming lines for the verses. We head home ready to fine-tune our ideas for a meeting at Ralph's in a week's time. We're feeling pretty inspired as we jump onto the bus and Ralph calls down the aisle to Ronnie, 'Any more animals dead yet?'

'Just the dog we hit on the 12.30 to Cronton,' says Ronnie.

TWENTY EIGHT

Observations From A Hill
Family. Family Entertainment. Reprise Records.

I've climbed up to the top of Pex Hill on my way to school. I'm a lonely figure following a lonely path with my guitar over my shoulder, and I feel pretty self-conscious as if I'm sailing uncomfortably close to pretentiousness. I just need to have a second look in the light of day to see if Jackie's magic is suffering from a hangover and how I feel now her dreams of the town are not hidden from the shelter of night.

It's a sobering view. There's no sign of life amongst the tired shops that wind down Widnes Road towards the murky, grey outline of the waste tips which mask a clear view to the Mersey and the docks. There are a few muffled sounds from the river struggling to penetrate a thin, industrial fog and seagulls swoop in and out of view between its weak, yellow layers.

The Swinging Sixties never touched this place, and the energy and enthusiasm which flashed onto our TV screens disappeared when the set was turned off and the little white dot faded into the blackness. Still, I'm glad to be miles from London and the draw of some impossible dream. It's home, and I'm looking through Jackie's eyes at the few square miles into which I've packed all of my eighteen years.

I unfold the piece of paper onto which I've scribbled the lyrics and chords and weight it down on the grass with a couple of stones. I blow onto my fingers to warm them and check the tuning on the guitar before playing the song through. The last note rings out across the fields fading into the sounds of traffic rumbling along Cronton Lane.

'Fuckin' smart sound, Phil.'

I turn sharply. It's Miffer, silhouetted against the light that's lifting the cloud on the edge of the ridge. He should be in London forging his rock career but he's returned, and the drumsticks poking out of the top of his rucksack tell me he's not on a flying visit. He has the look of a man who's not slept for weeks and has just crawled out of a nearby hedge.

'Great to see you back, Man! Are you just up for a visit?'

'Am I fuck!' Miffer sits wearily on the grass, drags a can of Long Life out of his rucksack, and sits back. He downs it in one and wipes the froth from his lips in the manner of a man who's refreshed and about to embark on an epic story.

'Had to come up here to empty my fuckin' head, get away from London and my mate Fred.'

'Doesn't sound like you're going back.'

'Look, I love the guy, but if he thinks the road to becoming famous is not helping to load the van, travelling around in taxis when we're not pickin' up any money from gigs, writing pop songs with too many key changes and boasting all the time that he's going to be a bloody legend, then he's on a different road to the one I'm travelling. The three of us were ok when we could sit around getting our sets together with real music. We knew where we were going. Fred's on a different path. He's got one vision. I have no fuckin' doubt he'll get there, but it won't be with me, Tupp and Mike.'

He sits on the grass, leaning forward as if being drawn by a magnetic energy. He gazes into the distance, the epitome of what we're trying to capture in our songs; the desperate wanderer returning back to his pubs, clubs, and well-trodden ways. He already looks more comfortable since he sat down and gazed across at the familiar landscape of home.

'Joe said you weren't keen on London.' It sounds trite, but it's the only thing I can think of to say.

'Look. Man. Everyone knows I'm highway-driven bluesman focused on horizons which I think are realistic and achievable. I do not drink Jasmine tea and ponce around in fur and satin and have delusional fantasies about where my life's going. I like to drink pints in pubs with others who like to do the same and talk about blues riffs, blues singers and moments in our lives when we've lived the blues and managed to crawl away

187

from wasted situations with only our drumsticks for company. I was serious. I was ready to see it all through, but the others will have to go it alone now. Ibex is finished. Fred's sorted a new drummer. Long live Wreckage.'

As the words tumble bitterly from his mouth, it becomes pretty clear that London has tasted Miffer and spat him back out without any edges or corners chewed away from his northern façade. Beneath the surface, though, is a self-deprecating anger that he allowed himself to be persuaded to head south in the first place. He mumbles on about rich hippies, dilapidated dwellings, watered, down beer and lack of money.

'What you gonna do? Find a band up here?'

'No chance of that, mate. I need some serious bread. I'm packin' in drummin' for a bit. Just been down to the dairy to try and get my milk round back but that bastard Dave Shuttleworth's taken it, so I'm lookin' to get a job labouring on the construction team on the M56. Twenty-five quid a week!'

With that, he pushes himself to his feet, takes the empty can and boots it into a field of sheep. They scatter away bleating.

'See you around, Phil. Bloody great to be back in the real world.' He takes his rucksack and moves off down the hill.

I pick up my guitar. I'm not sure whether Miffer listened to the song or if his offhand comment was an expression of empathy with Jackie's vision. Whatever, he's returned, the living embodiment of Ralph's dead man's ghost, except he'll find what he's looking for even if his milk float's been hijacked by a lesser mortal.

'Hey, Mick. Why the name change?'

He stops and turns.

'We might not have seen eye to eye on everything, but Fred and I were pretty close. When I told him I was coming back, he begged me not to leave.'

He looks past me into the dark clouds gathering above the ridge, takes a deep breath and steadies himself. 'The last thing he said to me was, 'If you go, all we are left with is wreckage'.'

He rubs the back of his hand across his eyes, turns into the wind and heads off down the path, the points of his compass drawing swiftly together. In a few hours, they'll be snapped shut locking him back into his old familiar world.

TWENTY NINE

Sing Me A Song That I Know
Blodwyn Pig. Nice Enough To Eat. Island Records Sampler.

I've fine-tuned 'Compass Point'. I'm pleased with the result and I make my way over to Al's humming the song over in my head. Walking through the streets to the tune is sort of inspiring as if I'm living in a film with its own soundtrack. The power of music and images makes me feel upbeat about actually living here, and I'm seeing the place in a new light. Maybe not so much as to make me dig in my heels and put down roots but I'm definitely feeling differently about the town. There's love and life here, and warmth and pride, and I think Jackie has done it proud. In a few minutes, I'll hear Al sing the lyrics to my chords and I'll get a real sense of performance.

Al's finished his own lyrics and his sister's helped put some chords to them on her piano. It's called 'Shadowlands' and has a subtitle 'A Drifter I May Be'. It's a narrative thing, the sort of track which could be part of a concept album. I catch sight of *On The Threshold Of A Dream* propped against the side of the piano.

Al sings it through unaccompanied. It's actually pretty good and tells the story of a guy who disappears into a grey, empty existence but drifts back through time and space to his spiritual home. Al says it can be interpreted on multiple levels but the main thing is that it's got a catchy flow and a good hook line which repeats in the chorus; 'Colour my life with dreams of home.'

By the time we're on the bus to Hunts Cross we've sung both songs through so many times we're word perfect. We even get a round of applause from a few pensioners who get on at Tarbock Green.

'Didn't know the Merseybeats had re-formed,' says an old guy, and offers us a few coppers. We politely refuse and shut up, with self-doubts creeping in as to whether we'll hit our intended audience.

Ralph pulls open his front door. 'I'm a dead man, lookin' for my home.'

'Miffer's back!'

'No friggin' surprise to me,' says Ralph. 'It's the pull of home. It's what we're all about and why we are heading for success instead of disappearing into obscurity. The ties have pulled Miffer back where he belongs, back to his true self. Now he's escaped the life others expected of him and he's sheltered in those familiar sounds and places of home. There'll be Blues Night at the Labour Club, factory hooters calling through the early morning mist, the lap of the ship canal against the wall lulling him to sleep and the soporific journeys on Ronnie's bus. All the important things you don't get when you're miles away and the pace of life is a flashing blur that collapses time so you don't know what's happening from one day to the next. This is what he's missed, the unique character of the North. Wild open spaces, big skies, and wind-whipped estuaries; milk, beer, banter and the blues. Have we got all these things in our songs, Men?'

'Nothing about milk,' says Al.

THIRTY

I'll Be Long Gone
Bozz Scaggs. Bozz Scaggs Album. Atlantic Records.

Steve Rothwell is not a teacher. Well, not in the mould of the most of the Wade Deacon staff who mainly teach to the top of the A-stream with the rest of us swimming or floundering behind. The hall is all colour and cooperation and I'm taken back to junior school and Mrs Barnes' classroom; a protective, warm hive where pupils were encouraged to talk and co-operate with each other. Starting the Wade was a seismic shock to the system, being herded like cattle into different groups, told not to speak unless spoken to and threatened with all sorts of punishments before we'd had the chance to do anything wrong.

That's what teachers became to me during the first five years, cloaked Mandarins of death stalking the classrooms and corridors with a licence to inflict pain and suffering on all but the chosen few. I wonder how Steve got through the WAB's interview process and whether he's a sign that the system is mellowing, touched by the permissiveness of the Sixties, which might eventually be filtering into Wade Deacon's stronghold of standards and traditions.

All the cast members are here and Steve has assigned us jobs. He says by creating the set we immerse ourselves into the world of the characters and it helps us to empathise with their situations. Most of the girls are seeing to costumes and Billy and Graham are having a fitting of their stuffy suits bought from a jumble stall on Widnes Market. Judith is sat at a desk near the stage designing the programme, drawing a picture of an isolated manor house on the front and producing a resume of the plot and the cast list in perfectly neat handwriting. Some of the Art A-level pupils are painting the set which consists of a Thirties drawing room with French windows exiting into a garden with hills in the background. Rob Morrell and Dave Sapp, from the Lower Sixth, are sat at the back of the hall at the sound and lighting desk scribbling the different changes onto a script and organising the music and a few sound effects. At the side of the set are chairs for the on-stage audience which will include the two critics, Moon and Birdboot. There will be no set changes as the action runs for an hour, straight through with no interval, and is a complete play within a play. The whole thing seems to be suddenly coming to life.

Steve wants me, Al and Ralph to do a last round-up of props and has given us a list to check through. After the wheelchair fiasco, Mugga is banned from doing anything practical but has been assigned by Steve to make the tea for about twenty people which has to be replenished every thirty minutes.

The majority of the props are straightforward acquisitions: notebooks for the critics, tennis racket and ball for Cynthia, a duster for Mrs Drudge, a torch, glasses, whisky decanter and various other bits and pieces for the table. There's an old Bakelite telephone needed, which Ralph reckons his grandad's got stuffed in his loft, and a gun for the shootings at the end which will echo to sound effects created by Rob and Dave. This afternoon Steve wants us to make some mock footlights which will run across the front of the stage giving the set a Thirties feel. He's suggested we go down to Woodwork to see if there are any spare lengths of timber we can 'borrow' for a few days. He seems to have no fear of Slugger Sidebotham, the buffalo-faced head of department, by sending us into his domain, unsupervised, to remove some of his precious planks without permission.

I like Steve's bravado. It seems to be just one step removed from the numerous prankish tricks we have somehow got away with over the years, and I'd love to strip Slugger's room of every last splinter just to see his face when he arrives on Monday morning, dropping his redundant chisels and bevel gauges to the floor with shock. Mugga has been relieved of tea duties to come with us so there's an even number to carry back the planks.

In the corner of Slugger's room is Eric, a length of thinly sawn plywood with a crosspiece bolted across the end to make a sword shape. It's a bit like a cane but the surface area is wider and the whip on the flexible shaft guarantees that its swing from Slugger's hand meets a boy's buttocks, hands or legs at maximum velocity. The aftermath can be devastating with red weals rising swiftly from the point of contact. Eric rules the classroom, employed for even small misdemeanours, from whispered words to lack of attention. We've all met Eric during our younger years. Slugger is one of the most hated masters.

Ralph sidles over to Eric and removes him from the wall. 'Listen, Men. We can't take wood from here. If Slugger gets wind Steve will be the first teacher ever to meet Eric at a Monday morning briefing. The caretaker will let us have a few lengths from the side of the cricket pavilion.'

'I puckin' hate Slugger,' says Mugga, and heads over to the tools cupboard where he takes out a hammer and six two-inch nails. He turns Slugger's chair upside down on the bench and hammers the six nails through the underside of the seat so their slightly protruding points will produce a scattergun attack on Slugger's backside when he slides into it on Monday morning.

'Puckin' sort him out.'

Ralph replaces Eric back on his hook. 'Men, we were never here.'

On the way home I buy a copy of the *NME* to see if Ralph's vision of the new wave of music is being shared by the mouthpiece of the music industry. The front's disappointing, just a picture of Lulu sitting on some grass looking as if the photographer's just leapt out from behind a bush and scared the life out of her. I can't find much inside to convince me our new direction is going to hi-jack the pages in the coming months and replace the acts tipped to invade the charts with their new releases.

Englebert Humperdink, the Foundations, Stevie Wonder and Desmond Decker, are all the tastes of Young Reg and Sheila and the top thirty is still dominated by middle of the road pop and the occasional bluesy tune by Fleetwood Mac and the Stones. An advert for the first album by Crosby, Stills and Nash, fills one of the inside pages. They are sat outside a whitewashed wooden house on an old settee and look like a cleaned up version of Free who have jettisoned their image of decadence and mystery.

I'm just about to shove it into my bag when a small piece of text catches my eye. It's in the section where readers are invited to send in their reviews of concerts they've seen and have a go at dabbling in the style and voice of the music critic. There's a couple of decent reviews of Family at Leeds University and Pink Floyd at the Electric Garden in Glasgow but tucked away in the lower left corner is a small heading which reads:

Wreckage, The Noisy Common Room, Ealing Tech.
31st October.

I'd been told by some girls I met in the Kensington Pub that this band was worth two shillings out of my grant and that I was going to see an exciting new talent worthy of comparison with Ten Years After, Humble Pie or Spooky Tooth. After two or three numbers, of what can only be described as anarchic and rampageous prog-rock, most of the audience drifted out to the film room or started talking and playing table football. There seemed to be a lack of creative connection between the band and their overly-flamboyant lead singer. Despite trying to maintain the attention of the audience by cavorting around the stage in an outfit seemingly lifted from a pantomime props

195

department, he succeeded only in driving us to the sanctuary of the bar where we could shield ourselves from the musical onslaught and enjoy the free booze. 1/10. Ready Steady Steve.

I flick back to the Crosby Stills and Nash advert. They look relaxed, laid-back, comfortable and in control; three guys about to embark on a journey of discovery before heading home with only an acoustic guitar between them. I feel a monetary pang of guilt for inwardly doubting Ralph's vision. He seems to have called it right. There's definitely a feeling in the air that new musical fashions are muscling out the old established scene of the Sixties The piece in *NME* seems like an epitaph for Wreckage, suggesting their roots are about to be ripped up and swept away.

THIRTY ONE

You Can All Join In
Traffic. You Can All Join. Island Records Sampler.

'These are friggin' perfect for the Conductors and Clippies Competition,' says Ralph as the train rocks along towards Sankey Station. But Al's a bit sceptical about heading off into Liverpool to attempt to light up Lime Street on a frosty, November afternoon.

'Three songs aren't really enough, Ralph. We can't just go out busking and play them over and over again.'

'Not a problem. We'll just add the ones from the St Mary's gig and that'll draw people in. Then we'll hit them with our new anthems.'

There's quite a gathering at YPF. Geoff and Jackie have come to hear 'their song', most of the cast of *Hound* have come, and Jean has brought a few of her rock mates along, which is a bit unnerving. This time, there's no Marshall Amplifier and no drum kit, and Jean's even persuaded Des to put the heating on. The ragged curtains have also been replaced, courtesy of some of the takings from the autumn fair, and the place has a bit of an intimate music venue feel about it.

Jean has been down to London to see John and she's changed a bit. I mean everyone changes a bit after they've been to London and she looks like she's been doing some London shopping. The Afghan has gone and been replaced by a long mac-type thing with a really thin waist which then flares out over her shiny black boots. I like Jean, but I always have the feeling that she's just politely accepting us for what we are and that she's mentally about five years older rather than a year younger. A few chairs have been scattered around the stage and she's sitting at the front with Carol and a couple of other hippie-style girls who look like they've set up as an impromptu *Juke Box Jury*. I gaze across at her, attempting an un-cheesy smile. She leaves the judges and heads over.

'Looking forward to this, Phil. Anne says Ralph is taking you in a new direction.'

'How's Tupp?' This is my standard ice-breaker with Jean and I need to deflate her expectations about what she's about to witness.

'Well, he's ok, I think. He's working in a record shop in Piccadilly to make ends meet. You know Miffer's packed it in but Wreckage is still going. They've had a couple of gigs which I think were ok but I don't think you'll see them again. In fact, Freddie's up at Geoff Higgins' place in Liverpool at the moment, picking up the last of his things to take back to London.'

I'm not sure about Jean's statement that I won't be seeing them again. Has she read this week's *NME* and is hinting that a final split is on the way or just suggesting that I'm too much of a closeted home-loving type to venture out of my local circle into something I just can't cope with. Whatever she means she knows I'm not Tupp and that, even though I might be heading out of town in a few months, the security and stability element of my life has to come with me. I look at Jean's mates. I'm definitely not their type. I don't have any devil-may-care bravado but perhaps it's something you just wake up with one day, Maybe suddenly your eyes zap open and you realise that there are going to be no more days like the several thousand you've just lived. Then you head off in search of adventure, excitement, and challenge; like Tupp.

'Hear you've changed your musical style.' She raises her eyebrows and smiles.

'Yeh!' I try to sound nonchalant and clutch at a chance to challenge her musical knowledge. 'We're going for the more progressive, folk-type stuff now, like James Taylor and Neil Young.'

'I've heard of Neil Young but not the other one,' she says doubtfully, as if he's not passed her quality control test. 'I believe you're doing some songs about home.'

'Yeh. We're writing our own material now, just like Mike and Freddie.'

I think this sounds like a pretty cool reply as if we're on a par with what's going on in London and Widnes has actually started to break into the scene and begun to creep out of the languid haze of the Fifties.

'Well,' says Jean, 'They're going for a different sound now. Freddie thinks that the music scene is changing fast and that songs have to be more melodic with different phrasing and chord structures; changing key now and then, that sort of thing. Do any of your songs change key?'

'No, we're keeping it simple.'

'Well, Widnes is a pretty simple sort of place. John says London's a place where you have to change and move quickly otherwise you're left behind.'

'Well, we're probably not going to London.' I try to make it sound as if we had a plan to head off there but we've decided it has nothing to offer us. 'So we're just gonna see what happens around here and then take it from there.'

'Sounds good,' says Jean. 'Think Ralph's ready.'

Ralph has appeared at the front of the audience with an acoustic guitar strung around his shoulder held up by a fancy guitar strap which has a look of Nashville about it.

'Right folks,' says Ralph. 'We're Western Highway. Thanks for coming. Al and Phil and I have decided to move on from Moonshine and we've been working for weeks on new original material. We'd like to play just three of the songs for you tonight, then we'll head off to The Chapel House for a few pints and anyone who fancies coming can tell us what they think. The songs are inspired by where we grew up and the need to find home after a tough time. The first song is about Widnes and it's called 'Compass Point'. It's about discovering the place you love is right there in the palm of your hand.'

We head straight off into the number. I'm concentrating on the chords but with half an eye on the audience. Al's vocals are impressively in-tune and, after they've taken in the first verse, there's a definite nodding and an almost discernible rocking from side to side. 'Compass Point' is flowing and the lyrics seem good sung to my chords. I'm buzzing and the song comes to an end too quickly. The last chord fades and Al turns to us and then back to the audience. 'Ok, 'Compass Point'. Thanks.'

Everybody claps politely but it's a bit like the clapping you get when you're down to the 'W's at a school awards evening. Al moves on quickly.

'Ok. Next one's called 'Shadowlands'. It's inspired by the mystery of the North East where I grew up.' Someone claps loudly and we move into the first verse. It's not as upbeat as the first song but the looks on the faces seem to suggest there's a definite engagement. A couple of Jean's mates lean forward in their seats as if they're a bit more interested, either in the song or in Al.

At the end, the clapping's a bit more encouraging, and I can pick up a few positive words from the whispered conversations between the girls. 'Dead Man's Ghost' keeps the momentum going and there's even a bit of clapping along when it hits Ralph's gritty chorus.

'They were good,' says Jean, as we sit together in a quiet corner of the pub. 'I like the themes. Got me thinking about John.'

'You mean will he ever drift back home?'

'I think he'll be the one who's the exception to your philosophy. He'll be back for Christmas but I can't really see him staying. There's nothing in Warrington for him. John Donne wouldn't have thought much of him.'

She finishes her drink, swirls her scarf around her neck, and gets ready to leave. 'I like the idea of taking literary themes into music. Your songs were good. Keep your fingers crossed that Donne comes up in the mocks. Bet you know him inside out now.'

I smile and shake my head, 'More into Hardy really.'

'Judith said so. Glad you've found someone to replace Miss Motown. Who was the guy you mentioned with Neil Young?'

'James Taylor.'

She pulls her purse out of her bag and quickly counts her money. 'Nearly two quid. Ok, I'll give him a go but you'd better not be wrong.'

THIRTY TWO

Jesus Is Just Alright.
The Byrds. Ballad of Easy Rider. Columbia Records.

'We'll be judged by the public,' says Ralph, as we head down Widnes Road on the bus, ready to set up outside the market. 'You get all sorts down here on a Saturday morning so it'll give us some idea of the scope of our appeal.'

Ralph has a brought a bucket for appreciative listeners to drop their money into and we set up outside the entrance on Alforde Street half an hour before the Market gets underway. Ralph reckons that by midday we should have earned a few quid each and, if fate is kind, a visiting A&R man from Island Records will have snapped us up along with a batch of second-hand singles, a new mop and bucket and a couple of best sellers from Marsh's Book Stall. We've added 'Roll Over Beethoven' and 'Eve Of Destruction' from the autumn fair playlist to split up our own songs but we can ditch them if it looks like the level of interest in our numbers is rising.

I'm feeling pretty optimistic about it all until I see a milk float speeding silently round the side of the town hall. It's Dave Shuttleworth en route to the market to deliver milk. We've not seen him since the St Mary's gig and I've no idea what his reaction to us is going to be.

As the float slows to a halt I notice a girl next to him. At first, I think it must be just someone helping him out with the deliveries, or someone he's giving a lift home to after an all-nighter down by the Mersey, but a second glance confirms that it's Lisa Wilcox looking cool and fresh for the day. She hops out of the cab and runs around to Dave grasping him around the waist and leading him across to us.

They listen as we play through 'Dead Man's Ghost'. As the last bars fade, I decide to get in the first word and pre-empt

Dave's inevitable tirade which would drive shoppers away from us and around to the side entrance.

'Hi Dave, Lisa. How's it going?' I decide to hit the deep end. 'Look we're sorry about the gig and leaving you to drum for hours.' I look at Ralph. 'Not that we meant it, we just got wrapped up in ourselves in The Chapel House and sort of lost track of time.'

Ralph backs away twiddling the machine heads on his guitar but Al takes up my attempt at reconciliation.

'Yeh, Man. You know what it's like. You have one pint and it turns into two or three and the next thing five minutes has turned into fifty. Still, all things have a great ending, eh. Nice to see you and Lisa are together. You make a cool couple. Opposites attract and all that.'

'Yeh, thanks, Man. And, no problem, we're not opposites anymore. Lisa's sort of shown me the light. Hope you guys do really well with the new band. Great song! Really cool number! Total forgiveness and all that!'

'Oh, for fuck's sake,' laughs Ralph. 'She's not turned you to friggin' God?'

'Rot in Hell, Ralph!' It's one of those out of character moments you get with girls sometimes but Lisa's venom surprises me. 'Blasphemy is a mortal sin. Didn't you learn anything in RE?'

Ralph stares at Dave. 'Yeh, Satan himself masquerades as an angel of light. The same colour as friggin' milk. *Corinthians 2*! Have you never read it?'

'Oh just...!'

'Cool it, Lisa,' says Dave. 'Forgiveness! We should show tolerance to non-believers.'

Ralph is unfazed. 'So you're giving it all up, Dave? Quite a change from being a beer-swilling, girl-snatching, sex-crazed, rock drummer.'

'Yeh, well, Man, Lisa's made me think a lot since the concert. Better things in life than fame, success, wealth and milk! Been a big gap in my life. Tired of searchin' all the time,

205

wondering about what I'm lookin' for. Jesus has the answers. After the concert, I was in a dark place. Now I see the light. Give him a try.'

'So you're givin' up milk as well as the debauched lifestyle,' says Ralph. 'Must be friggin serious.'

'Milk has carried me to sin,' says, Dave. 'The milk float has been the Devil's ride. I'm jacking it in at Christmas. End of a lonely journey. Play us another song, we'd like to be with you.'

Ralph is about to pack up and go, but there are other people gathering, so I give Al the nod and we break into 'Shadowlands'. Ralph is a couple of beats behind but after spluttering a few expletives under his breath he catches us up.

Lisa and Dave last about half the song. Dave nods and smiles and is led away into the market. We complete the final two verses but everyone has disappeared and the empty streets offer up no applause.

I'm about to play the opening chords to 'Compass Point' when a forceful arm grabs me around the neck and a hot, sweaty voice growls in my ear.

'Do you do puckin' requests?'

'We do requests,' says Ralph, 'Bog off back home and do some rehearsing for your part in *Hound*.'

'Puckin' do that every night,' says Mugga. 'Twelve puckin' hours which is more than you lot put together. Come on, play us a puckin' song: 'Tossing' and Turning' or 'Catch The Puckin' Wind'. With that he lets rip a venomous fart which rumbles and echoes along Alforde Street, reverberating off the walls of the town hall, and creating a noxious barrier between the road and anyone wanting to seek sanctuary in the market hall.'

'Mugga, you are an animal.' Ralph is the only one of us licensed to criticise his teammate. 'You should be taken to the vets and put down.'

Mugga laughs off Ralph's comments and hitches his trousers up so that they tighten obscenely around his crotch. 'Need a

206

new singer, boys, someone who can look good and pull the birds with a bit of raw sex-appeal?'

He sings a few bars of 'Tossing and Turning' with the predictable pelvic thrusts drawing worried glances from a couple of pensioners who pretend they've not cast eyes on his gyrating pelvis and head quickly into the market hall.

'See you for rehearsal on Sunday, boys. Hey, Phil, don't fancy swapping parts, do ya, so I can snog that sexy bird of yours.' He laughs menacingly and ambles off down towards The Black Cat.

Ralph shouts after him, 'You could stay on her farm, Mugga. You and the pigs would go well together.' Mugga's only reaction is to direct a V-sign to us from under his arm as he trundles off into the distance without looking back.

By 11.30 we've got 13/6d in our hat and performed the set five times. We're cold and bored and the whole thing is becoming a nightmare *This Is Your Life* with everyone you don't want to come into contact with turning up so you're at the point where you'd like to smash the big red book over Eamon Andrews' head. To top it all, as we're just about to pack up, Young Reg and Sheila appear like insipid phantoms out of the early winter haze. They are wrapped together huddling against the cold heading straight for the market without a sideways glance. Sadly, as we're about to creep away, Sheila spots us out of the corner of her eye and pulls Reg to a full stop. She twists round, mouth half open, and, holding her Mum's shopping basket at arm's length, wafts it in our direction as if she's flagging down a runaway train.

'Awwwh, Reg, it's Phil and his friends. Look they're a pop group. Do you do requests?'

'We do requests,' says Ralph, 'Just....!'

'Shut it, Ralph! Sorry, we're just packing up. Been here all morning! We've written a few songs about home, sort of in the style of James Taylor and Neil Young.'

'Oooh, my Mum loves him, doesn't she Reg?'

What really annoys me about Sheila is that every comment she makes has to be confirmed by Reg as if he has one brain that serves for both of them. Still, I'm a bit taken aback here as Sheila's Mum is about mid-40s, secretary of the local Women's Institute, and seemingly has a knowledge of Neil Young.

'Really, so she's got a copy of *Everyone Knows This Is Nowhere*?'

'Don't know about that, but she likes to listen to him on the wireless, doesn't she Reg?' She gives an annoying, junior school giggle. 'What's the recipe today, Jim?' She pauses as if there's been a sudden short circuit in her brain cells. 'Oh, silly me, it's Jimmy, not Neil, isn't it, Reg? Oh, I am a card!'

Reg grabs her by the arm and hurries her away towards the market entrance. Still giggling, she plants an enormous, sloppy kiss on his left cheek as they stumble through the doors.

THIRTY THREE

Rope Ladder To The Moon
Jack Bruce. Songs For A Tailor. Polydor Records.

It's only the second time I've been on the train to Liverpool since the Sink Club concert. I sit clutching my guitar looking out of the window as the train speeds through the outskirts of the city. I remember Freddie's mesmeric performance on stage with Ibex and try to mentally compare our progress since that night. I'm not sure whether we've gone backwards or forwards or whether I'm just being drawn along by Ralph's larger-than-life character into something that is wasting my time.

Ralph is one of those pupils who just passes exams without seemingly breaking sweat over reading and revision or, in his case, drawing. He's probably the best artist in school and Liverpool Art College would no doubt snap him up without caring too much about his academic grades. Al has a similar talent and I know behind his laid-back façade he grafts away in his room into the early hours of the morning leaving himself plenty of social time after five or six hours sleep. I scraped through the Eleven Plus and I've had to work hard to keep up with the pace of the grammar school. Still, I'm on course to get decent grades but there's the potential for plenty of slippage if something else takes over my life.

Then I think of Freddie and he only has one way to go. Filtering back up from the south has come an image of someone with unshakeable self-belief who knows exactly what he wants and, in the most charming manner possible, will circumnavigate anyone standing in the path of his dreams. Substitute our personalities and he'd still be singing blues with Ibex and I'd be Widnes' leading singer-songwriter putting the town on the map and creeping through the inside pages of *NME* heading for the front.

Spatters of rain hit the carriage window and the afternoon seems to be ebbing away. There are lights shining in the houses on the estates and wind is whipping up from the Mersey, rippling across the grass and stripping the last of the autumn leaves from the trees alongside the line. Lime Street Station is cold and cavernous with the echoes of men and machinery bouncing off its arched, glass canopy. We head through the crowds of shoppers and find a spot near the entrance, sheltered from the wind by the curve of the station building.

My only immediate ambition is to make a pound each which would sort out my Christmas present expenses: a packet of Condor tobacco for my Dad, chocolates for my Gran and a bottle of sherry for my Mum. It's a big ask seeing as we'll have to make £2.6s.6d to reach the magic figure and that doesn't include the train fare to and from Widnes. The wind seems to grab my fingers as I struggle with the guitar chords and Al's voice is getting a bit croaky. After playing the set through twice we've got another fifteen shillings which is enough to retire to the buffet for a break, welcome warmth and serious reflection.

'Shall we head in for a coffee?' Al mirrors my thoughts. It's been a long day and I've got a date with Judith to look forward to tonight.

'No, Men! Just give it another hour and then we'll call it a day. We've been getting some good reaction from a few people.'

Ralph is always the optimist. His 'good reaction' is a couple of wolf whistles from three girls we recognised from the third year and a donation of a shilling from an old lady who said she liked our tunes but we should be wrapping up warmer in cold weather. We carry on, the thought of an evening with Judith warming me up, and a promise from Ralph that if we sing the set through three more times we can catch the five o'clock train out of the city.

We start off again with 'Eve of Destruction'. I'm so cold I have to keep my head down to stop my face smarting in the wind. I'm not taking much notice of any people who may be hanging around but, halfway through the song, I raise my head enough to notice the bottom of skin-tight jeans tucked into the top of a pair of smart, white leather boots. Through stinging eyes, I see a thick fur coat topping the faded, blue denims. It's buttoned tight and, as we finish the song, Freddie turns into the wind to get his masses of black hair away from his face before turning back to us applauding and bowing simultaneously. He reaches out and clasps Al's hand shaking it politely and patting him supportively on the shoulder.

'Great to see you guys again. Do you remember me? We met before the Sink Club gig in the Philharmonic. I was with Tupp and the rest of the band.'

It's perhaps a sign of Freddie's modesty that he feels it conceivable that once met it's possible for him to be forgotten. He shines out of the cold, November afternoon looking a bit out of place in the dim, northern sunlight which is quickly disappearing behind St. George's Hall.

'Guys you look freezing. Let's grab a drink. I've got an hour before the London train.'

It's a welcome offer and Al and I need no convincing. We escape the elements and settle into the corner of the station bar. Ralph brings along the hat and the money is spent on three whiskies and a gin and tonic for Freddie.'

Thought you were in London, Man,' says Ralph. 'We've seen Miffer. Didn't work out for him then?'

Freddie rolls his eyes to the ceiling and smiles. 'We wanted different things. I didn't want to continue singing blues and that scene is finished in London unless you want to play the backstreet pubs for the rest of your life. Mike's keen to move on and we've been writing some stuff. We've got a couple of gigs before Christmas so we'll see how it goes.'

'What are you doing up here?' says Ralph.

212

'Just collecting some stuff from Geoff Higgins' place on Penny Lane. Cool place to live, eh? I'm heading back for good now. What about you guys? I didn't hear any blues even if it's the sort of day you'd want to sing them.'

'Great minds, eh!' Ralph slaps Freddie hard on the shoulder. 'We know it's all changing as well. Blues is finished up here too. Doesn't all happen down there in the Smoke. We're just testing the water, getting ready to move on. You've always got to be one step ahead if you're gonna make it in the music business. We're writing our own stuff too. Sort of progressive folk thing. Neil Young! James Taylor! It'll happen big and we'll be there.'

Freddie looks surprised but there's an interest. 'I've heard of them. I've seen the Neil Young album hanging around the flat somewhere. So what are your songs about, then?'

Al and I look at each other. 'They're about home,' chips in Ralph. 'You know, the need to go back to re-engage with your roots and realise what part the place has played in the development of your character and your life.'

'We looked Zanzibar up on the map in Geography,' says Al. 'You must feel the need to go back there sometime.'

'Lots of happy memories!' Freddie's eyes sparkle in the gloom of the station bar. 'Different place to London. Love to go back sometime. Maybe when I'm famous.' He laughs as if to acknowledge the cliché. 'Hey, I used to be in a band at school, just like you guys. They were called The Hectics and were my good friends Bruce, Ferrang, Derrick and Victory. We used to listen to songs on the radio and try to copy them. My favourites were Little Richard, Fats Domino and Cliff Richard. We knew all their songs.' He suddenly gulps down his gin and tonic as if he's had an idea he's in a hurry to carry out. 'Listen, I've got plenty of time before the train goes, why don't we go back out and do a song together. It'll take me back to St Peter's. Do you know any Little Richard?'

213

I exchange glances with Ralph. My ability to contribute to the group is based on prior knowledge of the songs and hours of practice but before I can say anything Ralph chips in.

'Great idea, Freddie. We can do 'Whole Lotta Shakin', can't we, Phil? We can do it in G, C, and D. Same chords as 'Roll Over Beethoven'. Come on, Men, let's get out there and rock.'

'What about me?' says Al.

'You're on drums,' says Freddie and, as we scramble out of the bar, he grabs a metal waste bin emptying its contents onto the station concourse.

'Ok,' says Freddie. 'I'll take the lead and you guys follow. Just play the single chords in the intro, follow my prompts, and we'll let it rock.' He grabs the hat from Ralph and strolls out into the crowds of shoppers heading along Lime Street. He's about five yards away from us, his fur coat shining in the lights from the station, when he hits the first notes. The effect is startling. The swathe of shoppers slows down with a fair number coming to an instant standstill. Freddie flings the hat back which lands in front of Al who is desperately trying to keep time with me and Ralph. Suddenly the whole thing is rocking along and Freddie seems to have captured the crowd who are clapping and tapping their shopping bags in perfect time to his vocals which slice through the damp air.

As Al beats the rubbish bin a loud honking, in perfect time, blares across from some cabs on the taxi rank and two of the cabbies are out dancing with each other twirling, twisting, and nearly choking on their cigarettes. Freddie has cornered a group of grannies and is twirling them round in turn, inviting them to 'shake it' which one of them does almost obscenely as her tights wrinkle and start to descend down her chubby, red legs. Leaving the grannies, he heads over to pretty, middle-aged women and in seconds they are bumping their bottoms together and the crowd is going wild.

He shouts across to us, 'Repeat the chorus till I tell you to stop.' We nod obediently and the pace takes up again with the taxis honking wildly and two policemen, who have been drawn by the commotion, beating the top of their helmets to the crazy rhythm. Within seconds, he's turned the concourse into an outdoor dance hall. Strangers have grabbed each other and, out of the corner of my eye, I see one of the grannies propelled underneath her partner's legs, sliding on the damp pavement giggling like a teenager. I glance across to Al. The hat is bulging with coins and people are throwing in more which hit the pile and bounce and roll around our feet. Suddenly Freddie is in front of us rising like a conductor, nodding at each of us, and orchestrating the finale as we hit the final chord.

The cheering is rapturous. A taxi driver drops a ten shilling note into the hat and shakes us by the hand. There are shouts of 'More! More!' and I can't imagine what's coming next.

'Bloody Hell. My train's in five minutes.' gasps Freddie, looking at his watch. 'Never stop believing in yourselves!' he shouts, as he turns and dashes off into the station.

We turn and look at the sea of faces peering at us waiting for the next move.

'Thank You! Thank You!' says Ralph. 'We'd like to follow on with one of our own songs we've written inspired by Widnes.'

'Bloody woolly-backs!' shouts a voice from the back. There are audible sighs of disappointment and the crowd starts to quickly disperse.

THIRTY FOUR

Bringing On Back the Good Times
Love Affair. Single Release. CBS Records.

Despite having a total of over £5 in the cap, Al is despondent. He's been plunged into self-doubt, drifting away through the mist of the carriage windows into some world beyond the damp, desolate spaces which speed by as we leave the centre of Liverpool. We pass the crumbling terraces, boarded up shops, and corrugated iron workshops of Toxteth and Edge Hill and it's clear he's at a low ebb. He has no girl and no persona at the front of an exciting new prog-folk group. Frontman bravado has slapped him in the face and it's anyone's guess if he'll ever recover.

I can sense what will happen now and it'll be no fun if my best mate drifts back into his pre-Moonshine world, seeking solace in King Crimson, The Moody Blues and Quintessence. In the run up to Christmas, I'll be climbing mountains and he'll be somewhere underground peering up at the world wishing he could hibernate away and awaken in spring for some new personal renaissance.

I nudge Ralph who, as usual, is drifting off to sleep, drawing his attention to the watcher hunched in his seat, forehead in contact with the carriage window dissipating condensation around his head.

'Big Al,' says Ralph. 'Great drumming!'

I jump in before Ralph can do any more damage. 'Look, Man, our band is not about someone like Freddie. That was just a one-off, and we all played a part in it, but we're more laid-back than that and we're not heading down the same highway.'

Al drags his head away from the glass. 'I'm finished guys. I can't compete with that performance.'

'We don't wanna be like that,' says Ralph. 'Girls would be fed up with it after five minutes. We're all the things they want us to be, Man; deep, thoughtful, philosophical, hitting at their hearts and minds not sliding them across a pavement on their arses.'

'Actually,' says Al. 'I do want to be like Freddie but it's just not going to happen. He's an enigma. He's travelled from the other side of the World to be here and he knows where he's going. Everything else in his life comes second. It's not the same for us; we've not even reached the first step in Freddie's life journey. We're still stuck in the school life he left years ago and we've got exams, expectations, and not even the bottle of Tupp and Mike to throw it all in the air for a different kind of life. I've hit reality guys. We're not gonna make it anywhere in the music world. We've got more chance of Tom Stoppard turning up when we do *Hound* and getting us into RADA.'

He returns to the carriage window staring into the night hoping that out of the swirling darkness might come a small thread of undiscovered inspiration to get his ambitions back on track. There's seemingly nothing to say to each other and the silence is only broken by the sound of Ralph counting out the takings and arranging them in three equal piles on the carriage seat.

'£1.15s.6d each, Men! Impressive for just one performance. We're like The Beatles after 'She Loves You' hit the charts. Performing for a pittance one week and serious cash the next.'

'It's Freddie's money, Jean'll have his address,' says Al, but Ralph is not to be moved.

'Bollocks, Man! We invited him into our band. He was a guest. Ok, we'll send him a fee, fifteen shillings, which still leaves us over one and a half quid each and the next prize is even bigger. Look, Al, if we win the competition we're on Radio Merseyside and it could be the big stepping stone to fame. I bet Freddie and Wreckage have never reached out through the airwaves to thousands of listeners. One last go and if we balls it up we'll disband and go back to listening to Joe's stereo. You heard what Freddie said, 'Never stop believing in ourselves'. If we don't believe we can do it no one else will. See you on Monday, Men, and we'll sort out a rehearsal schedule.'

The train pulls into Hunts Cross and Ralph drifts away in the thin, yellow light of the station approach. As the train continues on its short journey to Hough Green, I try to think of something to bring Al back to reality.

'We're probably not gonna win this competition, Man. We'll give it a go for Ralph but then it's time to move on.'

There's almost a pang of guilt as he takes my guitar, drops onto the platform, and makes his way towards the exit, his body hunched in defence against the sharp, November wind. I need a plan to get him back on track, so long as he doesn't turn the key in his bedroom door and hang a 'Do Not Disturb Until Spring' notice up on the outside.

I've arranged to meet Judith at Warrington station. She's been helping on the farm all day so she'll be tired. We'll just go somewhere quiet and romantic to talk and I guess we need to plan Christmas which is pretty exciting. On one level I'll be disappointed if we don't get one last go at taking the first steps to stardom. There are things it would bring which I'd really enjoy, like being invited onto *Desert Island Discs* by Roy Plumley and chatting about songs which connect with your emotions so strongly that they bond into your soul leaving musical markers which are there for the rest of your existence.

For good or bad, a few songs have been sewn into my memory over the last year and maybe there's a Bizarro Roy Plumley out in the galaxy somewhere inviting you to choose songs you wouldn't take to a desert island because the pain is too great as soon as the needle drops. Maybe, as time heals the wounds, the songs can be reclaimed and I could reach a point where I could float a message out in a bottle reading,

'Lost on an island, please bring Marvin and Tammi with you on the rescue ship'.

Luckily, I've been able to transfer 'My Girl' from Lesley to Judith so the good feelings far outweigh the pain which I'm sure is ebbing away even though 'Ain't Nothing Like The Real Thing' and 'You're All I Need' are immovable, glued into July 1969, and destined to stay there as the years speed forward.

There a few others rooted in my head. 'I Remember You' by the genteel Frank Ifield is July 1963 and my first girlfriend, Sue Yarwood, the spindly-legged, red-faced, compulsive hair-tugger who first raised awareness in me that there was an opposite sex. She'll still be planted there when I'm sixty even though in my mind we'll still be thirteen, picking blackberries, roaming the woods and chasing bob-seeds in the countryside north of Hough Green. That was before they slapped a Liverpool overspill housing estate on the land covering the newts, ponds and badger setts under a grey concrete carpet with the sounds of police sirens replacing the calls of blackbirds, warblers and night owls.

The train lurches into Warrington Central and, after the steam clears from the platform, I can see Judith sitting on a bench waving at me from underneath a giant poster of The Western Isles.

We decide to give the night out in Warrington a miss and jump on the next train to Padgate. Judith suggests The Farmers Arms, which is halfway between the station and her house, and the last train back to Hough Green is just after closing. It's a big, old building with gabled roofs and small, cosy rooms. We find one that's empty with a log fire crackling in the grate. The landlord's started to put some Christmas decorations up and I don't want to leave. It's just ten days to the production and we'll both be glad when it's over.

The tickets have almost gone. A lot of them have sold in anticipation of our kiss, but prudently Steve has banned the sale of tickets to pupils outside the sixth form unless accompanied by parents so at least a mature audience shouldn't be too fazed by it. Judith's parents are coming but not mine; I haven't even told them about it. The thought of them seeing me kiss a girl in public is slightly unnerving even though it doesn't seem to bother Judith.

I wonder about life after *Hound* and whether it will change anything. I've never spent a Christmas with a girlfriend so I'm not sure what to suggest. Should I offer to take her to the theatre or go carol singing or take her out to a club? It would have been easy with Lesley. We'd have flitted around the pubs and clubs sinking deeper and deeper into our one-girl, one-guy world fuelled by alcohol and the lyrics from a thousand soul anthems. I look across at Judith, the light from the flames flickering like my thoughts.

'It would be great to do a few special things at Christmas.'

Judith smiles warmly. 'Definitely! Our family has loads of traditions and things, probably because we're farming folk,' she laughs. 'That sounds really old-fashioned, doesn't it, like Padgate is stuck in the Middle Ages and we do lots of weird things that people who don't understand our life might find a bit strange. We can have a night out with Janice and her boyfriend, the girl who was at Young Farmers. You'd get on well with her. We could go to a film and then maybe out for a Chinese meal afterwards.'

'Great, and we can go out into Liverpool with Al and his girlfriend.' This is a bit of a gamble but I have the bones of an idea hatching inside which will almost certainly get Al back on track and save his Christmas.

'Yes, I like Al,' she says. 'Is he going out with anyone I know?'

'Possibly! She's in the sixth form. He's only just asked her. He did tell me her name, but I've forgotten it.'

'That's good,' says Judith. 'Means we can both get to know her when we go out. It's better than being the outsider having to fit in with people who know each other really well. You get all those in-jokes and references to things which you don't understand.'

'Yeh, you'll have to fill me in on Janice and her guy.'

'I'll wait on that one. She changes her boyfriend every week. I never know where she's up to. Anyway, I was thinking maybe you'd like to come over to ours on Boxing Day. We have a sort of family tradition. We have some lunch and then walk over to my Uncle Harry's pub, The Packhorse, in Culcheth. It's about eight miles there and back but it's the sort of thing you need after slouching around for a couple of days. It's the oldest pub in the village. A bit like The Pure Drop, I suppose, all oak beams and secret passages. But I guess your family has its own traditions. They're hard to get out of.'

My family doesn't have any traditions and I usually spend Boxing Day watching TV, counting my present money, and brushing away the boredom until normal service is resumed. I have a big problem here, though. I've promised Al and Joe I'll go to watch United with them. They're at home to Wolves and going to football with your mates is the nearest I get to any sort of regular commitment.

'Brilliant !' I just can't turn Judith's offer down it would send out all the wrong messages. This is a girl who's saying she wants us to be still going out in six weeks' time. I've never been here before and it's sort of exciting and scary at the same time.

Suddenly, the whole run-in to Christmas is turning into a social wonderland. There's the production, Tuesday nights at Young Farmers, and a visit to the Odeon in Warrington. There's her grandad's birthday party on December 1st and our Christmas shopping trip to Manchester. Suddenly, I'm in a world which didn't exist before and if Steve Rothwell hadn't got the job at school, and Ralph hadn't driven us to the drama group, and Tom Stoppard had decided to be a bricklayer instead of a playwright, none of this would have happened. The Wheel of Fortune has spun and left me the right way up and I just want to say a big thank you but I don't know who to.

She's also really supportive of the group and wants tickets for the Clippies and Conductors Night because we sound folky and that's her kind of music. As I head back on the train, there's that Hardyish sense of time beating to a common pulse. Suddenly, all the things that I've been at odds with in my life seem unimportant, swept away into dark corners by fresh new beginnings.

'

THIRTY FIVE

Chasing Shadows
Deep Purple. Deep Purple 111. Harvest Records.

My Mum has always been into music. Her house is full of LPs
and she has a state of the art Marconi stereogram with a soft
close mechanism on the lid to stop the needle jumping. It has
a radio inside with three tuning bands but she only ever has it
on the Light Programme to listen to programmes which fit into
the social class to which she now believes she belongs.

In front of the radio is a compartment for LPs. We had
regular family gatherings before she left home and a lot of the
songs in her collection still float around in my head, pin down
the happy times of childhood, and have a decent chance of
making it onto my desert island. I pull out a few and read the
track lists on the back covers. The memories of spinning Babs
round to Elvis's 'Rock A Hula Baby', competing with Geoff to
be the first to remember the words to Lonnie Donegan's 'My
Old Man's A Dustman', and learning to play along to songs
by Bobby Darin and The Everlys, take me back to the lazy,
hazy days of Nat King Cole's summer when you could rhyme
'weenies' with 'bikinis' and wonder if one day you'd ever get
to eat a pretzel.

I pick out *Doris Day's Greatest Hits*, the girl all mums would
like you to bring home to tea, eventually marry and live
happily ever after; the American Dream entering Widnes via
Burtonwood airbase. Life would be that idyllic summer.
Everyone would smile through pearl-white teeth and the
smoke from endless barbeques would chase away the dark
clouds of pollution from McKechnie's and the Everite.

Track 1 is permanently engrained in my memory. 'Whatever
Will Be Will Be' by Doris Day was sung endlessly to me by
my grandmother. Al's in a que sera sera phase at the moment.
There's the issue of him not having a girlfriend, and he's

inevitably seeking solace from the philosophical lyrics of his record collection. 'Everything passes! Everything changes!' is his quote of the moment. He's dug it out from a Bob Dylan track somewhere but the phrase seems blindingly obvious to me. I mean some things never seem to pass and change like Geoff and Jackie's love and the poor state of the beer at the Hammer and Pincers, but, generally, everything changes to some extent, sometimes quite quickly, like my feelings for Lesley, which have totally gone.

After all the anticipation and excitement of the weekend, Sunday always lets you down. The shops are shut, and the pubs don't open until seven o'clock, so I usually walk round to my Mum's as there's nothing else to do really. We have a coffee and I tell her my news from the week. She asks me if I'm ok and seeks my assurance that the red eczema marks on my arms are not caused by injecting a cocktail of drugs. I play with Rolf, their evil Jack Russell terrier, gauge whether I've stayed enough time to make it count as a social visit, and then head off, always with some money that Mum's slipped into my hand when her husband wasn't looking.

Sunday's deflated, depressing atmosphere doesn't inspire me to think that today is the day for Al's new beginnings. There's also the barrier of his soft arrogance to get through which makes him believe that, even if he does nothing, things will just happen and sooner or later his next girlfriend will just be dropped onto his doorstep by the Gods.

Predictably, in the aftermath of Freddie's mind opening performance, he's immersed himself in his character for the play, boringly over-analysing Stoppard, and cherishing the Theatre of the Absurd as evidence that life is full of hopeless situations, trivial dialogues, and proof of the meaninglessness of human existence with no happy endings.

After tea we head off through the Sunday night silence of the estate. I've a plan to get him a girl but it's too important to be discussed around at his house or in the Tavern where there'll be too many distractions, so we're making for The

Prince Of Wales down on Gossage Street which, on a Sunday evening, should be empty.

The Prince is actually a second-hand vintage control desk from a spaceship which has passed through the hands of intergalactic junk merchants and been finally offloaded to Greenhalls Brewery who are happy that it's built-in chameleon mode has allowed it to take on the outward appearance of a seedy, town centre pub.

At weekends, entering this piece of space debris takes you into a world of flashing lights where your brainwaves are sucked mercilessly into a stroboscopic netherworld while your eardrums attempt to fend off the throbbing sound from the central control unit; a large metal carcass cunningly disguising itself as a Wurlitzer Hi-Fi Jukebox.

We don't talk much on the way. I can sense Al's mood because he doesn't ask me questions about Judith, the future of the band, or Christmas, but I'm confident that by the end of the week, normal service will be restored and he'll be looking forward to extracting himself from the depths of side two of *On The Threshold Of A Dream*.

Luckily the back room at the Prince has been subject to a short-circuit in space technology, and it remains detached from the future, sitting comfortably in the past with nicotine-stained walls, tired tables and assorted ashtrays waiting to be relieved of the dog ends of unfiltered cigarettes. Al slings his feet onto a wooden stool and whips out his copy of the play, turning swiftly to the back and pondering over the final lines.

'So, I'm Inspector Hound, you're Simon Gascoigne, and at the end of the play we end up in the audience in place of the theatre critics watching the action. We've stepped out of reality and are sitting back watching our world from a distance. Have you ever felt like that in real life?'

'How can it be real life?'

'You know what I mean, just a feeling that you've detached yourself from your life and are looking at it from the outside.'

'Yeh, probably! Well, I sort of looked at myself after Lesley and I didn't really like what I saw. But that was after, not at the same time. Guess we need to swap places. I mean I'm looking at you now and I'm not seeing what you see.'

Al goes slightly on the defensive. 'So what are you seeing?'

'Well, you get introspective sometimes and shut everything out. You're heading up to Christmas and it'll be all bright lights and couples and you'll be just stuck in the corner like a decorative gnome. Look, I've got a sort of plan. I know you can't be bothered going out and trying to find someone but I've a sort of idea of how the girl could come to you.'

'Really?'

'Next Friday is the first dance rehearsal for the school social. The first dance is always the progressive barn dance. The girl who you end up with at the end of the dance is your partner for the rest of the session. It's a sort of dare. Put yourself in the hands of the Gods: chance, fate, destiny, whatever you want to call it. You end up with a girl for the afternoon and you have a couple of hours to chat her up. Christmas sorted!'

'What if she's already got a boyfriend? And worse still, what if she's not very attractive?'

'No, Man, Anne and her mates will try and arrange it so you have a reasonable chance. We can have a quick scan around the line and push into what looks like the best position. I'll be next to you so if I get someone better we can do a quick swap at the end. Two chances! What do you say?'

Al's mood lightens and there's a definite interest in offering his immediate future into the unpredictable hands of fate and chance.

'Ok, but if I end up with anyone already in a relationship, then forget it, and I don't want Lisa Wilcox after being handled by Dave Shuttleworth.'

'Yeh, well, half the girls in the sixth form have been handled by him so you might not have much choice.'

'Well as long as I don't know about it.'

227

There's a flicker of the old Al in there somewhere and, once he's got a girl, we can head full belt, with confidence, to the Clippies and Conductors Night. I decide it's a good moment to tell him about Boxing Day, and the invitation to Judith's, but just as I've summoned up the mental courage, Joe and Alison appear in the doorway and the moment's lost.

'Didn't expect you two in here. Tavern shut is it?' says Joe.

'No, just fancied a change of scene. Trying to liven up Sundays.' This seems a bit flat as we're the only four in the pub but Alison has a bit of news from London, relayed via Jean, and seeing as Freddie has just entered and disappeared from our lives in a flash, we're both interested.

'Mike's definitely continuing with his Art course up here,' explains Alison, 'so it looks like the end for Wreckage. Tupp's reason to go for a job at HMV is to keep him in touch with the music industry but he's made a definite decision not to come back even if Wreckage splits, which looks likely. They've got a couple of gigs left before Christmas but then it's probably over. Anyway, you should step into their shoes. Heard he played with you yesterday.'

'Think we played with him,' says Al. 'No secret then, eh. How did you find out?'

'More people in the audience than you think,' says Alison. 'You were probably too immersed in it all. Carol was shopping with her mum. She said you were with some outrageous guy conducting the onlookers. Had to be Freddie. Where did you go afterwards?'

'Oh, he headed back to London after picking up stuff from Geoff Higgins. I went to Padgate to see Judith, which reminds me, seeing as you're both here, I won't be at the United game on Boxing Day. I'm going over to a family do at her place.'

A silence descends on the room. It's as if I've just severed an invisible chord that binds me to Al and Joe.

'You can't be serious,' says Joe. 'We go to see United over Christmas. That's what we always do. How can Best, Law and

228

Charlton come second to a girl? Sold out! What do you think, Morefield?'

Al just shakes his head from side to side.

'Wait until the boys hear about this,' continues Joe. 'You've only known her five minutes and suddenly your mates are kicked down the social ladder. She'll respect you more if you tell her you can't come because you'll be at the match. It'll give her the right message. Show her where she is in the pecking order of things.'

I shrug my shoulders. It's a pretty defining moment and threatens our football fellowship but over the last few weeks my attitude to life has definitely changed and being with Judith has been enough.

'Sorry, guys, I'm not going. United are going to be one voice short in the Stretford End, but you can do me a favour, Joe. Sing along with the crowd for me like you never do.'

'I think you're doing the right thing,' says Alison. 'You both obviously like each other a lot. You can go to United anytime.'

Joe's not impressed and becomes embroiled in a discussion with Alison. I don't take much interest, except to notice he's coming a pretty poor second as the argument develops. Al and I finish our pints and head out into the November night. There's a definite feeling that summer has gone and the cold of winter is starting to freeze the memories of the days with Lesley. I think about the Blackmore Vale and the lush green summer days, winding lanes, close-knit villages and the freshness of everything. A feeling of resentment creeps in with the realisation my time with Judith is inevitably going to be played out through a drab, grey winter relieved only by the short burst of colour created around Christmas.

At this moment, I hate myself for spending the summer of '69 on a girl with whom I was never destined to have anything more than a superficial relationship. I'd seen Judith before the summer but didn't have the confidence to make a move for her. Now we could be six months into our relationship and we'd have a golden summer of memories fizzing about inside

229

our heads having walked and talked for hours in the lanes around Padgate and Fearnhead. For a brief second, I cross the line between love and hate for Lesley and have a feeling of time slipping away and the need to grab the present. I think of Geoff and Jackie who are living proof that lasting relationships can be forged in your teens.

'Wake up,' says Al. 'We're halfway home and you've not said a word. You're right to see Judith. We can go to the match anytime.'

'Don't you think it's strange I've not seen Lesley since summer? I mean you'd have thought I'd have bumped into her somewhere. It's not as if school's a massive place.'

'Fate, Man,' says Al. 'Keeping you apart while your thing with Judith gets going. Anyway, you're over her. You wouldn't want to see her again, would you? You've moved on and she's a soul girl. She'd never move into the world of James Taylor and Neil Young. Once a bopper, always a bopper. She'll be bopping until she's ninety whereas you will be the cool, ageing rock star sitting on a porch strumming your guitar and telling tales of world tours and hotel-wrecking sessions. She'll have been living out her boring life in Warrington listening to the same songs over and over again. Anyway, sounds like a cool idea for Friday.'

I walk home and decide to check with my inner feelings that Lesley has been consigned to the past and anything connected to her will extract no emotion from any memories which might occasionally jump into my head. I pull the box of singles down from the top of the wardrobe, flicking through the barrier of rock and blues labels and eventually reaching the brown, starry Motown cover which is dusty and creased at the back of the pile.

The room is uncannily silent. My Dad and Gran have been asleep for a couple of hours and there's just the hum of white noise which is left when everything else has settled down into the night. I turn the volume down and slip 'Ain't Nothing Like The Real Thing' onto the turntable. The intro chugs away until Marvin breaks the instrumental with his serenade to Tammi. The record plays through and the needle clicks, returning the silence. I open the curtains. Outside it's pitch black except for the harvest glow of the moon splashing a yellow haze across the western sky. It'll be shining across Widnes, Long Barn and the hushed sleepy hollows of the Blackmoor Vale. I take the record from the turntable, slip it back into its sleeve, and drop it into the waste bin.

THIRTY SIX

Yester-Me, Yester-You, Yesterday
Stevie Wonder. Single Release. Tamla Motown.

School has that end of term feeling and you can tell that things are winding down. Teachers are beginning to see the light at the end of a long term and the pace of the work has slackened as staff apply the brakes to the hard pursuit of academic excellence which has dominated the autumn term. For two weeks lessons are suspended for the Upper Sixth, to provide us with study time for the A-Level mocks.

There's a buzz about the school social which was born out of desire in the Fifties to allow some sort of proper and controlled interaction between the male and female pupils who were otherwise discouraged from any sort of social contact for the other eleven months of the year. The event will take place at The Queens Hall and is strictly organised along the lines of a traditional tea dance. There's a buffet, followed by two sessions of ballroom dancing separated by an interval of fifteen minutes when we are allowed four or five records from the current top twenty. Live music is provided by The Al Rath Band who are brought out and dusted down once a year for this particular occasion.

Leading up to the event, Friday afternoons are given over to ballroom dancing practice. The sessions are led by Frank Murphy and Iris Bunn, two teachers who are well into their fifties and who demonstrate with gusto how to master a progressive barn dance, the French Tango, and the Gay Gordons with an energy that is conspicuously lacking in their teaching. Over the period of the rehearsals, every pupil will be given a dance card to complete for the evening. No one can have the same partner twice, and the cards will be inspected before the event by form tutors whose duty it is to keep a strict eye on the proceedings throughout the evening.

The last waltz is the dance which really matters because, by the end of the evening, the atmosphere has usually got a bit heady and, after the band plays 'God Save the Queen', you are in possession of your partner for a trip to the chip shop and a romantic walk home.

It's the dance filled in first by most pupils. In the past, Frank's instructions in the first session to, 'Take your partners!', had been met by a cavalry charge across the floor where boys attempted to grab the girl of their dreams and scribble in their names on their dance card before the besieged females had time to protest. After complaints from the girls' school council, Frank and Iris now concentrate the first rehearsal on the progressive barn dance which gives the girls breathing space and the chance to spot and evade any undesirables.

Frank arrives first and ushers us into the gym.

'Right, fellows!' Frank has a lilting Irish accent which creates a relaxed and comfortable atmosphere evoking images of slippers, pipe and Val Doonican's rocking chair. 'The ladies will be with us presently and we will start with a progressive barn dance.' He moves over to the heavy, wooden record player and takes out a copy of *Jimmy Shand Plays Old Time*, wipes it with his white handkerchief and places it carefully on the turntable. 'Fellows, while we await the arrival of the ladies, would you please form yourselves into a circle so that we are ready.'

We line up in a ring around the inside walls of the gym, probably about a hundred and fifty of us in all. I try to work out Al's chances of ending up with someone. On pure physical attraction I reckon about ten to one but then she has to fall at his feet in the sequence of a dozen or so changes and I lose the ability to finalise the calculation.

Anyway, we plan it as best we can. The girls are brought in by Iris. They show less embarrassment, are confident and more self-assured. I notice Anne on the far side shuffling what looks like a group of girls into a cluster within the inner line. I start to worry about timing and turf Widge and his mate out of the circle to take us closer to them. The strategy is in place and all we need now is the luck of the Gods. The faces of Anne's group aren't immediately recognisable as the glare of the low sun streaming through the gym windows casts a monochromatic haze over the far side of the room.

Iris builds up the atmosphere.

'Ladies and gentlemen, in a moment I will refresh your memories as to the finer points of the progressive barn dance. At the end of this dance, you will be with a partner. You will keep this partner for the rest of the rehearsal. Thank you.' She delivers a few crisp pointers, takes a few questions from the girls, and we are off.

The girls on the inner circle start to move around. I start with Alice Wilson, the Head Girl. She is totally unsullied; a shining example of everything your mum would want you to bring home for Sunday tea and she has personality; bagfuls of it. She is bright, bubbly, intelligent and self-confident but not in the running. She frightens me to death and she would strip Al's persona to the bone before he had time to say, 'I think, therefore I am.'

And so they pass on, Jean England, too tall, Annette Miller and Judy Davidson both spoken for. Each one handed on with a resigned shake of the head until the music passes its midpoint and the dance is coming to an end. In resignation, I glance at Al and then back down the line of girls. I reckon we have three or four changes left, Sue Strong, Alison Fisher, Claire Hewitt and, in the whirl of dancing, I have to blink and check that it's true. Four changes down the line is Lesley and suddenly I don't know whether I'm praying for the music to stop or continue in the hope that we'll be together for the rest of the rehearsal.

As the music reaches its climax she arrives, dropped into my arms like some treasure returned after a fear that it had been lost forever. I have about twenty seconds to say something appropriate, something that might bring us back closer even if the final gap is unbridgeable. The last time I'd held her was at

234

the bus station in Warrington after she'd finished with me and I'd begged her to let me walk her home. I'd held her with unreturned tightness, not wanting to let go as she tearfully got onto the bus. Now she is back and there is no resistance in her arms.

'You, ok?' We say it together and laugh and half the time has gone. I pray for the music to stop. The last bars are playing and I hold on tight. I glance at Al, who is with Claire Hewitt, and I swear the nod is there and that he is almost pushing Claire away before the tune gives out.

The song continues and Lesley has gone to Al who avoids my gaze. The music stops and they are together for the rest of the session. I stand watching them, holding an unknown girl in my arms. They are smiling at each other and Al has a look I've not seen for months. They are chatting and laughing and deliberately not looking back at me. I turn back to my partner for the afternoon. It's Brenda Clegg, Tommy's girlfriend. She stares into my eyes.

'Who are you fuckin' looking at?'

THIRTY SEVEN

Get Ready
The Temptations. Single Release. Tamla Motown.

What is worse? Your best friend going out with your recent ex, or refusing to go with your mates to Old Trafford and ditching them for the girl of your life? I don't actually know what happened after the dance rehearsal except that I caught a glimpse of Al and Lesley scribbling on their dance cards before I headed off home to do some English revision.

I've had a couple of days to think about it all but tomorrow's the dress rehearsal for *Hound* and I've been too immersed in A-level stuff, and the trials and tribulations of fictional characters from the nineteenth century, to think deeply about anything in real life.

My Gran has rescued 'Ain't Nothing Like The Real Thing' from the metal bin in the garden. The sleeve's covered in blood-red tomato stains as if Marvin and Tammi have been stabbed through the heart. It's back on my bed like one of those nagging thoughts which drifts in and out of bad dreams. I pick it up and drop it out of my window onto the concrete porch where the rain batters down soaking the vinyl and washing away the memories.

I haven't seen Al since the dance rehearsal; he's been away on an Economics trip to London, which arrives back this evening. The cast is meeting up at the Tavern for a drink and a pep talk and some last-minute pointers from Steve. I've heard, via Anne, that he's asked Lesley out, which I suppose I can't really argue with. I mean it was my plan and she's probably the sort of girl you'd want on your arm when you've had an empty space in your life for a while. And, as I need to keep reminding myself, I'm over her, so I have no reason to have any feelings about who she's moved on to.

It's early evening and I jump off the train. I see Al leaving the coach and heading up towards the pub. I pick up my pace, catching him just past the cemetery.

'So how's it going with Lesley?' I try to sound nonchalant but what I really mean is, how can you be such a hypocritical bastard when you spent most of the summer criticising me for going out with a bopper and ditching my friends, but our friendship's too important for such recriminations, so I leave it at that.

'Cool,' says Al. 'I wouldn't have asked her out if you hadn't got over her. Got a date next week if that's ok.'

'No problem with me, Man. Pity the Sink's a rock venue now. Where are you going? Babalu, soul deck?'

Al looks at me as though I'm talking about a different world.

'No, Man! Pictures! *Easy Rider* at the Plaza.'

'Right! Hendrix, Steppenwolf, The Byrds. A spiritual, drug-fuelled journey about wandering hippies. You really know how to read a girl.' I am laughing so much inside. She'll be out of that cinema, and out of his arms, faster than Peter Fonda's motorbike.

'She's up for it,' says Al. 'New experiences, new highways! We all need those. If it all goes ok it'll be smart. We can head out in a foursome; get to a couple of films and concerts. What do you think?'

'Maybe,' I say. 'Judith's got some family stuff planned and I might be over in Padgate quite a lot.'

What I really want to say is, 'Yeh, we'll go out as a foursome every bloody night of the Christmas holidays so Lesley can see how blissfully happy I am,' but it won't come out.

Al sighs at my disinterest. 'Look, I think we should talk about it but let's leave it until after the production. There's too much in our heads at the moment.'

We're the first in the pub. Bernice has died her hair orange and has the look of the Fifty Foot Woman, elevated behind the bar glaring down at us with her one eye.

'Two pints of Guinness, Bernice. Nice hair !' says Al.

Bernice doesn't take the sarcasm. She hits the buttons on the pump and reaches down below the bar.

'Don't want any crisps, Bernice, I've just had tea.'

'Not getting you bloody crisps. I've got this for you.'

She pulls out a warped vinyl from under the bar. Remnants of the brown label are clinging to the wet grooves and a tomato stain is still visible on the label.

'Found this in our garden this afternoon. Looks like it was washed off your porch. Assume it belongs to you. Didn't have you down as a soul-type. Maybe it's your Gran's?'

'Do I look like a bloody soul-type, Bernice? Shove it in the bin will you?'

'Can't do that,' says Bernice. 'House rules! Only waste from the pub can go in our bins.'

I grab the single from her and head out of the door where I hurl it like a black discus out into the night. It's caught in the wind, lands on Upton Lane, and is splintered into a hundred pieces by a passing car. I stand there staring at it wondering how something I once loved could become such a focus of despair.

Suddenly a hand slips underneath my arm and pulls me around. Judith wraps me inside her coat and kisses me gently. 'Just practising for tomorrow night,' she smiles. 'Just six more of those and Simon and Cynthia won't be part of our lives anymore. It'll just be us.' We stand hugging each other in the doorway. Anne smiles and winks at me as she squeezes past and, just for a moment, I have a feeling that this is something more than I ever thought it could be and that Herbie's relentless ramblings about fatalism being a negative force in people's lives might just be wrong.

I never expected that I'd ever be drinking in a pub with a teacher but the Doc's 'new breed' obviously doesn't give it a second thought. Steve fits into our circle like he's one of us and we laugh and talk about the same things. I wonder if the

WAB knows about this and then decide he's not the sort of person who would care so long as Steve was doing the best for the school and playing the game right. There's something I need to check with Steve, though. I'm still worried about the kiss and whether the WAB and Thackara actually know it's going to happen up there on stage with an audience of governors, parents and a Widnes Weekly News reporter out beyond the footlights.

'It's all down to the Magic If,' says Steve. 'Stanislavski believed that performance should be believable for an audience, so everything on the stage has to be as real as possible. He asked his actors to pose questions to their character. So, what if the cleaner, Mrs Drudge encountered a stranger in the house while she was cleaning one day? The actor answers the question and incorporates the answer into their acting which becomes believable for the audience. So, if Lady Cynthia encounters Simon, the past lover she adores, alone in the drawing room, she'd want to kiss him, wouldn't she? It's got to be real on stage otherwise the audience's belief is not as strong.'

'But do the WAB and Thackara know it's going to happen? I mean it'll be the first public, live kiss in the history of the school.'

'Well,' says Steve, 'I've talked to him about Stanislavski and Stoppard and the trend in theatrical movements. He's pretty knowledgeable about it all, and they've both got a copy of the script and the cast list, so I assume all's ok.'

'Assume' is not one of my favourite words at the moment. I mean I assumed Al would not pursue a relationship with Lesley and I assumed Lesley and I were destined to go out for ages. I assumed Matt Busby would have bought loads of new players after winning the European Cup but I've been wrong on all three. In fact, most of the assumptions I've made in life have turned upside down, so the nagging worry still rumbles around but, as Steve's the director, I assume he'll be the one to take any flack.

The cast is pretty excited and we all sit around drinking and conversing in character with the rest of the pub giving us strange, pitying looks. Jean has brought a camera and we pose in twosomes and threesomes. I feel suddenly glad that these moments are being captured in time. For the first time in months I feel really happy and thirsty for life and the dry empty feelings from the late summer days have gone.

Steve's got the last few tickets and I notice Al buying one. It's no guess who it's for and in a way I'm glad. The audience will see a fictional couple in a staged embrace in a time and place far removed from the echoes of the cold school hall. Lesley, though, will see the reality of me and Judith embracing way beyond the realism demanded by Stanislavski, and I wonder how she'll feel as she peers out of the darkness mentally crossing the fourth wall.

We're almost there. The dress rehearsal has passed without a hitch and the stage crew are complimentary about what they've seen. Steve is running on adrenalin. It's his first school production and a lot of the staff members have bought tickets. Herbie has surprisingly offered to run front-of-house and the Doc is coming to sit alone in the balcony at the back of the hall, following the action with a braille copy of the play specially ordered for his collection.

Steve has drilled the usual things into us after the rehearsal: move into the lights, project your voices to the back wall, be on cue and the strategies for forgotten lines. There's no prompt, Steve has demanded that we learn the complete scenes that we're in so we can help each other out on stage or just improvise. Mugga has asked if he can take one of his Gran's sleeping pills before the performance to add to the realism demanded by Stanislavski. Permission has been refused, but only on the grounds that we'd have to pick him up and carry him to the front of the stage for the curtain call.

'Wouldn't that be more realistic?' says Al. 'I mean if we just dragged him across the stage at the curtain call and flopped him in front of the audience and rolled him off the edge then they would actually believe he was dead.'

Steve is not for agreeing. In fact, he's against a curtain call but he's been overruled by The WAB who wants the audience to show its appreciation for a jolly good show.

Before we leave we get everything together. The stage is arranged for the opening night, props are checked and left where we can locate them, and the costumes are hung neatly backstage where they are overseen by Miss Thring, the needlework teacher from the girls' school. The lights and sound are checked and the programmes stacked neatly in the dressing room cupboard. There are chairs backstage with our names on and a few good luck cards pinned to the back of the scenery. Steve has arranged for the hall to be locked for the next two days, creating a time capsule ready for us to step into at 7.30 on Friday.

We sit on the front row of numbered canvas chairs. Judith and I are in the ones marked 'Reserved for Headteacher and Headmistress' and I suddenly realise how close the front row is to the taped 'X' on stage where Judith and I will stand to kiss. Almost touching distance: a small void for Thackara to leap into and shout, 'Stop this indecency, immediately!' However, it's too late now and everything around us is closing down. The props, costumes and make-up crew sit behind us and Steve thanks us all for the hours of hard work we've put in. The cast seems really small; just the eight of us carrying Steve's reputation on our shoulders. Well, nine really, but Mugga is still asleep on stage and it would be a welcome relief for everyone if the key was turned in the hall door sealing him away from the rest of the school until Friday.

To relieve the tension we've got a meeting round at Anne's to go through the songs for The Clippies and Conductors Evening.

241

I've asked Babs to come along to give her opinion, and Anne's asked her Mum, adding some empathy with the older clippies and conductors. We've also reluctantly asked Joe because he knows a lot about music and also, if we sound shit, he'll tell us and we'll pack up and go home.

For the interval, we've decided to do our three original songs plus 'Whole Lotta Shakin' because Al reckons he's got to see if he can give it a go before he packs in singing for good. 'Compass Point' has got to hit hard and show Widnes in a strong light and I'm getting quite into the Neil Young album and his double-tracked harmonies and melodic acoustic fingerpicking which drift you dreamily through a series of images of complex relationships and lost love. However, I'm not sure about our chances of blowing the clippies and conductors away. I think of Freddie and how he decides on the audience reaction he wants before he sets foot on stage. He sparks into action, drawing the attention of the crowd, controlling their behaviour and emotions with an invisible force, locking them into an unbreakable bond which only shatters once they escape, exhausted, into the night air.

Anne's Mum is supportive, although she drifts in and out while we're playing, supplying us with coffee and cakes. Even Joe nods away and, when we've finished, gives two lethargic claps, which I take as a positive endorsement that maybe we have something appealing to his musical taste which always has to be half a step ahead of Radio 1 mainstream.

'There won't be much competition,' says Ralph confidently. 'It'll be girls singing like Sandy Shaw or Cilla Black and a few crooning or country efforts from the conductors because that's the sort of thing you get down at their social club on a Saturday night.'

'You've never been to their social club,' says Al.

'No, but I've been on George Wakefield's run on a Monday morning and you get a whole friggin' playlist sung to you from Hunts Cross to Widnes. I know every bleedin' word to Matt Monroe's catalogue, including the lyrics he makes up himself.

If he sings 'From Runcorn With Love' once more I'll plant him. He even sings 'My Kind Of Girl' to the women pensioners and autographs the back of their bus tickets.'

'How's it going to be judged?' says Babs. 'If I'm reading it right, George must be the odds-on favourite.'

'No friggin' idea,' says Ralph, 'but if he turns up we'll have to find some way of nobbling him unless I can push him off the friggin' bus the week before.'

THIRTY EIGHT

She's Like A Rainbow
Rolling Stones. Through The Past Darkly. Decca Records.

The pressure of preparing for the production is helping to disconnect my mind from a maze of befuddled feelings relating to my best friend developing an unlikely attraction for my first love. I need to clear the air with Al and maybe offer sympathy for the immediate future. This will possibly involve him, cutting his hair, ditching his prog-rock collection, leaving the band and buying a suit from Calverts in readiness to join similarly diminutive people at the soul venues which are thankfully no longer part of my life.

There's a certain anger as well. I'm getting on with my life and have buried a painful chapter from the past but, following the dance rehearsal, there have been unwelcome flashbacks I have to come to terms with finally severing the ties but I'm not sure how it will happen.

I've decided to broach the subject with Al on Saturday after the second performance of the play. He's bought Lesley a ticket for this evening's performance and, true to form, he's persuaded Steve to let her have one of the VIP seats on the front row, rubbing shoulders with the WAB and Thackara. She'll be a stone's throw from where Judith and I will be standing over the taped 'X' which, according to Herbie's *Brewer's Dictionary of Phrase and Fable*, is the ancient symbol of disloyalty and betrayal.

Still, I have the consolation that I have the girlfriend that most of the sixth form want. I'm backstage looking at her. She is dressed in Thirties costume with a long cardigan and drop-waisted dress clinging to her figure. Her blonde hair is tied back into a ponytail and her make-up gives her a pale innocent look. She is a girl who would look beautiful in any age and a sudden resentment builds against Al and Lesley.

They're spoiling it all. I want to rid them from our lives altogether and head off to a place where memories can't touch us, but a glance through the heavy serge curtains reveals Lesley sitting on the front row a few feet from where Simon and Cynthia will complete their embrace.

I think about grabbing Judith and running out of the hall, down the front drive and onto a passing bus full of grey Widnesians. They'll turn and marvel at us in our colourful Thirties costumes, as we speed across the bridge leaving Wade Deacon, Lesley and life as I know it behind. We'll get off at the bus depot in Runcorn and stand hugging each other in the rain without coats or cares, the swirling waters of the Mersey creating an impenetrable barrier to any worries and doubts which are in hot pursuit. But the lights dim and the opening music filters backstage. I glance back through the curtains but my view of Lesley is now obscured by Moon and Birdboot who sit next to the two headteachers. Suddenly they are spot-lit and the play is underway.

I've never kissed anyone in front of adults before and even though it's acting, it's going to be uncomfortable. Still, I suppose it's going to be quite a moment in the history of the two schools. This is probably going to be the public confirmation that the permissive age has finally breached the two fortresses of single-sex education and brought them together in one electrifying moment of existential drama. From now on, everyone will be able to kiss each other publicly. The playing fields and bike sheds of Wade Deacon will become arenas of snogging with both headteachers looking out of their study windows nodding in satisfaction. Trouble is I suspect the WAB and Miss Thackara know nothing about Stanislavski and are expecting a polite whodunit, with any suggestion of contact between the opposite sex discreetly removed from the script. Moon and Birdboot are in full flow with the two headteachers smiling appreciatively on an intellectual level far above most members of the audience.

I prepare for my entrance, repeating my opening line over and over, correcting and re-correcting every tiny error of pace and intonation. I move into the wings next to Judith. She squeezes my hand, smiles, and I'm on.

The spotlights obliterate most of the audience but I can still make out the WAB and Thackara surrounded by a haze of light like two guardian angels. Moon and Birdboot are next to them, dressed like two trussed-up penguins in their critics' costumes, and I can tell they are keeping in character, pretending to scribble notes into their small, green jotters. The scene with Mrs Drudge goes well and there are some appreciative chuckles from out in the darkness. This is followed quickly by my scene with Felicity (Anne) who I'd loved and left at some undefined moment in the past. Then there's a brief period of dialogue between Moon and Birdboot before Cynthia enters. I move forward calling her name, making sure I'm fully lit by the main spotlight. Judith comes towards me, her eyes sparkling with the reflections of the lights.

I draw her close and we kiss. There is a definite intake of breath from the audience or possibly it could be a fart from the dead body which has lain in a creditable state of rigidity for over thirty minutes.

Moon and Birdboot deliver a few more lines while we hold the kiss and then there is our bit of romantic angst before the second kiss after which I'm able to take a back seat while Magnus and the others take over the scene. As I stand at the back of the stage watching the action, I notice an empty seat on the front row. Thackara has gone.

There is no interval in the play which runs on for another half hour. We take our bows to thunderous applause and leave the stage. I don't know if anyone else has noticed the early departure of Thackara, and Steve is so euphoric about the reception the play has received that I don't bother to mention it.

Saturday goes just as successfully but there's no sign of the WAB or Thackara. Steve has paid for drinks and sandwiches at the Tavern and we arrive at about nine o'clock. It's full of sixth formers who have been to the play and there's lots of laughing and congratulations. Then Steve arrives and he's looking worried. There was a note left in his classroom during the performance. It's from the WAB who's had a message from Thackara. All the girls in the cast are required to attend at her office on Monday. She wants me present and the WAB wants to see me before I go over.

'It's the kiss, Man,' says Al. 'You should have done a stage one. Stanislavski would have forgiven you.'

It's a long Sunday, like waiting for a filling at the dentist, knowing he's run out of anaesthetic and the only scenario involves fear and pain. Al is graciously keeping Lesley at arm's length. He says it's better we don't see each other in the short term and that if we can talk things through we should all be able to move on. He's invited me round for a game of Subbuteo which he says is an escapist form of counselling, and that we'll talk like two opposing managers in the dugout, locking horns during the match, but shaking hands at the end of the game and sharing a couple of pints in the players' bar.

'Think Judith, Man. You're on top of the World. You can be Real Madrid. I'll be Derby County seeing as they've just been promoted and don't really know what the future holds.'

Al kicks off. 'Look, Man. You've got to let go of all this. You've broken some of the connections, like ditching the music, but you've got to get rid of it all. 1-0. See, you're not concentrating on the important things in life. You can be side-tracked. It's easy for you to be picked off. You've got to break the old associations and immerse yourself in your new life. If Judith gets wind that you're still harbouring feelings for a lost love then you'll have blown it big time. You have the girl of everyone's dreams, even my friggin' dreams, and you're still vulnerable. 2-0. What a turn up we have here at the Bernabeu Stadium with the battling Derby County two goals up against the six-times European champions.'

I kick off and lose possession immediately. I'm firmly on the back foot and need to stem Al's tide.

'If you want the truth, Man, Lesley is over you, and that's your problem. Your visualisation of things is all wrong. In your head, you're representing you and her as it was. It's gone, disappeared. Pity about the dance rehearsal because I think you were almost out of it but you've got to stop looking back. 3-0. Jesus! Can you try and make a game of it?'

It's half-time and the Real coach has a lot to do to lift his side.

'So what happened to Lesley's Curtis?'

'She chucked him, Man. He was too much of a stereotype; just a shallow single-minded soul guy. There's more to Lesley than that. Look, it's the second half. Imagine you're walking down the tunnel, leaving the memories of Lesley behind in the dressing room. Step out into your new world, ditch the backlog of emotional conflict. The crowd is willing you on. You are not going back. At the end of the match, she will not be there. You only feel like this when you're away from Judith. Your life is on a permanent run of home draws in the cup. The crowd is behind you. Hey, good shot! 1-3 and all to play for!'

Half an hour later we're in the pub. Al won the match 3-2 but we're laughing and joking and the weight of the past has lifted. Al has done his post-match press conference and talked about the spirit of his opponent and how I can take heart from defeat and concentrate on the positives. I feel at one again with my best mate and now there's only the future which will be shining as brightly as the FA Cup if I can just get through the disciplinary committee meeting in Thackara's office.

THIRTY NINE

Good Morning Starshine
Oliver. The Cast of Hair. CBS Records.

'Come in, old Stephens. Please, sit down.' It's hard to predict the outcome of a meeting with the WAB. Whether you're getting brilliant O-level results, or you've let the school down, it's always the same welcome.

'You have a mission, old Stephens. Miss Thackara wants to see you. I don't know what it's about but I suspect it may be something to do with you kissing one of her girls in public. There may be bridges to be built and you carry the reputation of the school before you. Your appointment is at 2.30. See what you can do.'

He rises from his desk and opens the door. 'I very much enjoyed what I saw of the play and I have told Mr Rothwell as much. Report back immediately afterwards. I shall be here until well after lessons end.'

There are no further instructions and I don't know whether the WAB is angry, dismayed or unconcerned. I'm ushered out of his office and that is that.

At least, I've escaped from Kenny's Latin lesson. He's been covering Roman Gods and I'm looking at Thackara's heavy study door and thinking of Janus. It's shut and that's maybe a good sign. As the God of Doors and Passages, a closed entrance symbolises peace and maybe I can take heart from this and see it as a way of settling all my problems of the last few months and moving on.

I sit wondering about the consequences. They're unlikely to be anything long term as we're leaving in a few months so maybe she's going to pull the plug on Christmas and Iris and Bert will have to banish Jimmy Shand back into Pom Pom's music cupboard for another year. I don't know what to expect and it's different to sitting outside the WAB's room. Those experiences are always man to man; that's how the WAB makes you feel, always a meeting of equals, even though he wins every time.

A group of third years hurries past pointing and giggling, their laughter masking the comments whispered behind hands clasped to mouths. A few minutes pass and a group of lower-sixth girls approaches. One is Babs. She lets the others pass and sits down next to me.

'Great play, Phil. Really enjoyed it. Missed you at the family do over the weekend. I told your Mum all about it.'

'Really? What did she say?'

'She said...' Babs looks at me shaking her head. '...she'd have liked to have come but you never invited her.'

'I didn't think she'd be interested.'

'Phil, she's really proud of you. You shut her out. You shouldn't do that with family, they're too precious.' She reaches over and ruffles my hair. 'And if you escape from in there you need to bring Judith round over Christmas. I told her you'd found a lovely girl.'

Miss Thackara's door opens.

I'm ushered into her office. She's about late-40s, perfectly dressed in an expensive cotton suit with hair tidied formally into a bun. Her room is clean, organised, ordered. Anne, Judith and Jean are already here. I try to read the looks on their faces but their eyes just follow me unemotionally into the room. There's a smart, leather armchair facing the desk and, sweeping her arm in its direction, she invites me to sit.

I'm waiting for the black cap to be whisked out of her desk drawer but the look on her face doesn't give the impression that I'm about to be banished and an invisible force field erected around the sixth form block. She sinks back into her own leather chair, a smile breaking the girls' concentration. They laugh together and the room is suddenly rid of worry and fear, replaced by relief and puzzlement. This is not what I expected.

251

'I enjoyed the play immensely. I am so sorry that I had to leave before the ending but I had a governing body meeting to attend. The girls have just talked me through the conclusion of the drama. Stoppard is such a wonderful young playwright. You must have enjoyed working with the script.'

Her secretary brings in a tray of refreshments which is placed on the smart G Plan table. She beckons us to help ourselves, and I sit next to Judith warming my hands on a cup of fresh Lyons coffee.

Miss Thackara sips from her bone china teacup, breaks a Rich Tea biscuit in half and points it in my direction. 'I've invited you over because you and Judith seem to be the natural connection in all this. She smiles the kind of smile that suggests she's drifting back to her own youth and maybe the mystery, romance and excitement of a rambling holiday in the Thirties to remote places with her own Simon.

'I've been mulling things over during the weekend and I want this to be just the start of closer relations between the schools. Jean is already on the social committee, along with my head girl and deputies, and I will be asking them to organise a musical Christmas concert for the sixth form; something more modern than the school social. I've just spoken on the phone to Mr Bonney and we've agreed that the Queens Hall Event will be compulsory for years one to five only. You should be able to enjoy yourselves at Christmas listening to your own music with people of your own age. We have some money in the school fund and I understand there are some good local groups around. Beat and soul, I believe, are popular styles; whatever the committee decides. It will be ticket only, of course, we don't want undesirables to get in. I'd like you to join them in the planning if you have the time.'

The four of us sit in the girls' quad. I get the occasional shouts of, 'Give her a kiss!', from passing third years but I can handle it. Cynthia and Simon have done the impossible. They've freed the sixth form from the shadows of Iris and Bert's frumpy and fashionless world of order, deportment, and etiquette and possibly elevated the Christmas of 1969 into the realms of myth and legend. I'd wanted to kiss Miss Thackara, but I couldn't, even if that bounder, Simon, would have taken her in his arms and twirled her around in an exaggerated embrace.

The WAB is pleased, if not a little surprised. I get the impression he has difficulty reading Thackara but the positive development in relationships between the two schools has put a smile on his face. I think, like me, he feared the worst and, although he rules the corridors of Wade Deacon with the invincibility of Superman, perhaps across the short divide is his nemesis, a new woman of green Kryptonite, who could strip away his cloak of invulnerability with a bat of her eyelids or sharp intellect. I look across his desk at his wiry frame, gaunt features and his black cloak, perhaps symbolically shielding him from the assaults of the decade. I look at his feet and his carpet and the foundations on which he's standing and wonder if his slightly hunched back is a sign that everything's slowly giving way and crumbling. Maybe in a few years' time, he'll be gone along with Herbie and the Doc and all the other guardians of the traditions forged inside its rustic stone walls.

'You've been a credit to the school, Old Stephens. I must say I am not immune to misjudgement. The new creation has come. The old has gone, the new is here!'

'Sir?'

'*Corinthians 2*, Old Stephens.' He pauses thoughtfully, 'But you are perhaps unfamiliar with it.'

He reaches into his drawer and pulls out a handful of money.

'I believe this belongs to you, Morefield and Clayton. Old Branaghan has paid his share back and will not be requiring of the first years to supplement his income as long as I remain in charge of the school.'

He hands over seven shillings and looks me in the eye.

'Worthy causes, Old Boy! Worthy causes! You will arrange for this to be donated to a suitable charitable cause and bring me the receipt by Friday.'

He rises from his desk, moves quickly to the door and holds it ajar.

'Our impulses are too strong for our judgement sometimes. You will know that of course.'

'Sir?'

'*Tess of The D'Urbervilles*, Chapter 1. Good luck with the mock revision.'

FORTY

With A Little Help From My Friends
Joe Cocker. Single Release. Regal Zonophone Records.

The social committee is chaired by the squeaky clean, brand new, untouchable, head girl, Alice Wilson. I have only ever seen Alice heading for the bus home, carrying a huge pile of books, looking pristine and unflurried. She is a girl in control of her own life, at ease with her persona, unconcerned about developing into something different. She has the look of Samantha from *Bewitched* and a smile that says if I wiggle my nose you're history chum.

Her two deputies are from music's middle of the road. There is Maureen Parker (Judith Durham) and Sylvia Hartson (Petula Clarke). Jean is my Sandy Denny, cool, worldly and unflustered. We sit around a large, oval table and throw our ideas into the ring. The Thackara school of social intercourse goes for a local band, The Terry Dixon Four, who play their own versions of pop classics, appallingly, and a soul disco with a sprinkling of chart hits.

Fortunately, we are saved as, after an initial phone call, Alice discovers The Terry Dixon Four is booked and the committee has no Plan B.

Alice is worried. They have twenty pounds in the social fund to cover the cost of the band and the disco. I'm rolling ideas around in my head when Jean jumps in, 'My brother plays in a pop group. They're really good. I could check to see if they're free.'

'What are they called?' says Alice.

'Wreckage,' says Jean, 'but they're looking to change their name to something with more of a pop sound.'

'How much will they cost?'

'Twenty pounds, I could definitely book them for that. Phil will organise the disco for nothing.'

Alice looks me up and down. 'Do you know anything about Motown? Have you got any soul?'

I'm not sure if she's referring to my record collection or asking for a character reference but I try to sound credible.

'Definitely! Marvin, Tammi, The Four Tops, Temptations, Supremes. Got them all. My bedroom's packed with them.'

Alice continues to stare at me. 'You don't look like a soul person.'

'Oh, I firmly believe music should cross boundaries. I hate stereotypes. Soul! Rock! Pop! I love them all.'

I'm not sure they're convinced but they're the sort who'll agree to anything to give the impression to Miss Thackara that they've got things done and dusted without any protraction. Organising concerts is beyond their realm of experience and, so long as they can report back to the head with a positive outcome, they're happy.

I'm on the bus with Jean, heading for her house in Sankey and I'm thinking of Alice: the clean, confident, cardiganed. ambassador for Miss Thackara's school. In my mind I can see Tupp's flat, the darkness and the dirt, and all sorts of demons gleefully creeping out of the blackness, escaping up the M1 and defiling her world.

'Are you sure you're doing the right thing?' Deep down I know I shouldn't be saying this to Jean, reinforcing her image of me as a person unwilling to take risks, strike out and challenge the natural order of things.

'Trust in Freddie,' says Jean. 'Look what happened when he played with you. Alice and the others won't stand a chance.'

We look at each other and start laughing and I feel I've connected with her at last and that we're embarking as equals on a quest which might shake the foundations of Alice's world but will probably result in the best Christmas social ever.

Twenty minutes later Jean's on the phone to Tupp. Not on to Tupp's phone. It's a phone box outside the flat where he lives and she hopes someone will pick it up.

The phone rings for ages before it's answered. It sounds like a child at the other end and Jean's very specific with her instructions,

'Could you go to number 46, flat 12, just behind the phone box, ring the bell and ask for John Taylor. Tell him his sister's on the phone.'

There's a rumble and a knocking at the other end as the phone bumps against the metal money box and I can hear a dog barking and what sounds like a domestic going on at the other end of the street. The sound of a police siren rises and falls as it speeds by and I sit listening in the quiet security of Jean's hall

'I wonder if Dr Who listens like this when he lands on a new world, sticking his ear against the door of the Tardis just to see if he fancies a peek, before deciding whether or not he should hit the lever and head off somewhere else?'

Jean laughs. 'You're not going far, are you, Phil?'

Then there's more rumbling and rattling and the phone's picked up and Jean's into conversation with John. There's a lot of laughter when she asks about returning for the Christmas gig. Then there's more knocking as he heads back to the flat to check with the others and the ringing of fire engine bells and what sounds like a drunk singing somewhere in the distance.

'What did he say?'

'He likes the idea, mainly because they're short of money. They've only had a couple of college gigs recently. I think things are coming to a head. John says he's lucky to have that job in the record store.'

Then there's some scuffling and swearing and possibly the sound of glass breaking. Jean looks a bit worried until Tupp's voice is on the other end. I listen closely.

'Sorry, just getting the tramp out of the box. Thinks he fuckin' lives here. The guys say ok, so long as we can sort out a van. What's the date?'

'12th December. It's a Friday night. If you can get here for late afternoon the hall will be empty and you can do your sound check.'

There's a bit more laughter before Jean hangs up. 'Sorted,' she smiles. 'Just need you to DJ. Don't worry about the Motown. Guess you're over all that by now. What sort of music does Judith like, anyway?'

'Oh, folky stuff, I guess. Same as me, Neil Young, James Taylor?'

'Yeh, well you owe me, Phil. I bought that James Taylor album. It was, well. 32s/6d down the drain. I could have bought *Led Zeppelin II* or *Let It Bleed*.'

'Then you'd be left behind. Blues is on the wane. Just wait until Saturday. You'll be able to say you were there at the beginning.'

She smiles. 'That's what John said to me at The Sink Club, Phil. I've heard it all before.'

FORTY ONE

Trouble on Double Time
Free. Free Album. Island Records.

I have a sense that the next few hours are going to mark a turning point in my life. Ralph's breathed confidence into us and believes that going live on Radio Merseyside will bring the idea that we will be the next big thing around town to the near edges of reality.

We're the first act to arrive at the Queens Hall and the stage has been set up. There are three mikes at the front, a couple of large Marshall amplifiers with a smaller Orange amp for the P.A. and a large drum kit pushed towards the rear. At the back of the hall is a desk, with a cassette deck and a few tapes, which I assume contain home-made backing tracks for some of the acts. Al tests a microphone, which cuts the air with too much treble, but that'll probably change when the hall fills up. Ronnie Hurst pushes through the double doors dressed in his conductor's uniform as if he's just finished a shift.

'Goin' home to get changed, Ronnie?' says Ralph.

'Ha, nice one!' says Ronnie. 'Nice and clean this one. Sandra's pressed and ironed it and I don't wear aftershave when I'm working.'

'What's the format, Ronnie?' says Al.

'Right! You're on first because the audience knows you're here but the rest of the acts are a surprise. They'll wait backstage, do their turns, and sit at the front. There are three judges: Len, Sandra and Margaret, the canteen manageress. They'll mark out of ten immediately after each act and the scores will go straight up on that big blackboard over there so the tension builds with each act.'

Ralph grabs hold of Ronnie's hand. 'Best mates, Ronnie! Tell Sandra to give us a good score and I won't tell anyone the details of her night on Shuttleworth's milk float, circa 1967.'

Ronnie pulls his hand away sharply, looks deflated, and heads off over to the judging table where Sandra is neatly arranging the judging forms.

'Wasn't that a bit tight?' says Al. 'How do you know that happened?'

'I don't,' says Ralph, 'but that bastard has had about half the girls in Widnes so there's a pretty even chance it happened sometime. Anyway, they'll never split up.'

I glance over at Sandra and Ronnie who are in a heated discussion in the corner of the room and worry about the damage Ralph might have done. Sandra slams the judging forms down onto the desk and heads our way. A second glance confirms Ronnie has disappeared. She arrives red-faced in front of Ralph.

'Don't you ever make up stories about me, you bastard!' She winds her arm up behind her back bringing it with full force across Ralph's cheek. 'Don't you ever do that to us again! You've upset Ronnie so much he's gone home. I can tell you before you even come on stage you're getting sod-all from me!'

She storms off out into the foyer, slamming the door hard. After the echoes subside Al breaks the silence. 'Nice one, Ralph, we might as well pack up and go home now. We're only going to get marked out of twenty. That's ten points start to all the other acts.'

'Nah, we'll weather it. She'll calm down. We've got an hour yet. Three pints, Men. Come on!'

The hall starts to fill up. *The Real Inspector Hound* cast arrives as one and thankfully they've come as passengers. There's still an air of euphoria after the success of the play and the anticipation of Wreckage's appearance at school; a real Christmas night with great music and a sort of homecoming for Tupp and Mike. After the hugs and handshakes and the good luck wishes, they grab some drinks and fill up the front row. At the last minute, Steve comes in with his girlfriend and Mugga. 'Couldn't leave this one at home,' he smiles. 'Even the dead will be cheering for you.'

Len, Margaret, and the still fuming Sandra, settle behind their scoresheets. Compere for the night is the jovial Eddie (call me Mister Widnes) Worthington who must have been built along with the Queens Hall when it opened thirty years ago. He tells a few jokes and then he's into the introductions. After a few 'Hellos!' and 'Thanks!', he turns to us.

'Ladies and Gentlemen, or should I say Clippies and Conductors?' He raises his hand as if he's trying to levitate something, producing whoops and cheers from the mass of red, black and yellow surrounding us. 'It's no more than I can say other than we've got some great acts for you tonight with the lucky winner appearing on Radio Merseyside next week. There are six acts in total and a very eclectic evening we have in store. First on is the group who have also very kindly offered to entertain us in the interval. Ladies! Gentlemen! Clippies! Conductors! A big welcome to Western Highway.'

The front row leads the applause. The lights dim and we clamber up the wooden steps onto the stage. I can just make out Sandra who is gazing face down at the score sheet, pen in hand, and I'm sure she's moving it around in a circle over and over again. We've decided Al can introduce us and he steps forward taking the mike. He mouths something into it and the audience cover their ears from the feedback. The guy on the sound desk waves an apology and Al tries again. 'Hi. Great to be here. We're Western Highway and we're going to sing a track we wrote ourselves called 'Compass Point'. It's inspired by life in Widnes and is dedicated to Geoff and Jackie who are sitting over there.'

There's a rippling of applause and some shouts from out in the darkness. Jackie blushes and sticks her behind behind Geoff's back. Al counts us in and we're away.

The song goes well and I can even notice Anne, Geoff and Jackie miming along to the lyrics. Judith sits still at the end of the row smiling up at me. She's not a rock star's girl. She'll go home tonight with thoughts of Hardy, Keats and Shakespeare in her head rather than any evocative images our songs might create. We've talked about songs and how they can permeate people's psyche and she tells me she has a few desert island tracks and that one day she'll tell me what memories they evoke.

The last chords sound and there's a lot of applause, not only from the cast but from all around the hall. There are even a couple of shouts of 'More!' from out in the darkness but jovial Eddie floats across from the shadow of the wings over-exaggeratedly clapping his sweaty hands.

'Ladies and gentlemen. A big hand for our very own Western Highway! And now it's over to our panel of judges. What did you think about that stunning performance?'

Well, you can't fault Eddie for talking us up but the moment of truth is about to dawn and he's hovering with his piece of chalk next to the blackboard. I look across at the judges. Len and Margaret are engaged in what looks like meaningful discussion but Sandra is sitting straight-faced staring through us without any sign of emotion.

'Now judges, are you ready?'

The scores are revealed in turn. Len holds up a '10' which is greeted with rapturous applause which reverberates around the hall. Margaret breaths deeply, smiles and holds up another '10'. The noise levels rise with sprinkles of plaster filtering down from the mouldings on the ceiling. The tension rises and we wait for Sandra. Slowly, like a zombie rising from the dead, her arms lift into the air revealing a large zero marked in heavily over-scribbled chalk on her slate. There's silence and a few disgruntled mutterings which start to rumble round the hall getting louder like an approaching train and exploding into a chorus of boos and shouts.

Len takes to the microphone. 'Order! Order! Ladies and Gentlemen, please! Order if you please!' The noise subsides and the audience members focus their attention on Len.

'Sandra, it looks as if you've missed the '1' from the front of your '10' my dear.'

There are scatterings of applause and the audience glances as one towards Sandra. She carefully wipes the '0' away with her cloth and scribbles something on the slate.

'Thank you, Sandra!' Eddie breathes a sigh of relief. Sandra finishes scribbling and holds her slate aloft. In large capital letters is written 'ZERO' and underneath something which looks like, 'You bastard, Clayton'.

After about five minutes Eddie has managed to restore some order and the competition moves on but there's a troubled atmosphere, a gathering thunderstorm, with heavy threatening feelings rising around the room.

Next is Marion Crossley who scores 6, 6 and 5 for a calming performance of 'My Old Town'. Then there's Shelley Owens, the ten-year-old daughter of a bus driver, who gets a creditable 5, 5 and 5 for 'Pretty Little Widnes Miss', written by her Mum, but collapses in tears at the disappointment of not making Radio Merseyside. Annie Wareing, one of the bus cleaners, scores 4, 4 and 6 for a slightly out of tune 'Strolling Down The Albert Road'. So, after four acts, we're still in the lead and the tension is beginning to rise, and Judith has to pull her hand away from mine because I'm crushing it.

'Ladies and Gentlemen, four performances gone and just two more to go and the boys from Wade Deacon are still out there in the lead looking down from their compass point.' He laughs loudly in an attempt to take the audience with him but the front row is silent and tense and the rest of the audience too busy chatting to each other to take much notice.

'Now we are in for a real treat. It's your own, your very own, our very own, George Wakefield, the singing bus conductor, with one of his special compositions. It's inspired by Matt Monroe and titled 'Portrait Of My Town'. Please put your hands together for a very special talent.'

'We've got no chance now,' says Al. 'He'll bring the house down. Half the women here will be waving their autographed bus tickets.'

The lights dim and the hum of the audience fades to silence. It's a silence which stays and stays as George waits at the microphone for the opening bars. Ralph is hunched forward in his seat fumbling with something under his jumper. 'Get this to Anne,' he whispers, 'and tell her to put it in her bag.' He passes me a cassette in a plastic case with the name 'George Wakefield' barely visible in the dim light.

'Jesus, Ralph, where did you get this?'

'Lad on the sound deck. Barry Hartshead. Best mates!' says Ralph.

I can't get to Anne so I shove it the under my seat just as the house lights are raised and Eddie bounds across the stage. 'Ladies and Gentleman, a slight hitch, we seem to have lost George's backing tape for 'Portrait Of My Town'. We are running out of time, George. Would you like to sing it unaccompanied and the judges will take that into account when allocating their marks?'

'Bugger that!' says George. 'I'm off to The Cricketers.' He half stumbles down the wooden steps and exits from the hall. There are sympathetic 'Awes' from sections of the crowd but the main competition has gone and only one unknown act to round off the first half of the evening.

'What a shame! What a shame!' says Eddie. 'So now, Ladies and Gentlemen, let's hear your appreciation for the last act of the night who, like Western Highway, are going to play live. I give you the Dave Shuttleworth Blues Band.'

'The friggin' bastard!' Ralph is red-faced with fury. He tries to get up but Al and I hold him down. 'Leave him, Man. He's not gonna win. Remember, blues is dead and this lot here like country covers and songs about home.'

'Ok,' says Dave, 'Nice to be with you tonight and nice to see some old friends in the audience. We're a blues band and blues is more than music it's a way of life. This is a blues song

265

I wrote after visiting Widnes Market. It's called 'The Ballad Of The Dead Man's Ghost'. He jumps back to his drum kit, counts in the band, and the opening chords, sounding very similar to Ralph's composition, fill the room.

'The friggin', bastard robber,' splutters Ralph, 'but a good choice because after this number he's fuckin' dead!'

The number goes well and it's obvious Dave and his band have spent some time rehearsing it but there's a feeling that the audience is starting to get tired and the smell of the buffet being set up is drifting across the hall. Some of the conductors leave their seats and start heading for the bar and I glance across at the judges. Len is puffing out his cheeks and Margaret has her hands over her ears. The song grinds to an end and there's a smattering of applause. Eddie takes the stage for the last time urging the audience to wait before heading for the refreshments.

'A round of applause for all our acts, ladies and gentlemen. First class performances! May it be the first of many evenings Busking With The Buses!'

There's some cheering and stamping of feet and someone at the back has an old car horn which they honk furiously.

'And now judges, can I have your final marks for the Dave Shuttleworth Blues Band!'

It's one of those moments where noise seems to fade into the background and time seems to move in slow motion. Len holds up his slate first. There's a large white '7' filling the space. Three of those and Dave and his band will be blasting out across Merseyside next Tuesday morning. Margaret's next! She wearily raises her slate. It's a '4'! A large, white, gleaming '4' which shines like a triumphal beacon around the hall. The cast starts to mutter excitedly and Ralph and Anne hug each other in uncontrolled anticipation. There's just Sandra left. The gaunt, stone-faced Sandra who raises her slate without emotion to reveal a large '10'.

Emotions explode around the room. Dave hits his drums wildly in almost primeval celebration. I decide to grab Judith

266

and leave but we're pinned back in our seats as Anne heads for the judges' table. Seconds later she has her hands around Sandra's neck and the two of them are falling to the floor scattering seats, tables and drinks as they pull each other's hair and roll in pools of beer and squashed sausage rolls.

'Don't ever go near my boyfriend again, you cow!' screams Anne. She pushes Sandra's head hard against the floor sending globules of grey matter from a Holland's meat pie bursting around Sandra's ears and matting her hair with beef gravy.

Suddenly Dave is there trying to pull her away.

'Get off her, you bitch. She puts you to shame on the back of the float anytime!'

He's silenced by Ralph who flies through the air as if he's going over in the corner for a spectacular try, flattening Dave, and knocking the wind out of him, only to be dragged clear by the rest of Dave's band who in turn are set upon by Mugga.

There's pandemonium with women screaming and men swearing. Judith and I head for the door. In the street outside is Tommy, with five of the rugby team, heading for a night at The Black Cat. Seconds later Al, Steve and the rest of the cast come hammering out of the hall.

'What the fuck's going on?' growls Tommy.

'Mugga and Ralph! They're outnumbered in there,' says Al.

'Fuckin' great,' he snarls. 'Come on lads, snooker can wait!'

Judith and I are sitting in the quiet calm of Widnes Station. My flirtation with the rock music business is over and I feel glad. I've even left my guitar behind which I suspect is lying splintered across the Queens Hall stage. Still, Jimi and others have always gone through a guitar wrecking phase so I'm not that bothered it's been consigned to my music history. I can move into the run up to Christmas with no distractions and

267

just the Wreckage concert to kick start the best Christmas of my life.

'How do you feel?' says Judith.

I stroll to the edge of the platform and look down the line which narrows and vanishes into the horizon west beyond Hough Green. Tess says we should live the moment because all our yesterdays get smaller and smaller until they vanish beyond recall. In a few months' time, the friends, family, and places that have filled my eighteen years will no longer form part of my everyday life with some things disappearing forever.

Judith joins me at the platform's edge. The evening sky is ice blue with only the white clouds above the power station breaking the view to the east. It's a vista of Hardy proportions.

'I want us to have a really good Christmas. Just you and me, stepping back from mad ambitions and school work and enjoying the present.'

'Me too.' Judith puts her arms around me and pulls me close.'

'Whole week without seeing you. Seems ages and I can't make the concert on Friday. I got a letter this morning from Leeds, my first Uni interview, but I'll get back on the ten o'clock for a drink afterwards.'

'Don't worry, I've had enough of concerts and, anyway, it's mocks next week so I guess everyone's social life is on hold until Friday.'

'Let's do something special on Saturday to celebrate, just me and you.'

'We could get the train into Manchester, go Christmas shopping and get back for something to eat at The Farmers.'

'Yes, and I'll ask Mum if you can stay over, she won't mind.'

The train hauls into the station. It's packed with shoppers and Janice hangs out of the window calling to us both. I feel good that Judith's got someone to go back with and the long, dark walk from the station to Long Barn won't be undertaken alone. It's the first time I've felt like this. I mean usually, you just kiss and say goodnight and head off in different directions.

'See you next Friday just after ten. Good luck with the mocks.' She pulls me close, kisses me, and heads off into the carriage.'

'Ooooh! Lovebirds!' shouts Janice out of the window.

I smile as Judith drags her down into her seat and the train pulls away.

FORTY TWO

Ramble On
Led Zeppelin. Led Zeppelin 11. Atlantic Records.

'And now some news from Widnes. Police were called to the Queens Hall shortly after 9pm last night when fighting broke out between both men and women. A number of youths were arrested and taken into custody but later released after being cautioned. The disturbance took place during Widnes Bus Service's Clippies and Conductors Night which had to be abandoned following a disagreement over the winners of their Busking With The Buses competition. Our programme on the history of the bus service in Widnes, scheduled for December the 19th, has been postponed until further notice.'

The singer-songwriter dream has ended, brushed away with the broken glasses, trampled pastries and blood-stained beer mats. I'm back to my musical roots and the tracks on my record player are from Free and Hendrix, reminding me that the highways are still out there to be discovered. I won't be leaving Widnes for a career in rock. I've got a different sort of image which I can see materialising a few years down the line.

I'm in the modern version of Herbie's world, in a neat, terraced house, in a sleepy suburb, where the front room is converted into a study. There's an expensive stereo system, and a neat collection of albums, but most of the shelf space is given over to Hardy, Shakespeare, Pinter and the famous classics. I'm having friends round for dinner and we're talking about Literature and people and places and imaginary lives which have inspired our thinking. I've mapped out the start of the journey. There's an application form on my desk for teacher training in Manchester. If I can marry Herbie's intellect with Steve's youth and enthusiasm, I reckon I can make a half decent English teacher. Jean is right, I'm not going far. Distant enough to cut the ties but close enough to keep the wobbly part of the compass somewhere near Long Barn, just in case. On Tuesday, I'm going to run the idea past Herbie and see what he says.

In the meantime I've taken refuge in my bedroom, lying low for a few hours with Hardy, Shakespeare and selected poets, reflecting on the more philosophical elements of life before my English mock in two days' time.

Herbie has given us some sample questions to consider. I look at the first one.

Explore the relationship between Tess and the communities in which she lives. Would you say she belongs to them?

Herbie is right when he says the themes of great novels can transcend generations. Tess struggled with belonging from the moment she left her childhood behind in Marlott and Herbie suggests that she is on a restless journey struggling with guilt and fatalistic self-doubt as the omens of disaster gather around her. I'm not quite on that level but I can feel my ties starting to stretch and pull, straining the anchor chains and creaking towards breaking point.

I love our songs but there's not much for me to hold onto in Widnes. I had a momentary glimpse of belonging at Long Barn; a tiny window into how Tess must have felt in the safe, warm, sun-soaked home of Talbothays. I don't belong in my Mum's world and my bedroom is fast becoming small and claustrophobic when once it was much larger with room for me and my Dad to play with the Triang train set which buzzed around the floor taking us on journeys recalled or imagined.

Discuss the relationships between Tess and Angel Clare and Tess and Alec d'Urberville.

This is easier. For a start, the storyline has manifested itself in Widnes over the last twenty-four hours. For Angel, Alec,

271

and Tess read Ronnie Hurst, Dave Shuttleworth, and Sandra. The bounder on his milk float, instead of a pony and trap, and the sullied girl with a secret to keep, revealed to her love in heartrending circumstances.

I can't read the novel without a simmering anger towards Angel but I feel sorry for Ronnie and just hope he rises above Angel's character and presents Sandra with a promise of unconditional forgiveness.

There's no difference between Alec and Dave, they are both egocentric, despicable and conniving. I have a disturbing vision of Sandra being unable to suppress the guilt and worry and having to abandon her warm, all-encompassing world of 'Accounts' for somewhere like the dark, unforgiving front counter of the DHSS on Widnes Road. Her wedding night, and idyllic future, could be a dim and distant dream, the tinkling sound of milk bottles reminding her of the fragility of happiness and how it can be cruelly swept away by the whims of fate.

The English mock has gone pretty well and I've decided to hang around and gauge Herbie's reaction to my plan. He's in his room sifting through the pile of marking ready to transport them back to his house, where he'll no doubt carefully place them in order, with his A-stream protégées sitting at the top of the pile. He'll settle down in judicious satisfaction, safe in the knowledge that his hours of toil, in the spartan setting of his dusty classroom, have at least ensured that the trials, tribulations and tortures of his much-loved characters are safely planted into the minds of a new generation.

'Sir, can I ask your advice on something. I'm thinking of possibly going to Manchester to train to teach English.'

Herbie raises his head and his eyes cast me a languid look of suspicion through his thick, brown spectacles.

'I admire your ambition but there are certain qualities one needs to be a successful teacher, Stephens. Firstly, an extensive knowledge of the great canon of English literature. How many of the great writers are you familiar with?

It's a pertinent question. For all his appearance of Michael Henchard at his fate-trodden worse, he has the observational mind of Sherlock Holmes.

'Well, just the ones we've covered in Lit, really.' I actually want to say that the reason I'm thinking of teaching is because he's been an inspiration and that before I came into his class I didn't have much interest in reading. Now I ride with the thoughts, feelings and experiences of all the characters he's brought into my life. But I can't tell him. It's not the sort of thing boys say to masters.

'You will need to read extensively, Stephens, but filling your head with the knowledge of the great writers is only the beginning. Teaching is invariably a life's journey of Dickensian proportions. It embodies time spent in sombre places with a steady stream of hyperbolic characters and unrelenting social drama. Secondly, there's discipline. You need to make the podium your fortress, secure enough to withstand the onslaughts which come at you from every corner of the classroom. You need to fend off the enemy but at the same time push them back with knowledge so that they sit defeated in their desks yet enriched with the works of the great writers.'

He slowly guides his spectacles from the bridge of his nose moving them backwards and forwards as if to get me into a sharper focus.

'Have you got a Plan B?'

'Not really, Sir.'

Herbie picks up a *Real Inspector Hound* programme from his desk and there's a discernible mellowing in his eyes. 'Still, I enjoyed the play. I had little idea that you, Clayton and Morefield had such Thespian talents. If you are keen on teaching, have you thought about Drama?'

I shake my head. He lifts an exam script from near the top of the pile. 'There again, your English work has improved

273

considerably since September. Has there been a reason for that?

'A bit of a realisation I suppose, Sir. Time's moving on and I need to get some reasonable A-level grades, especially as I'm a bit unsure what to do.'

Herbie opens the drawer beneath his desk and pulls out three large books.

'Not all of us who wander are lost, Stephens. *The Fellowship Of The Ring by Tolkien*. Are you familiar with his work?'

'Only through Led Zeppelin, Sir. They sing about Mordor and Gollum on their latest album.'

Herbie looks as if I've just told him one of his precious treasures has been stolen.

He leans across the table, handing me Tolkien's trilogy as if he's passing a key to a world of knowledge and enlightenment.

'Led Zeppelin? The world is indeed full of peril and in it, there exist many dark places. Switch off your record player, read these over Christmas, and we will talk about your ambitions in the new term.'

FORTY THREE

Songs of Yesterday
Free. Free Album. Island Records.

School is almost finished for the weekend. I'm gazing out of the window to see if Wreckage's van speeds past on its way to the girls' school.

Being so close to Christmas, quite a few of the masters are spending the period after lunch in the Crown, the small pub opposite the school gates. A couple of lads doing S-Level Latin have ambled across so Kenny can check some verb structures after his game of darts.

This year there's no sound of Eric thrashing the Christmas spirit out of terrified first years. Slugger is recovering at home after impaling his backside on Mugga's self-fashioned chair of torment. There's been no suggestion of an investigation into the incident, suggesting that Slugger's unpopularity extends way beyond the confines of his personal torture chamber.

Half an hour later the bell rings and I amble across to the girls' hall. In Kenny's absence, I must have nodded off as the van's already there and Tupp, Mike and a couple of others are unloading a mountain of gear out of the back. There's no sign of Freddie outside but, as I carry a box of leads into the hall, he's there, sitting on the side of the stage, checking his appearance in an old mirror.

'Phil, great to see you. How did your gig at Lime Street end up?'

'Well, it sort of ended after you left and we've split now. Had a bit of a disaster at our last gig.' I hand him his cut of the takings. 'Ralph says to give you this and thanks for giving us a few minutes of what the future might have held.'

His face creases into a smile. 'So generous of you guys. The drinks are on me after the gig. Hey, where's your girl tonight?'

'Oh, she's at a Uni interview, might make it later. Maybe you could sign my ticket for her as a sort of souvenir.'

'Love to, Man! Great idea! What's her name?'

'Judith.'

'Hey, that could be cool.'

I'm not sure what he means but he grabs an old pencil lying at the side of the stage, scribbles on the ticket, and stuffs it into the top pocket of my Wrangler.

'See you after the gig and bring your girl. It would be great to meet her.'

The unloading of the equipment continues, with Freddie a disinterested spectator, but by half past six the stage is set, they've done a quick sound check, and the band members and their friends leave to go over to the Crown.

The hall is quiet, almost eerie, but the stage looks good with a new kit replacing Miffer's, weatherworn drums and cymbals. 'Wreckage' is painted neatly on the front of the bass drum and the polished guitars glitter in the shafts of moonlight which ease through the skylights above the main windows of the hall. The only blemish is the old school mike stand; it's a big black and chrome, metal monster with a heavy, three-legged base. It has the look of a second-hand lamp post and appears just as immovable.

I'm waiting for Babs. I only have a couple of singles but they'll do to check out the system. I click the turntables into motion, dropping the needles onto my two birthday presents. 'Hey Joe' crossfades with 'Do What You Gotta Do'. Jimi battling it out with The Four Tops like two of Superman's adversaries who are planets and universes apart.

'Sorry I'm late, hon.' Babs stumbles across the hall carrying a bag bursting with singles.

There's enough to fill the three dance floors at the Babalu but, after half an hour, we've sorted a pretty eclectic playlist and we're ready to go.

'Choose one for Judith,' says Babs.

'She won't be here till the end.'

277

'No, you pudding, I mean just choose one that reminds you of her.'

'No, we're not really like that. I've not really thought about it.'

'I'll choose,' says Babs, 'and you can tell me what you think.'

She takes a single out of the bottom of the bag. I'm expecting Motown but it's a plain, white cover with 'USAF Burtonwood' stamped on the front.

'Your Mum got me this. It's a bootleg. Not been released yet. I'm not playing Marvin's version, this is more you. She drops the needle and turns up the volume. Carole King's voice is instantly recognisable as she sings out the opening lyrics to 'Some Kind Of Wonderful'. It's a slow, melodic version of her song with the words sung clearly and with an irresistible sincerity.

Babs smiles at me. We both stand and listen as the lyrics fill the hall. There's just the piano, background percussion, and a girl singing about her guy but not having the words to tell him how she feels.

'Have you told Judith?'

'Told her what?'

Bloody hell, Phil, you're hard work. How you feel about her.'

I shake my head.

'Well, you daft ha'porth, tell her tonight, and if you can't, give her this as a Christmas present You can't just sit back and expect things to happen.'

Babs hands me the single. 'She feels the same, Phil. Just tell her, she wants to know.'

About half an hour before the doors open the band and their entourage return. Babs is drawn across to the girls and the talk seems to be about the fads, fashions and the trends momentarily appearing in a bubble of southern style.

I sit on a couple of raised rostra towards the back of the hall with an elevated view of the preparations. There's plenty of space on stage and the hefty mike stand is central in front of the drums which are set well back. Unlike at the Sink Club, Mike and Tupp will have breathing space so the stage is Freddie's and he looks at it thoughtfully, standing apart from the group, apparently unconcerned by the final sound checks and the taping down of yards of wire. There doesn't seem to be the urgency of the Sink Club and the energy and drive seem to be falling away.

There's no tape machine to record the proceedings this time. Tupp and Jean perch together on the edge of the stage; a picture most probably replicated on countless snaps tucked away in albums scattered about the Taylor household. As time moves on, the group and their entourage drift backstage. There are just a few minutes of silence before the heavy wooden doors crash open and the first pupils barge towards the front of the hall intent on securing a decent view.

It's a sell-out, security is tight, and Mugga is on the door providing a formidable barrier for any would-be gate crashers; but there's a poignancy to it all. This is our last Christmas social; the big goodbye. The final chapter in our journey from jelly-flicking first years to intelligent adults.

In the foyer, there's a non-alcoholic bar which sells mixers suitable for adding to the bottles of vodka and gin most of the girls have brought in their handbags. The atmosphere is building and it's different to the school dance. There are about two hundred sixth formers here hell-bent on having a good time. I drop the needle onto 'Nowhere To Run' and the evening is underway.

Perched up at the back I can see how the evening's developing socially. I'm semi-hidden behind miles of paper streamers and balloons which suits me fine. My girl's promised to try to make the last fifteen minutes and I'm happy just to enjoy playing the music with the power to choose the tracks. I've arranged to do the first hour and then hand over to

Dennis Jones. I've promised Alice an hour of soul and chart but I don't care what happens after that.

I mix up the music as the atmosphere builds. There are some great tracks to dance to in Babs' collection and I put on a triple run of songs from the summer charts. 'Bad Moon Rising', 'Born To Be Wild', and 'Honky Tonk Woman' segue together. The hall is packed and the place is rocking.

'My fuckin' favourite that one.' Two bodies have climbed up onto the rostra. It's Miffer and Dave. Dave has a bottle of Carlsberg Special in one hand and the keys to his milk float in the other.

'Give me a bit of space lads.' I try to usher them behind the balloons and streamers. 'How did you get in?'

It transpires that Mugga has had his comeuppance. Miffer was determined to see his former band and Mugga was no match for the two of them. He's in the toilets trying to stem a heavy nosebleed.

'We're not here to cause trouble,' says Miffer, as he sits under the balloons rolling a cigarette. 'Just wanna see the band and how good their new drummer is.'

'At least the bastards on stage won't desert him,' says Dave flashing me a look which confirms that I'm lucky to be alive. I try to change the subject, 'Where's Lisa, Dave?'

'How the fuck should I know,' says Dave. 'I only wanted her for a couple of dates. Had to pretend I was into all that religious crap.' He takes the cigarette from Miffer, inhaling slowly. 'It was worth it though.'

The hall is clouded in a sweaty haze but from the back I catch a glimpse of Al talking to a pretty cool-looking girl. She's wearing a full-length cotton skirt with sandals, tight sleeveless top, a headband and an assortment of rings and wristbands. There's no sign of Lesley. Dennis takes over, drops the needle onto 'Two Can Have A Party' and the dance floor fills. I do a quick scan of the hall, sure to see her somewhere with one of the Warrington bunch, but it's just a sea of swirling bodies and flailing arms.

Ralph joins us on the rostra. The lights dim, plunging the stage into darkness. There are a few shadowy movements and the odd flash of reflected light followed by seconds of intense anticipation. The first drumbeats punch holes in the silence and a spotlight cuts a sharp path of light through the darkness picking out Freddie who stands motionless in its dusty beam. Mike plays the opening riff to 'I'm So Glad' and Freddie is away, belting out the vocals, standing in an exaggerated pose, caressing the mike stand, and twisting a leg around the rigid, metal pole. He's glued to the spot, one hand clasping the microphone close to his mouth, the other gesturing, inviting, teasing, persuading the crowd to come to him, to reach out and connect with his vibrant energy which extends beyond the confines of the stage into the heaving body of the audience.

'Who the fuck does he think he is?' says Ralph. 'One of the great Cream tracks and he's fuckin' ruining it. No wonder you left, Miffer, it's fuckin' embarrassing.'

He's on a different wavelength to Anne, though. She's at the front of the stage with Jean and Carol. They're part of a mass of swaying bodies drawn into the music which is pounding off the walls of the hall.

We're into the second number. Freddie is finding his feet, but he's losing the ability to manoeuvre the mike stand. The bars of 'Communication Breakdown' pick up the pace and, in desperation, he gives it an almighty yank. There's a high pitched snap of metal as the three screws holding the lower part of the stand give way and the slim metal pole parts from the base. Freddie is as surprised as the audience but instantly he's in possession of a lightweight prop, with mike atop, and he's off, liberated from the dead centre of the stage. He clutches the mike and loose metal strut, throws back his head in a neck-breaking backwards jerk, lifts his right knee to somewhere close beneath his chin and starts to stalk the front of the stage in outrageously exaggerated movements.

The concert rocks along but problems are developing with the sound, with a buzzing noise coming from Tupp's speaker

281

and an annoying crackling from Freddie's mike. After a throbbing version of 'Crossroads' Tupp consults the members of the band and steps forwards.

'Ok, guys looks like my amps knackered so we're gonna do one more song and then finish. You'll all know this so rock your keks off and we'll see you soon. It's our version of 'Jailhouse Rock'.'

Freddie strikes an exaggerated pastiche of Elvis holding his mike aloft, freezing in a grandiose pose, before thrusting his hips in unison with Mike's opening chords. Drawn by his precocious arrogance the body of the audience sways and pushes towards the front of the stage.

'I'm off,' says Dave, jumping down from the rostra. 'Need to check the float. I left it parked outside.'

I have half an eye on the concert and the other on the clock. By the end of the song, Judith's train will be arriving and we'll be off and away from the sixth form crowd into a quiet corner of the Crown. The hall is a whirlpool of noise, spinning, swirling towards the magnetic light of Freddie's presence. The room seems to be getting smaller, hotter, as he absorbs the energy of the crowd and the back of the stage has become a black, muffled void, with the rest of the band driven into the shadows as the mike stand flashes like a sabre in Freddie's hands. I get a sense of a mental time shift as if Wreckage are about to be banished into Freddie's past and my own future is about to be bottled, shaken around, and spilt out into a world where a myriad of highways beckon me in different directions. I need to get out. Is this the turning point where I choose my road and leave fate, like Wreckage, abandoned and consumed in Freddie's fire?

I need to get to Judith and trust in Babs. I'm going to start by telling her I've missed her and then hold my breath. Six days have seemed like a long time. I have a final look out from my vantage point. I can just see Al and the girl standing aside in the shadowy outreaches of the hall; two indistinct figures almost invisible in the sparkling grains of light. I need to beat the crush so I head off down the side of the hall and out into the cold, empty foyer.

I'm just about to leave for the station when I'm grabbed by the arm from behind. It's Al's girl. I turn around and do a double-take. There's a moment of confusion before I realise, for the first time since the dance rehearsal, I'm looking into Lesley's eyes. They're the same deep brown, framed by her dark, spiralling hair, but the makeup has changed and, with the cheesecloth, denim and leather, she could have just stepped off my Woodstock poster.

My first reaction is to pull away. I don't want this but there's something deep within that makes me stop. Suddenly, we're both smiling half-embarrassed smiles and I'm shaking my head in mild disbelief.

'Sorry, I didn't recognise you. Some change.'

'Yes. Got a bit fed up of soul. Still like Marvin and Tammi though.' She pauses, dropping her head slightly and losing my gaze. 'They'll always remind me of you.' She hesitates before looking up. 'Hope you have a great Christmas.'

Suddenly she's pulling me close and my arms are involuntarily closing around her waist.

'Take care. Maybe we can all meet up for a drink after school's finished.' Her arms tighten and she kisses me slowly and gently. It's a moment frozen in time and one shared by Judith as she pushes through the door.

There's a sudden explosion of noise as the hall doors crash open and I'm lost in the chaotic mass of pupils funnelling towards the exit. Judith's gone, but there's a wall of bodies blocking my pursuit. It's five minutes before I can squeeze out into the chill of the evening. There's no sign of her anywhere, but Ralph is beckoning me, flagging me down like one of the Le Mans pit crew. I arrive in front of him with a dead stop.

'Big P, bad news! Ugly bastard syndrome!' I follow his eyes in the direction of the car park. The milk float has gone.

283

The hall is empty. The excitement, and the grumblings from Alice and her crowd about the band being a bit self-indulgent and the lead singer being, well, take your pick from weird, worrying, extravagant or existential, have long since drifted into the night. The mike stand lies broken on the stage next to the bass drum proclaiming 'Wreckage'; a fitting epitaph to mine and Judith's relationship, shattered and smashed by a tragic moment of chance of which Hardy would have been justifiably proud.

'Lost something, son?' The caretaker brushes a mound of streamers, trampled balloons and assorted beer bottles towards the bins.

'Yeh!'

'Want me to have a look round?'

'It's ok. It won't be in here.' I wander over to Babs who's collecting her records.

'So, where is she?'

I drop the single back into Babs' bag. 'Don't know. She wasn't on the train. Must have been late back from Leeds. Thanks for everything.' I give her a hug and head out into the night. The band members are loading up the van with a few old friends giving them a hand. Freddie is leaning against the driver's door pulling his velvet jacket tight against the cold.

'Hey, Phil, what did you think?'

I pat him on the shoulder. 'Great, you were amazing. Better than Lime Street.'

Freddie laughs. 'We're all off to the pub. Coming for a drink?'

'No thanks, I've gotta meet my girl. But good luck. Hope you make it.'

Tupp hoists the final amplifier into the van and slams the doors. The sound echoes around the emptiness of the playing fields before disappearing into the night. He starts the engine. Freddie jumps in and pulls the door shut. The van moves off flickering between the shafts of light from the hall windows. I turn and head out into the blackness making for the path across the golf course and the two-mile walk home.

FORTY FOUR

What Does It Take (To Win You Love)
Junior Walker And The All Stars. Single Release. Tamla Motown.

Saturday morning. I've not slept. I'm up early with nothing to do. It's just a week until the end of term and I should be looking forward to the best Christmas of my life but instead, I'm on the bus to Widnes hoping I'll meet someone I know to take my mind off things. I decide to get off at the town hall and walk the full length of Albert Road and end up in Calverts for a coffee, taking in the Music Shop to maybe buy an album to cheer myself up. The town seems cold and empty like my immediate future. The Christmas holidays will be blank days without Judith; a world plunged into monochrome instead of the green, reds and golds of festive cheer. I meet no one, it's too early, but the Music Shop is open. I search for an album that might lift me from the shadows but my emotions are flat and unresponsive. I'm hovering between self-pity and anger at Lesley for ending both relationships.

I'm the only one in Calverts. The smell of fresh coffee is uplifting but the Christmas displays have no meaning. After half an hour some familiar faces from school drift in and there are a few mumbled words of greeting and comments about the show. I'm about to leave when Ralph pushes through the door followed by Anne and Jean.

'Big P! Commiserations!' It's a daft word to use, it sounds like I've just lost the cup final or something. It's probably a bloke's way of saying, you dickhead, you've blown it but I'm your mate and I can't tell you that.

Anne is more open. 'Phil, I'm sorry. I phoned Judith this morning and tried to explain the context of it all but she wouldn't talk except to say she's got a date with Dave this evening at The Sink Club Christmas Charity Night. Dave's playing with a band.' Her frown turns into a half-smile and she touches my hand. 'If it's any consolation he just gave her a lift home last night. Nothing else happened.'

'Ok, thanks, I'll get a ticket and go and talk to her.'

'No chance,' says Ralph.' You know the size of that place; it was sold out months ago. You'll never get past those evil bastards on the door.'

The evening is drawing in and I'm alone back in my bedroom. The theme music to Coronation Street is playing on the radio. It's a bleak, wet, whimsical, depressing drone; the music of dreary streets and forgotten relationships. It's an ending sort of sound like there'll be no more episodes. No more episodes for me and Judith. Lesley has delivered the final blow and I'm down and out, flat on a canvas of lost hope, anger and despair.

I pick up 'Do What You Gotta Do'. It's pristine, played only twice, and now earmarked to be swept off to Blue Mountain Records. 'Don't Forget Motown'. I smile inside. It's forgotten me. There are no happy endings and the real things have disappeared. The guy at the Sink Club was right. The romance, the hope and the simplicity have gone. Soul is dead, disappearing into the cold, hard world of blues. Move on! Get over! Leave behind! Disappear down that long highway putting the miles between you and a love which was never meant to be.

I toss the record uncaringly onto a shelf where it flops against my pile of LPs dislodging a buff-coloured envelope which loops onto the floor. It's the present from Young Reg which has been there for three months, discarded, forgotten and unopened.

It feels empty. I slit it open using the stem of a Subbuteo goalie and two thin pieces of card fall into my hand causing a sudden shot of adrenaline as I gaze at the writing on the front.

Sink Club.
Christmas Charity Night.
Admit One.
Complimentary.
Liverpool Leisure Services.

I stuff the tickets into different pockets of my Wrangler top, grab some money, and run. Fifteen minutes later I'm on the 9.30 train to Liverpool, out of breath, heart pounding, but now in limbo for the next twenty minutes; a time to just sit and collect my thoughts.

Can a splinter of time really change the direction of your life? Maybe there's no such thing as fate and Thomas, Herbie and Al have got it all wrong. Is it that our lives are really fashioned by the merest fragments of eternity? Unpredictable moments that change your destiny in the blink of an eye? Irrespective of how it's all been orchestrated, thanks to Young Reg and the random trajectory of a Four Tops record, I've got the Sink Club Tickets, and my immediate future, clasped firmly in my own hands.

I will the train to pick up speed. The carriage is almost empty with just the sound of the engine as it hums and rattles its way up the long slope towards Hunts Cross. Outside there's darkness with occasional sparks of light the only reminder of a world out there living another Saturday night. There are people in their homes, pubs, cinemas and darkened streets unaware of the stakes riding on the inconspicuous journey of a two-car diesel as it twists and groans on the metal matrix of rails leading into Lime Street Station.

I hit the Sink Club running and stumble down the steps into its dingy half-light. A cloud of smoke hovers above the audience who are packed at the front of the stage. Dave's band are on and the first familiar chords of 'Toad' leap from the speakers drowning out the spontaneous applause and exaggerated whooping.

My eyes struggle to focus through the sweaty haze. Dave is here. Judith must be here somewhere but there's no sign of her and Dave's drumming is getting incessantly louder and the guitars haven't even broken off yet. Then, yielding to the force of his double-four onslaught, the mist parts momentarily and she's there at the back of the hall, half hidden by a pillar blocking out the worst of the sound.

In seconds, I'm in front of her. I'm about to try and speak through the layers of noise but as I open my mouth Judith's finger is pressed against it and she's mouthing back to me, 'Sorry!', and we're holding each other for the first time since Widnes Station. Seconds later we're heading towards the exit with Dave embarking on his ten minutes of madness. The rest of the band members have exited backstage but we have to pass their amps and sound deck on the way out. Their mixing guy has also gone for a break and I can't resist yanking the guitar leads out of the mixer and pulling the shiny, steel wires out of their sockets. Dave is consigned to another marathon stint and maybe there's a Lisa Wilcox somewhere in here but Judith and I flee the storm out into the cold, December streets.

Snow is falling as we skirt our way through the backstreets down towards the waterfront. At the Pier Head, there's a busker wearing a John Lennon cap huddling under a doorway sheltering from the flakes slanting obliquely through the street lights. As we pass he breaks into the opening chords of 'Here Comes The Sun'. We both stop and break into laughter. I grab a handful of money from my jeans and spill the coins out into his collection box.

'Eh, top, mate. Happy Christmas.'

We walk a few more steps and Judith turns me around, pulling me inside her coat and wrapping us both in its fleecy warmth.

'Here's to Christmas.' She kisses me softly and we hold each other as the wind whips flurries of snow around our ankles. The Royal Iris drifts out from the landing stage, the reflection of its red and white Christmas decorations throwing a starburst of celebration onto the river.

'Last train to Padgate, then?'

'What, both of us?'

'It's ok. Mum knows you're coming. I told her last Saturday, remember!'

We walk up towards Lime Street, leaving our footprints close together in the falling snow.

'How did the concert go?'

'Different! I know Alice and the committee were expecting something a bit more straight and Freddie was, well, just outrageously flamboyant. I got him to sign my ticket for you. Not sure what he wrote.'

Judith takes the crumpled piece of card and holds it under the streetlight.

'*To Jude*,' she laughs. 'Nobody has ever called me that, I'd hate it.'

'What else has he put?'

'Oh no!' She smiles and shakes her head. 'He's written, *Remember me. I'm going to be a bloody legend!* What a dreamer!'

She drops the ticket into a litter bin and, arm in arm, we head off for the train.

Ibex

Mick 'Miffer' Smith emigrated to America some years ago but still keeps in contact with friends through regular visits and phone calls to the UK. John 'Tupp' Taylor never returned home and runs a successful music management company in London. His sister, Jean, still lives in Warrington. Mike Bersin completed his art degree, went on to work for Radio Metro in Newcastle, and, until recently, continued to play blues with his band, The Proper Boys. Freddie, of course, went on to become a legend and arguably the greatest frontman in the history of rock music.

Thanks to:
Molly Page, without whose inspiration this book would not have been completed.
Jean Taylor, John 'Tupp' Taylor and Mick 'Miffer' Smith for providing facts about Ibex and Wreckage.
Geoff Haynes and Carole Page for their help and support.